"The doctor studied the young circle. It was impossible for him to imagine what was going on in his mind, yet he knew he was looking at an exceptionally strong person. One of the few that was okay within himself.

Billy looked up and walked over to the doctor's desk, "Thank you, sir, for being so honest. I'm sure it wasn't easy to tell me."

Billy held out his hand; the doctor did the same. The handshake was firm. Billy turned and left the room as the doctor went behind his desk to sit down. He sat back in his chair in wonder at how the human condition could allow one man to completely fall apart at the kind of news he had just given Billy, and how some, like Billy, could just accept the knowledge of their fate and go on.

He was sure that Billy had understood what he was telling him. Was he in denial? Some, maybe, but he didn't think that was the case. Instead he realized he had just met a remarkable person."

Just Another Marine

"She had to see. Slowly, almost fearing what she would find, she leaned over the back of the bench. The tears again flowed freely when she found the key was still there. She would never be sure when the idea she had entertained so positively about ending her life faded away, and yet it was as gone as yesterday's sunrise. She just sat on the old bench with what she was sure was an idiotic smile, aware that somehow Grandma's old key bench and the providence which had arranged for it to arrive today had put her world squarely back on its feet."

The Key Bench

A TALL BOOK
OF SHORT STORIES

STEVE WHEELER

A Tall Book of Short Stories. Copyright © 2016 by Steve Wheeler. All rights reserved under International and Pan-American Copyright Conventions.

ISBN-13: 978-1533185372
ISBN-10: 1533185379

Coke is a registered trademark of The Coca-Cola Company. Goodwill is a registered trademark of Goodwill Industries. Rolodex is a registered trademark of Sanford A Newell Rubbermaid Company. Harvey's and Harrah's are registered trademarks of Caesars Entertainment Corporation. Ford is a registered trademark of the Ford Motor Company. Hard Rock Cafe is a registered trademark of the Seminole Tribe of Florida. Budweiser and Bud are registered trademarks of Anheuser-Busch InBev. Giants is a registered trademark of the San Francisco Baseball Association LP. IHOP is a registered trademark of Dine Equity.

Editing and book design by Carol Callahan

Printed in the United States

Acknowledgments

To Diana, for inspiration

TABLE OF CONTENTS

Patsy 1
The Killing of Al Baloney 15
Eighty Years 22
Indecision 35
The Meter Maid 41
The Key Bench 44
Reminders 52
The Coach 56
The First Day Alone 68
The Letter Writer 72
Road 18 92
To Find Love 95
The Dice Players 133
November 1944 141
Fate 142
A Rolodex of Memories 190
Just For a Day 194
A Million Times 215
The Anniversary Card 220
A Written Mystery 229
Just Another Marine 232

Patsy

***IF.* NOW, THERE'S** a word. If only I was tall. If only I was rich. If only my nose didn't take a sharp right halfway down its length. If only I had been there when she was.

Chris Andrews sat on a bus bench outside the Ryman Theater, waiting for the doors to open, impatiently. His guitar leaned against his leg in its case, held together with duct tape, looking like a lot of others in the town of Nashville.

His was a story told a million times of the overwhelming desire to be a musician, to play and be recognized in the Mecca of country music; to stand on the stage of the Ryman Theater, the Grand Old Opry and just play. It was here she had sung. It was here she had been revered.

CHRIS DIDN'T KNOW when Patsy had become a part of his life. It must have been the first time that he heard her sing. The record belonged to his sister; so he appropriated it and played it till the sound got bad. He had money from his paper route, and that got him a lot more of her records.

He had been playing the guitar since he was five and started getting lessons from his uncle. He knew that he didn't practice enough. He just couldn't get really interested, so he did only as much as he thought he had to. That all changed when he found Patsy.

He started learning all her songs, which he wanted to play as well as the musicians that accompanied her and, with that, his practice began in earnest.

His uncle remarked as how he was really beginning to pick it up and started showing him more difficult things to do.

By the time he was seventeen, he was an accomplished musician, and there was not a song that she sang that he didn't know by heart. The amazing part of his love of Patsy Cline was that she died the year before he first heard her sing. He knew it was stupid, but he asked God if some day he might meet her. He also started writing songs just meant for her voice. He would hear the feeling she put into the words.

HE LOOKED UP as the door to the theater swung open in time to see an old gentleman hook the door back. He made his way across the street and into the lobby. The ticket booth was not yet open. The old man that he had seen was just going in the door to the theater.

"Excuse me, when will they be selling tickets?"

The old man turned slowly and looked at him—a smile flirted with his lips. "We're not actually open today. I just like to let a little air in the place. There's a show tonight, though."

Chris knew that the disappointment must have shown in his face when the old man asked, "Make the trip just to see this place?"

"Yeah, pretty much."

This time the old man did smile, "My name is Gabe. You are?"

"Chris, Chris Andrews."

"It's nice to meet you, Chris. I don't guess it will hurt if you have a look around. Just don't make me have to find you, OK?"

"Hey, thanks a million. You just holler when you want me out of here."

The old man just nodded. With a knowing smile on his face, he turned and went into the theater.

Chris couldn't believe his luck. He entered the theater through the same door the old man had taken, who was nowhere in sight.

It looked just as he knew it would, and it even smelled just as he thought it would. He looked at all the rows of benches shining from all the times they had been sat on. The floor was also wood, made of long planks, a path worn in the aisle from many, many peoples' steps.

He followed his feet as they moved of their own volition toward the front of the stage. It was somehow smaller than he had pictured. He slid onto the bench at center stage, lost in what felt like a dream. He sat there—how long, he had no idea.

HE WAS STARTLED back to reality by the old man's voice, "Are these yours?"

He held in his hand a few pages of music. Glancing at it, Chris recognized his handwriting and one of the songs that he had written just for her.

"Oh, yeah, those are mine. Thank you."

"You dropped them by the door. I like the song, by the way."

"Thanks, I wrote it for her." The words slipped out unexpectedly.

"Her would be?"

'Well, uh, uhm; it's kind of crazy, but I wrote it for Patsy Cline. She's dead but…"

"Yes, I know."

Chris smiled at the old man. "Think I'm a little over the edge?"

"No, not really. Lots of people do things like that. Did you ever see her perform?"

"No, I really wish I had though."

The old man heard the longing in the young man's voice. It had a desperate quality, of something unfulfilled.

"Perhaps someday you will," he said softly.

Chris looked at him, a sound of awe in his voice. "Wouldn't

that be something?"

The old man rose from the bench. "Stranger things have happened. It seems the Lord has ways of making dreams come true."

CHRIS STARTED WANDERING around backstage, looking into the dressing rooms and finding it strange that they were not as glamorous as he had imagined. The working part of the stage with all its lights, pulleys, ropes, curtains and scenery made him wonder how it all worked. When you watched it on television, it all looked so simple.

He finally worked his way back out to the front of the stage and once again found himself sitting on the bench at center stage. He moved to the end and leaned against the side 'til he found a comfortable position, and just let his mind wander. He could see her there in the middle of the stage, the mike in her hand as the band began the song he had written just for her.

He knew he was dreaming, and he didn't want to wake up. She was singing his song, and it sounded just the way he knew it would. Somebody was poking him. Reluctantly he pulled himself awake. "What?"

"So…you *are* alive."

"Yeah, I think so."

He opened his eyes, or at least he thought he did. He closed them tight again and then opened them: she was still there. His head swiveled rapidly both ways. Yep, he was still in the Ryman Theater, but this was impossible. Once again he closed his eyes and shook his head, then looked up; she was still there.

"You all right?"

"Uh, yeah."

"I'm Patsy Cline. Are you the guitar the agency sent down to play for me while I practice?"

"Well, uhm, uh, that is," *Don't blow this chance stupid*, he thought. "Yes, ma'am."

"Well, forget the 'yes ma'am' stuff. My name is Patsy, and you are?"

"Crisssss." His voice broke as he spoke. "Uhm, Chris, ma'am, uh, Patsy."

"You do have a problem spitting words out, Chris. Well, come along."

She stopped at the top of the stairs. "Chris, it would help a lot if you brought your guitar along."

He looked at his empty hands. "Yep, right." He grabbed his guitar from the bench and followed her on stage.

"Are you familiar with my music?"

"Oh, yes ma'am, Patsy. I know it like the back of my…" She was looking at him funny. "Yes, ma'am."

"OK, let's start with *True Love*."

He started to play, and she stopped him immediately. "Chris, not so softly; I like to hear the music when I sing."

"Sure."

This time he played at a volume she liked, and she winked at him to let him know. When she finished the song, she smiled. "That's a good song to start with; it lets me warm up slowly. How about *She's Got You?*"

He was still having a hard time with his voice, so he nodded and started to play. He was completely unaware of how he was playing. He didn't care since it was all a dream anyway. He just feared waking up and being disappointed.

The music of her voice filled the stage, rising and falling with the notes of the song. He played as though he had accompanied her all his life; easily without thought or effort, fulfilling one of his dreams. They did three more songs before she signaled a break.

"Chris, I usually practice with a piano for accompaniment but I really enjoyed our practice. I want you to know that I think you are really talented."

"Thank you, Patsy. I think that's as nice a compliment as I've ever been given, especially coming from you."

"Listen, I have to go and make a couple of calls. I'll be back in a bit."

"I'll be here."

"OK…is that yours?"

He looked at where she pointed and saw that his music had fallen out of his guitar case again. "Oh yeah, thanks."

"Is that a song for me?" she kidded.

Chris was feeling a whole lot better than he had at the start of the practice, comfortable and confident. Yet he still felt himself turning scarlet, despite knowing that it was all a dream.

"Now that I think about it, I might have had you in mind when I wrote it."

"Well?" she said.

He picked up the sheet music and handed it to her. She glanced at it briefly while making small noises as though she were humming the tune to herself. "I'll bring this back after I make my phone calls. OK?"

"Sure."

With that Patsy turned and walked off the stage toward the dressing rooms.

Chris suddenly felt a strong call from nature and dashed off to the bathroom he had seen in the lobby. He passed a few people and thought how real can a dream be.

WHEN HE RETURNED to the lobby he got a Coke from a vending machine, then made his way back to his seat at the front of the stage. He let himself imagine that she would like the song yet at the same time he knew that he was an amateur, a wannabe, a beginner at best, but still, the thought was nice.

Comfortable, and with his heart not pounding like it intended to break all his ribs, he relaxed in his seat, letting the sounds of the theater lull him along in what he knew had to be a dream. There was a smell to the theater that brought along with it all the memories of people laughing and tapping their feet, singing along as they watched their favorite singers on stage. There was a palpable scent of all the times the floors had been waxed and polished, along with the scent of pine cleaners used a thousand times on the benches. He could not imagine any place that had a warmer, more welcoming ambiance than this old theater.

"Dreaming, are we?"

This time her voice didn't startle him like before. "I hope not, but somehow I know I am."

"This place can have that effect on people. I think people that love country just have to see the Opry or they don't think their lives are complete somehow."

"How about you? Did it have that effect?" he asked.

"I think for me it was different. I didn't want to just see it; I wanted to be on its stage since I was a kid. I wanted to be where all the great ones had been. I thought it would never happen and then I got lucky and won a talent contest, and the next thing I knew, here I was."

"Maybe I should enter a talent contest."

"You play the guitar well enough. Do you sing?"

"Like a song bird...with a bad sore throat."

"Like I said, you play the guitar well enough."

"Thank you."

"I'm meeting someone for a late lunch and then coming back here to get ready for the show. Would you like to join us?"

- - - - *PATSY* - - - -

"You know, I think I'll just hang out here for a while, but thanks anyway." He was sure that if he left this building it would all come to an end. He wanted to have this magnificent dream for as long as he could make it last. *God*, he thought, *I hope when it's over I'll remember it.*

HE WAS AWARE of more and more people being in the theater. He could hear some of the conversation and laughter as the people that work here got busy with preparation for that night's show. He glanced at his watch and couldn't believe that it was already after five in the afternoon. He wondered if time really went faster in a dream. He had read somewhere that most dreams only took seconds.

He felt like he was welded to his seat, so he forced himself to get up and walk to the lobby. The hunger in his stomach yelled at him to get something to eat.

He walked over to one of the guys straightening and cleaning the lobby and asked, "Is there anything to eat here in the theater?"

"Nope. You work here?"

"Uh, just for today."

"Well, go through that door; there's an ice box usually has some sandwiches in it. Mindful you watch out for bread that's green, OK?"

Chris smiled. "Thanks for the warning."

The roast beef sandwich tasted good and it was fresh. He got another Coke and again went and sat down in his usual spot. The place was really filling up with the people that worked in the theater and he was having a good time just people-watching. The show he knew started at eight, so he would have to move before then. He couldn't help but wonder who these great seats belonged to.

THE NEXT TWO hours flew by as the activity increased and more and more he could see that it took a lot to put on a performance for television. He was enthralled with all of it.

He picked up his guitar and walked out to the lobby. The coat check was open, so he thought it would be a good idea to leave his guitar there and pick it up later.

"Can I check this here?" he asked the girl.

"Sure." He started to hand the girl the guitar when a voice behind him made him stop.

"Are you Chris?"

He turned and looked. The guy was six foot six if he was an inch, with thinning hair over a hawk-like face.

"Yes, sir."

"Patsy said I'd find you somewhere out here. I'm Dave, Patsy's musical director, piano player and factotum. You know, I do whatever it takes. Anyway, she said she'd like to see you, oh, and bring your guitar."

They walked through the backstage to the dressing rooms and entered Number One. Patsy was sitting at a dressing table applying her make-up. She turned as they entered.

"Hi, Chris."

"Hi, Patsy."

"Chris, do you like working out of the agency?"

"Well, I, uhm, you know, it's OK."

"Well, I'll tell you. I got the strangest phone call from the agency apologizing all over the place for not getting someone out here to play for my practice. Said they got hold of an old gentleman, and he said he'd let me know, but said he thought it was already taken care of. You know anything about that? Oh, and by the way, just who are you?"

Chris didn't answer for a moment. He just sat there trying to think of how to explain, and being sure that he had a very stupid

- - - - PATSY - - - -

look on his face.

"I got to Nashville last night. This morning I came here 'cause it was the main reason that I came to Nashville in the first place. I got here early and found the theater locked, so I went across the street, sat at the bus stop and waited for it to open. Finally an old colored gentleman opened the door. I asked if I could take a tour, and he said no because there was a show tonight. He must have seen the disappointment in my face and said I could take a look around, but not to get lost. He said his name was Gabe. I spent the day just being here."

Patsy and Dave could see the wonder in Chris' face that only happens when a dream comes true.

"The place is magical like no place I've ever been. You can see the paths worn in the wood floors where thousands of people have walked. And I could just imagine them leaving with smiles on their faces talking about the show they just saw. You know the place smells, but it's a good smell like old wood and polish. You know it's just something special. Anyway I came from Texas just to see this place and Nashville. Thought I'd show some of my songs to whoever would look at them, and that's how I ended up here. I guess I fell asleep. Next thing I knew you woke me up. That's the whole story, except that when you asked me to play, I sure wasn't going to miss the chance."

Dave glanced at Patsy and saw her eyebrows rise as if to say, 'What do you think?' Dave lifted his hands palm up and shrugged his shoulders. Then he said, "That's quite a story. Patsy said you knew her music dead on. Why's that?"

"If this sounds corny I can't help it; I just love all her music so I learned to play it."

Dave nodded, "This old guy, Gabe, what's he look like?"

"I don't know, an older black guy maybe in his sixties or seventies, average height; one thing though, he has white hair, really white hair."

Patsy looked at him and said, "I've been around this place for a long time, and that doesn't sound like anybody I've seen or know."

Dave echoed her thoughts. "That's even stranger than you knowing her music so well."

Chris smiled. He knew that they believed him.

"Patsy showed me your song; it's good. We ran through it a few times with the boys, and it works well with her voice, even the words sound good. A nice thing about it is that it's a good melody and easy to play."

Patsy said, "I know that this is sudden, but we'd like to introduce it tonight, if it's all right with you?"

"You're kidding, right; I mean you're not serious?"

"I'm serious," she said.

"Patsy, there is no one in the entire world that I would want to introduce that song besides you. It's just that, I can't believe that it's true."

Dave smiled at him and said, "Believe me, if she says it she means it."

Glancing at his watch, he said, "Patsy, it's getting to be that time."

"Chris," Patsy said, "We're going back to my house after the show, and you should come along so we can work out how you get paid for your song; besides, it will be fun. Oh, and I had them hold that seat in the front row where I found you. That's as close as you can get without being on stage."

Chris started for the door to the dressing room when Patsy's voice stopped him. "Chris, there's no title on the music sheets. What do you call this song?"

Chris turned to her. He had never written the title, yet he knew exactly what it was. "It's called *If Only*."

HE WAS IN what he considered his seat next to a man dressed in, of all things, a full buckskin outfit down to the boots with a ten-gallon hat in his lap. The show flew by. Minutes went by in the space of seconds; funny, wonderful musical seconds. And then she was on stage.

He was aware that he was focused on her alone, as though she was there by herself. The music started, her voice singing a love ballad so easily, and everyone in the theater knew she was singing just to them.

"Thank you, ladies and gentlemen, thank you. We are going to do something that we very seldom do. Tonight we're going to introduce a brand new song that we just found today. It's by a very talented musician and composer that I know you will be hearing from over and over in the future. The song is called *If Only*."

She smiled at Chris as the music started then lifted her voice to his song. Chris listened with more than his ears. He was hearing the notes from her voice with his heart, his soul, his very being. She sang it as he knew she would, flowing from note to note, singing the words just as they were meant to be sung. Chris, with his eyes closed listened to the last note knowing within that, if he never wrote another thing, it wouldn't matter. This had been the culmination of all he had ever hoped for.

BUT ALL DREAMS must end. "Whaa, uhm, uh..."

"Chris, wake up. It's time for you to go."

The last note was still lingering in his ear. He didn't want to give it up. His eyes opened reluctantly to find Gabe looking down on him with a bemused smile on his face. He slowly turned his head to look around. He was where he had sat down, still on the bench next to the stage.

"Having a dream, were we?" Gabe asked.

"What makes you ask that?" Chris said.

"I have never seen a nicer smile on someone sleeping in all my days."

Chris knew he must have been smiling. How could he have been doing anything else? "It was some dream, Gabe. I was here with her. I actually played guitar for her and she sang my song and...and it was all special. I was afraid when I woke up that I might forget the dream, but now I know I never will."

"Well, it's time for me to go. People are arriving to put on tonight's show." He said this as they walked to the entrance to the theater. Chris walked out the front door, then turned and looked at Gabe.

"I want to thank you, Gabe, for letting me see the theater. I'll never forget today. Gabe, is that short for Gabriel?" Chris asked.

"That's right, Chris; it *is* short for Gabriel."

"Well, thanks again, Gabe."

"You're welcome," he paused, "ya know, Chris, it might not all have been a dream."

CHRIS FOUND HIMSELF back on the same bus bench that he had sat on that morning waiting for the Opry to open. He opened the guitar case and saw immediately that his music was gone; he must have dropped it in the theater. It was already getting dark and a little cold. He watched as people flooded into the Ryman Theater. How long he sat on the bench he didn't know. He saw a cab approaching, got up and waved it down.

"Where can I take you, my friend?" the cabbie asked.

"I need to find an inexpensive place to stay. It doesn't have to be cheap, but not the Ritz."

"I know just the place." The radio was on, tuned to a country station. Chris heard a song he liked. "Could you turn that up a little? That's a good song."

"Sure."

They listened to the end of the song.

"How about that music? This is Dan 'The Man' Martin on WCCM, which stands for country-country music. We have to say it twice 'cause that's all we play. Who wants to hear anything else anyway? OK folks, I have a rare and wonderful treat for everybody who ever loved country. A recording of the wonderful Patsy Cline lost for years, a song apparently recorded at an Opry appearance, has just been discovered. I know you're gonna love this one, folks, and remember you heard it for the first time anywhere on WCCM. It's titled *If Only*."

The Killing of Al Baloney

MY NAME IS STEVE. I'm just a kid. Not a real little kid, I'm nine, and I'm really scared. My dad is gonna kill a guy. His name is Al Baloney.

I don't know what else to do, so I'm writing it down so I won't forget. I'm so mixed up now that if I don't write it down, I'll never remember any of it right.

It all started last Friday night when my dad's friends, Phil and Charlie, came over for an early spring barbecue. It was cold, and the wind was blowing as they stood around the barbecue having a beer. They were kidding my dad about having a barbecue two months before spring really got here. Then they said it was time to do the thing, and this time they would use a heavier iron to do the job. I didn't know what they were talking about. The next thing I heard was Charlie saying, "This time, Steve, we don't want any excuses like last year. This time you gotta get Al Baloney."

My dad's name is Steve too. Why does he have to get this Baloney guy?

I NEVER HAVE any trouble sleeping, but that night I didn't sleep at all. I kept seeing my dad with a big iron in his hand raised above his head like he was gonna hit somebody. I couldn't see who it was 'cos I don't know who Al Baloney is. That has to be who he was gonna hit. I mean it is, isn't it? Heck, my dad likes just about everybody. I wonder why he hates Al Baloney so much that he would, you know, kill him.

OH BOY, OH boy, oh boy. Now what do I do? I mean, that night I had it figured out pretty good. The answer was right there in front of me. TELL MOM. But now I don't know what do, 'cos Saturday morning I heard Mom and Dad talking about it. "I gotta do it," Dad said, "This time I'm not gonna miss; this time I'll get Al Baloney or die trying." Then I heard Mom say, "You'll get 'em this time, don't worry."

YOU CAN SEE why I'm asking what should I do now. If my dad does what he says he's gonna do, he'll probably go to jail. I don't want him to go to jail. If he does, I'll probably never see him again. I love my dad. I don't want that to happen and what would happen to Mom? They love each other. She'd be lonely and have nobody but me. I'd try, but I don't think I could take care of us. Heck I don't even have a job. I'm in grammar school. There's gotta be an answer. Dad always says there is an answer for everything. I just gotta think some more.

I CAN'T THINK straight 'cos I'm so scared. Then last night Phil came by and said that Wednesday would be the perfect day for getting Al Baloney, and if Dad needed help he and Charlie would be right there. That means I only have three more days left. I think I'm going to go crazy if I can't find some way to stop my dad.

    I watched a movie last week where this guy killed another guy and they sent him to the big house. I don't want my dad going to the big house. I can't imagine where that is and, besides, I thought they sent you to prison. Maybe the big house is even worse.

    On Tuesday Phil said they are going to leave early in the morning. Maybe I can fix it so Dad's truck won't run, and then he couldn't do anything. I don't think that would work. Nope. Dad can fix anything; I heard Mom say so. I wish I was older maybe then I would know what to do.

    I finally got up the courage to ask my friend Petey. He's

eleven, and he laughed at me. He told me it was all my imagination, and that my dad wouldn't hurt anyone. But I know what I heard. Sometimes Petey isn't too bright.

BOY, THIS IS scary. I've never been up this late, it's almost two in the morning, and it's cold here in the garage. I know that if I'm going to do anything, it has to be now. It's Tuesday night, so it's now or never.

SHOOT, what do I do now? I can't get the hood open. How does Dad lift it so easy? Wait a minute! WOW, I've got it! I'll let some air out of his tire. I know you can't drive with a flat tire.

OK, that should be enough; the rim is almost down to the floor.

I'm really tired. I think I'll get in the back of the truck and rest for a few minutes, then I'll go back to my room.

STEVE SAID, "For crying out loud, Charlie, will you at least try to be quiet? My wife and kids are trying to sleep."

"Sorry, Steve, ya' gotta remember I don't have any of those, so noise at four in the morning at my house is no big deal."

"I know Charlie, but I'll bet your neighbors think it is."

Phil said, "Steve, if it doesn't bother Charlie, he doesn't think it should bother anyone."

"All right, all right, let's just get going, OK?"

They had put all their gear in the truck the day before, but Steve looked in to check on it. He thought he saw something that didn't belong under the tarp when Phil said, "Hey Steve! You know you have a flat tire?"

"What! I can't believe it! I would have noticed that when I put the gear in the truck. I'll be damned. I think I'll just put some air in it and see what happens."

The three men stood staring at the tire after Steve put the

air in it. They listened for any telltale hissing and watched for the decline of the rim. After ten minutes they decided it looked fine now.

Steve said, "OK gents, let's roll." He forgot about the lump under the tarp.

THEY MADE GOOD time driving up the coast and got to the point almost an hour before low tide. By the time they had their gear on, it would be good and light. Steve walked to the back of the truck and threw back the tarp. To the amazement of all three men, there was his son asleep in the pile of their gear.

"Why in the world did Stevie get in the back of the truck?" Steve asked.

"Maybe he thought it would be fun to come along," Charlie said.

"Or maybe he was sleep walking," Phil chimed in.

Steve shook his head. "Stevie would have asked if he wanted to come along."

"Well then, the only thing to do," Charlie said, "is ask him."

I CAME AWAKE with a start wondering why I wasn't in my own warm, comfortable bed. Then I remembered climbing into the back of Dad's truck. Oh golly, I'm in trouble, looking at the three men staring at me.

"You all right, Stevie?" Dad asked.

I was scared to death that Dad was gonna be real mad. "Yeah, Dad, I'm OK."

"What are you doing here?"

"I…umm…I don't want you to do it, Dad. I don't want you to kill anybody. I don't know what Al Baloney did to you, but I don't want you to kill him. I don't care what he did; you just can't do it. I didn't mean to listen when you and Charlie and Phil were talking, but I did and when I heard you talking about killing Al Baloney, I got really scared. But I didn't know what to do about it and then I fell asleep in your truck and …and that's why I'm here."

IN A MOMENT of clarity Steve realized what had happened. He remembered his son near the barbecue, and it was clear what he had overheard.

At that moment his friend Charlie said, "What are we gonna do with the kid?"

Steve didn't speak for a moment, then said, "He'll have to stay here. This has to get done." He looked at his son and said, "Stevie, you will stay in the back of the truck. You do not get out under any circumstances. DO YOU UNDERSTAND?"

I WAS SHIVERING and didn't think I could even talk. Dad looked at me again and said, "Do you understand?"

Somehow I managed to say, "Yes, Dad."

"Good, now lay down in the truck, wrap up in that blanket and get some sleep. We'll be back when this is over.'

Dad turned to Phil and Charlie. "I'll be back in a minute." He walked off around some of the big redwood trees and was back in a couple of minutes. "OK, let's get this done."

I watched as the three men picked up their gear and headed for the beach. I hope that Al Baloney didn't show up.

CHARLIE TURNED TO Steve. "Aren't you worried about Stevie being alone in the truck?"

"There is a woman in her car on the other side of the tree from where we're parked. I asked her to keep an eye on him; she said she would be happy to."

As the three men headed down to the beach, Steve explained

what he thought was going on. He knew that little Stevie had overheard them talking about getting 'Al Baloney,' and had jumped to the conclusion that they were going to kill someone.

I MUST HAVE fallen asleep because the next thing I knew I woke up as Dad, Charlie and Phil got back to the truck. They were dragging a really big black garbage bag; it looked heavy.

"Dad…is…is that him?"

Dad looked at me and didn't say anything. He nodded at Charlie, "Show him."

I turned away. I couldn't look.

"Stevie, you wanted to know what this was about; now turn around and look."

I turned around in time to see Charlie lift one end of the bag. I couldn't believe my eyes when all these weird looking shells tumbled on to the ground.

"What's that?" I stammered.

"That's Al Baloney," Dad said.

I couldn't say anything; I just stared at the pile of shells.

Dad came over to the truck and picked me up in his strong arms.

"Stevie, that's abalone, not Al Baloney. When you overheard what we said at the barbecue, you should have just asked me what it was about. Instead you got all worried and upset thinking I was going to do something terrible. If you ever think that I'm going to do something I shouldn't because of something you overhear, please just ask me to tell you what's going on, and I promise I will. OK?"

I still couldn't talk, so I just nodded my head.

Dad, Charlie and Phil put the abalone back in the bag. They talked about what a good day it had been and how calm the ocean was today. I listened to all of it until I fell asleep leaning against my dad.

We were almost home when I woke up. I felt better than I had in a couple of weeks. It just seemed, you know, easier to breathe.

We were pulling into the driveway at the house, and I saw Mom waiting in the driveway with a worried look on her face. I knew it was because of me. It would have been worse if Dad hadn't called to tell her everything was OK.

I turned in the seat and looked up at my dad as the truck came to a stop in the driveway.

"Dad?"

"What, Stevie?"

"I knew you wouldn't do anything bad."

"Thank you, son, that means a lot."

Eighty Years

A SLIGHT GROAN escaped his lips as he swung his legs over the side of the bed. He sat for a moment with his left hand out behind him until he felt comfortable, then he slowly pushed himself to his feet. He turned to look at the girl who was still asleep in his bed. Even after all these years he still thought of her as a girl. His girl.

His first few steps were a little uncertain. He reached the kitchen, turned on the water for his instant coffee, pulled the bread out of the cupboard and started putting the light breakfast together; the same one that he had been eating for years. Today was a big day, and he wanted to enjoy all of it, start to finish.

He took his breakfast outside to sit at the table on the back porch with its wonderful view of the mountains.

He ate his grapefruit sections slowly, enjoying the half bitter taste they made in his mouth. He mixed it with the cinnamon toast and washed it down with coffee. He wondered if a nutritionist would approve of his breakfast.

HIS APPEARANCE BELIED his age. He still walked at a decent gait with a good stride and, much to his delight, there was still a little color in his hair, which he wore short. When people looked closely they could see the many lines in his face. He liked to think the lines came from laughing and smiling too much. Around the house he did all the little things that needed doing, but for any heavy stuff, he had his neighbor Jim come over and take care of.

He was an interesting person because he was an interested person. He still read a great deal, from newspapers to novels to biographies, to almost anything he found at hand. This had become easier when he finally admitted that he needed reading glasses, but he decided they made him look distinguished and not necessarily old.

He sat back in the chair, holding his coffee cup with both hands, and enjoyed the warmth the cup gave his fingers. The sun was just beginning to paint the mountains with the light pink orange color telling anyone who rose early that another day was just beginning. This, he decided, was going to be a beautiful day.

SHE ROLLED OVER in bed to find him gone which was no surprise at all. When he retired she thought that they would spend some mornings in bed together. It turned out to be seldom, very seldom indeed. He ran on an altogether different clock than anyone she knew, and it wasn't remotely in tune with hers. At times she wished it was.

The thought of getting up crossed her mind, and she let it slide away. The bed felt very comfortable, and she couldn't remember any reason she had for getting up. There probably was one, but remembering things lately had become more and more difficult.

She had no doubt that he was out on the back porch. No one she knew liked to watch the sunrise the way he did. He told her that their back porch was the perfect place to watch the sunrise. It faced due east, and they lived on a small knoll that got them just high enough to see over the valley and the town below. He said it was like watching one of those giant movie screens. He swore that sometimes the rays of the sun touched him before the sun came over the mountains. He didn't know how that could happen, but he swore it did.

She rearranged the covers, letting herself sink deeper into the comfort of the bed, half mad that she was awake and madder still knowing she wouldn't go back to sleep.

The last few years it had become one of her small pleasures to stay in bed for a while when she felt like it. It wasn't that she needed the rest; Lord knows she didn't do that much these days. It was more because she could, and it brought her a conspiratorial pleasure; even if the conspiracy involved just one person—her.

She grabbed his pillow and put it behind her head, then slowly pushed herself up to a sitting position. Reaching behind her she pulled a book off the shelf, deciding that a little reading before she got up would start the day off nicely. Her choice in reading more than any other was a good mystery, a real who-done-it.

Halfway through the chapter, a line in the book reminded her that there was a reason to get up and get going today; it was her anniversary.

They hadn't really planned anything for the day though he had promised that he would make her favorite dinner. This was a day more to think about all the wonderful years and the delightful things they had done together, and their children. A slight expression of pain crossed her face at the thought of the children. She shook her head and let it go. Carefully she sat up, letting her legs go over the side of the bed. Her walker, which she hated, stood sentinel at the edge of her reach. She could damn well walk without it, but he insisted she use it after she fell a few months ago. If she didn't, he would nag her until, in frustration, she gave in.

The shower felt wonderful. The water was just the right temperature as it ran on her back and shoulders. She looked forward to her morning shower and was so happy that she didn't need help, as so many of her friends did. Today she would dress a little nicer than most days. After all, it was a special day.

"You gonna be in there all morning?" His voice startled her.

"I'll be out in a few minutes, don't rush me."

"If I didn't say something, you'd stay in there half an hour."

"Just for that, I'll stay in a little longer."

"Oh, brother," she heard him say as he closed the bathroom door.

HE MADE HIS way to the kitchen and put the kettle on again. He got another mug and put decaf instant in it—for her, caffeine was a no-no. He did most of the cooking in the house as he enjoyed it, and she didn't. Most mornings he would cook her a light breakfast of eggs and toast, even though the doctor told her that the eggs were not really a good idea.

In no uncertain terms she explained to the doctor that, at her age, it was pretty silly to start worrying about it. The doctor just smiled and shook his head. He knew a losing battle when he faced one.

He heard her behind him and turned. "My goodness, don't you look nice!"

"Why, thank you sir. It's very nice of you to say."

She had on a pair of Levis and a nice white sweater with a small bright red bandana tied in the back of her hair. She put silverware on the table along with a napkin, and took the salt and pepper from the cupboard.

"Are you going to join me for anything?"

"I think I'll have another piece of toast. The first one tasted good. You should have joined me earlier. The sunrise was spectacular."

"You know you always say that. I swear you do sometimes even when it's foggy."

"Perhaps." A thought worked its way across his face. "I guess it isn't so much just the sunrise I like; I think maybe it's just that it's a new day, a new beginning, you know, a new start. The beauty of it is you never know at the beginning what that day is going to bring."

A LITTLE LATER, "My goodness it's ten o'clock. Do you have to shop for dinner?"

"No, my dear. I shopped yesterday."

The fact that he was still driving amazed him and most everyone he knew. Every year the DMV made him take a written test, an eye test and even a driving test; every year he passed them. He had spent some of his younger years driving for a living, which he had truly enjoyed. He always thought that this was the reason he still drove well enough to pass the tests.

"You have anything you want to do today?" he asked.

She knew by the tone of his voice and the way the question was asked that if she didn't, he definitely did. "No, not really, why?"

"Well, it is a kind of special day you know."

"You're right. I think earlier, when I was in bed, I was feeling a little down. I thought about today and our reason for a little celebration, and then thought of the kids. It made me feel a little maudlin. What did you have in mind?"

"I thought we would take a little drive. Have a look at how much the world we grew up in has changed."

She smiled to herself in wonder that, at this age, he still wanted to know and see what was going on in the world.

"That sounds lovely. What time?"

"Let's say one o'clock, okay?'

"Fine."

HE WAS SURPRISED when she said, "The car seems to be running well."

He glanced at her briefly. He knew she didn't know an engine from a motor. "Yes, it does. That kid Craig at the garage is a good mechanic."

They were on their way to wherever the drive took them. He told her it was one of those days when you should let your heart lead the way.

"My, aren't you poetic today?" she replied.

He had taken the road that went around the backroads as he didn't feel like driving in any traffic if he could avoid it. They had both been born in the small town where they still lived and had, except for a few occasions, spent their entire lives there.

Their children had also spent their lives here, though both son and daughter were now deceased. Their son died in World War II on an island called Kwajalein while serving in the Marines. Their daughter Joan had died just two years ago from ovarian cancer. The loss of their son had been hard; the loss of their daughter, terrible.

They didn't know as many people in town as they once did, with old friends leaving or dying and new younger people moving in. In truth they had outlived most all the friends that they had grown up with.

THEY DROVE IN comfortable silence, not needing any conversation to interrupt as they watched the countryside drift by.

"Well, will you look at that?" he said.

"What?"

"The old Samson place, someone's torn half of it down."

"Marie, that's my hair dresser, told me some rich stockbroker type bought it and is going to completely redo the place. Make it as nice as it was years ago. Remember how nice it was?"

"Yeah, now that you mention it, it was getting pretty run-down. Should be a nice improvement for the whole town."

They came around a small hill, and the lake came into view. The lake was a place they knew well, and it had played a large part in their lives. It was where they had met all those years ago. It was also the place that he had chosen to propose to her.

"You know you're nothing but an old sentimental fool... thank you."

To her, the smile on his face was as sharp and attractive as the day she had met him when he was seventeen. Then, the smile was because he was attracted to her. *Now*, she thought, *it might be because he was still attracted to her.*

HE PULLED THE car up to an overlook at the south end of the lake and got out of the car without speaking. She heard him open the trunk, and then he was at her door opening it for her. In his right hand was a small picnic basket.

"Hungry?"

"When in the world did you have time to pack a basket?"

"While you were being lazy, lounging around in bed."

"I'll have you know I was not lazing around. I was contemplating the day."

"I see. Well, let's go sit at the bench and have a little lunch. I'm hungry."

"Me, too."

There was light-heartedness about her as she took the lunch out of the basket and spread it on the table. First the tablecloth and silverware, then one by one, all the things she loved at a picnic, right down to the fried chicken and the Greek olives.

She couldn't help thinking that one was never sure when they fell in love that it was going to be the kind of love to last a lifetime. There just wasn't any way to be sure; yet when he got down on his knee at this very spot and told her that if she would be his wife, he would love and care for the rest of their lives, somehow she knew. She just knew.

"So, who put the basket together for you?"

"I'll have you know I did it all by myself."

"John?"

"Okay, Sue; I might have had a little help. Jennie across the street provided the chicken and the potato salad and the rolls… and the chips and dip, but I did the olives, the wine and put the basket together."

They ate in quiet companionship, slowly, savoring the good food, being together and enjoying the memories that this place always brought to them. The ospreys were sailing high over the lake, majestic in the silence of their flight. He was amazed for the hundredth time when one folded its wings and plunged into the water, rising again with a fish in its talons. He turned and looked at his girl. "The day would not have been complete without coming here."

She didn't give him an answer, and he had expected none. To anyone watching, they would have been two old people having a picnic together, but at this moment neither one of them felt the least bit old. As if by mutual consent, they both moved at the same time to start cleaning up their picnic. They had stayed longer than he had planned and, after all, he still had a fine dinner to fix. However, before that there was one more place they had to go. After everything was packed, they walked to the car at a leisurely pace.

"I wondered if you would bring me here today."

"I have been kinda planning this day for a while. It didn't seem proper to have our day and not come by here. You have to admit that this place has been good to us."

"Umm, yes. This is another one of the spots that has been important in our lives."

He looked at her again with the same smile that seemed to have been on his face all day.

"How well do you remember our first anniversary?"

HER MIND WENT back to their first house not far from where they were now. She had been in a terrible mood that day and didn't know why. When he came home it was obvious that he was in no better mood than she. They barely talked and after they had a couple of drinks, the bad moods seem to deepen. What exactly started the fight she didn't remember, and, when they had talked about it later, he said he didn't either. But fight they did, yelling at each other, then screaming at each other until she could take it no longer. She fled from the house and just ran down the road until she came here.

It was a small bridge over a small creek. You could see for a half mile down the river's tumbling length until it made a soft turn and disappeared. She couldn't remember how long she stood at its rail listening to the creek below, the anger passing out of her as the water passed under the bridge.

She was aware that he was there before she saw him or heard his voice.

"You come here often?"

"Sometimes…I call it my wishing bridge. Silly, isn't it."

"What were you wishing for now?"

"That we never have another fight like that."

"I like that wish. Think it will help if I wish that too?"

"Couldn't hurt."

He walked up beside her, but made sure they didn't touch.

"Did you make the wish?" she said.

"Yep, and I added something to it.'

"Really!"

"Yep, I wished that you would forgive me for being such an asshole."

She nodded her head. "You're no bigger an asshole than I am."

She turned and took his face in both her hands and gave

him a kiss that he remembered to this day.

That first time wasn't the only time they had come to the bridge after an argument, but there never was an argument quite as bad as that first one. It was a place that they found helped them work things out. It somehow eased them out of whatever the argument was.

"Oh, yes, I remember…I'm getting a little cold. Shouldn't we be heading home?"

"At your service, young lady," he said as he escorted her into the car.

THIS TIME HE took the road that led them through the heart of their town. They thought of it that way, with both of them having been born and raised here. He knew that in the early afternoon the traffic was usually not too bad. Most of the streets were tree-lined with some almost covered side to side with branches, like driving through a living canopy.

The street that they had followed into town came to an end at the town square. He was right about the traffic. There were few cars and even fewer people to be seen on the sidewalks. They drove to the right in order to go round the square, taking a left at the next corner. On the right was the old El Camino Theatre. Built in the late twenties, its architecture was very dated and still as pretty as the day it opened.

As they passed, Sue glanced at the billboard. "Now, what in the world is that all about?"

"What?"

"The billboard."

"New picture?"

"No, it's not for a new picture. You had something to do with this, didn't you?" she said accusingly.

"Now, Sue. What are you talking about?"

"It says, 'Sue owes John a dollar.' Now, what is that all about?"

"I knew you'd forget."

"John, pardon my French, but what the hell are you talking about? And how did you get Jerry to put that up on the billboard?"

"Jerry was easy. I told him I wouldn't do anymore electrical work for him."

"You haven't done any work for him in ten years."

"Well, actually he volunteered. And as far as the bet goes, I knew you would forget, what with your memory and all these days."

"John, if you don't tell me what in the world you're talking about, I think I'm going to get very mad."

"Today's our anniversary, right?"

"Yes, yes, today is our anniversary."

"Do you remember this day forty years ago?"

Thinking, she very slowly said, "Yes."

"Joanie had that wonderful party for us at her house with just about all our friends joining us with a marvelous barbeque and too much to drink and eat. Then we rolled the rug out of the living room and danced till everybody finally gave up and went home."

"Yes, I remember all that."

"Good. Well, on the way home we were talking about how wonderful the day had been. How lucky we were with family and friends and the good fortune we had for all those years. I said, 'Wouldn't it be wonderful to celebrate again in forty years?' and you said, 'There wasn't much chance that would ever happen.' So I say to you now what I said to you then. 'I'll bet you a dollar that we do' and you said that you wouldn't have to worry about paying off that bet. Well, well, guess who owes John a dollar?"

THE MEMORY OF that conversation came flooding back as he

finished speaking. At the time she had been amused at his optimism, thinking the whole world was his oyster and time for them would go on and on.

They drove along for a while, while she thought about the years gone by—the memories rich and caressing. He was doing much the same, only he was thinking about the years to come.

When they drove up to the house they noticed a note tacked to the front door. Sue took the note off the door and started to read it as she walked into the house.

"It's from Mike and Peggy." She read out loud, "Dear Grandma and Grandpa: Don't know what you were up to today, but we brought you dinner so you wouldn't have to cook on this special day. The food is in the oven, and the wine is in the fridge. If you feel like company, please give us a call."

Sue spoke as she opened the oven; "Now wasn't that nice of them? Peggy is so much like Joanie, and she couldn't have been luckier than when she found Mike.

"John, will you look at this! There is enough food in this oven to feed an army."

She opened the fridge. "There are five bottles of wine in here! John, why don't you give them a call?"

The smile on John's face was exuberant. "Get the feeling they were planning to have dinner with us?"

John dialed the phone, and Peggy answered immediately.

"Hi, sweetheart…No, we're fine, we just went out for a ride… Yes, we would love to have company; there is enough food here, according to Sue, for half the town…Okay.

"She said they would be here in a couple minutes."

When they pulled up to the house, the two of them had been too lost in memories to notice all the cars parked on the street. Now John looked out the front window to see what looked like half the town coming to his front door, led by Mike and

Peggy.

THE PARTY WAS momentous to say the least, and all those who showed up didn't stay too late in deference to their hosts' age. All of them knew that it was very unlikely they would ever attend another eightieth anniversary party.

When all the guests were gone, and they made sure everything was cleaned up, John and Sue went into the living room and sat on the couch.

"What a day!" she said.

"Amen to that."

"Are you tired, John?"

"I think I'm too excited to be tired. How about you?"

"The same."

They sat for a while, her hand held lightly in his. It was bedtime and they both knew that they should be in bed, yet neither wanted to give up the day. He was ninety-seven and she was ninety-five, and for this moment they were very young.

"You know you never did pay me the dollar you owe me."

There was a smile on her face as mischievous as he could ever remember seeing.

"Maybe you can take it out in trade?"

Indecision

SHE WALKED SLOWLY down the tree-covered trail, her head bent over her chest and her body shaking slowly from her sobs. Her feet followed one another as if with a mind of their own. She stumbled yet was unaware that she almost fell down. It was getting cold on the mountain; she didn't notice. When she left the city she had had no destination in mind; it was as if the car found its own way here.

A small tree branch hit her on the forehead and, for the first time in the last hundred yards, she looked at her surroundings. She was on a part of the trail that was completely covered over by branches with thick brush blotting out any view off the trail; it was like being in a cocoon. It was also cold and damp. *This is the kind of gloomy place I belong*, she thought. *Cold, damp, almost dark, miserable, just like me.* In better times this mountain was one of her favorite places to be; she loved the clean air and the strength it seemed to give her when she came to hike.

A small, harsh, choking sound ripped from her lips as once again she started to sob. Her head was down as she stumbled further along, finally bumping into a rock and sitting down. She was barely aware of the pistol that hung from the fingers of her right hand. She was so tired. She leaned back against the rock and closed her eyes. It didn't matter that she was tired; nothing mattered. She put her cold hands in her lap and looked at the pistol. She snorted a derisive laugh. How appropriate that he had bought her the pistol, for protection he had said. The only protection she needed was from him and his cheating ways.

She suddenly sat up, startled and not at all sure where she was. Her head moved in jerky movements as she looked around.

Must have fallen asleep, she thought, *so tired. He isn't worth it; he isn't worth anything.* Yet she knew that made her worth less than anything. Stupid, it was all so stupid. Getting off work early and flying home in anticipation of surprising him. They hadn't even gone to the bedroom; they were grunting and humping on the couch, not even aware of her coming through the door. She stood frozen, unable to go any further into the room, unable to leave, unable to speak until the scream pushed out of her mouth. She saw their heads swivel toward her, the quick look of guilt crossing their faces. Her fiancé and her good friend. She remembered no more. The next thing she knew she was on the mountain walking down the trail with the gun from her glove compartment somehow in her hand; her life over.

SHE WAS AWARE that suicide was a stupid thing. She had never been able to rationalize what would make people take their own life. She could now. The scene in the living room started to push its way back into her mind. She forced it out of her thoughts. She wanted nothing in her mind, no thought, no reason, nothing…nothing.

She looked at the pistol. She knew it was time. The tears were still coming from her eyes as if there were no end to the supply. Angrily she wiped her cheeks with her arm, again thinking he wasn't worth it. Curiously she looked at the gun. It looked harmless, so small. She took a long, deep breath and raised the gun to the side of her head.

"Are you going to do that here?"

She was so startled by the voice that she almost fired the gun. If the trigger had been easier to pull, she would have been dead on the spot. Her head whirled around trying to look everywhere at the same time. She saw nothing but the trees and the bushes. Had she imagined it? Was her mind playing tricks on her? Slowly this time she carefully looked at her surroundings. He was standing in the shadow about twenty yards away. His clothes blended well with the surroundings. She could tell he was tall, but in the shadows and the gloom she couldn't determine his features.

"Don't come near me."

"Lady, I'm not getting anywhere near a woman with a gun in her hand. I just thought if you were going to do what you looked like you were going to do, it would be better if you did it somewhere else."

"You're not going to try and stop me?"

"Lady, I could care less what you do, but this is my favorite place to come to think, work out problems. If you blow yourself away here, the place will get all messed up. I mean with the coroner's wagon and the clean-up crew, forensics, not to mention nine million cops and rangers, it would take years for the place to recover."

"I don't care about any of that."

"Yeah, I suppose you don't…Uh, well I'd sure appreciate it if you take a moment to give it some thought."

"I don't have a moment, my life is over." In the back of her mind, crazily, the thought of moving somewhere else was stirring.

"Okay if you must, I guess you must. Will you wait just a couple of minutes though? I want to move up the trail a little ways so I don't have to watch."

"Don't leave." She didn't know why she said that, yet for some obscure reason it was important now that he stay.

She looked up at him. He was standing there on one leg with the other resting against a tree. He wasn't moving nor did he say anything; he just stood there gazing at her with an odd expression on his face.

"So is he worth it?"

"You don't know anything about it!" She almost screamed.

Again he was silent.

"You knew the girl he was with, didn't you?"

It felt like he had hit her in the chest. "Shut up, just shut up."

She looked down into her lap; the gun was still in her hand. *Why am I talking with him? I need to end this.* She started to raise the gun. She glanced at him and could see that he had still not moved; he wasn't going to try and stop her.

"Well, did you give it some thought?"

"What?"

"Moving away. Not messing up this nice place."

"Go to hell."

"Will you be there waiting for me? I hear that people that kill themselves go there."

Suddenly she was sure she didn't want to go to hell, the thought almost abstract. What difference did it make? She was already in hell.

"Mind if I come over there and sit down?"

"You stay away from me."

"Mind if I sit on that log across the trail from you?"

"I don't care what you do. I thought you wanted to leave so you wouldn't have to watch?"

"I thought so, but I now realize that I have a morbid curiosity. I never have seen anyone die up close."

"You're sick."

"Maybe so, maybe so. There is one other thing. They say that suicide is always messy, so maybe I could clean you up a bit. Then it won't look so terrible when they find you. That's always hard on the family."

He said this as he slowly crossed over to the log directly across from her and sat down.

"Nobody will care."

She knew it for the lie that it was when she said it. This would just about kill her mother.

"They'll care; nobody raises someone without caring. Family always cares."

THEY SAT THERE across from one another without speaking for some minutes. He had an expression of exasperation on his face, yet there was a kindness in his eyes. She couldn't think clearly; her mind was bouncing from thoughts of her family to the scene in the apartment to the pistol in her hand. She didn't want to think anymore at all.

"Not as easy as you thought?"

Her head was again hanging down with her chin almost against her chest, and the tears were once again falling in her lap. The strangled "No" that escaped her lips was barely audible.

"You could change your mind, you know."

"Nothing...there's nothing." Her voice was just a whisper.

"There's always something. Once I was going to do this. Somehow something worked its way into my head that I was being really, really stupid, so I didn't. Don't mind being stupid sometimes, but really, really stupid, that bothered me."

Again they sat in silence. He watched her patiently, fully aware of what was at stake. Her body was shaking less as the sobs and the tears began to subside, yet her head was still down, and she seemed to be transfixed by the gun she held.

"Why aren't you trying to stop me?"

He breathed a sigh of relief. The moment was past; she was coming back. "No point; if you really want to kill yourself, and I stop you now, you'll just find some other way to do it later. Now can we move down the trail? I really don't want you to mess this place up."

The laugh that escaped her lips was a little hysterical, but he thought it was the nicest sound he had ever heard. "Will you stop it about this place?" she said.

He laughed too as he walked across to where she sat on the rock and very gently took the gun from her hand. He slid it into his jacket pocket. She didn't notice.

He made no moves; just stood there in front of her waiting. Her breathing slowed down, the ragged sounds of her crying all but gone. Still he waited. Finally she lifted her head and looked up at him the expression on her face of pure pain. He reached slowly and gently, putting his hands on her shoulders and helping her to stand up. He enfolded her in his arms, and they stood together that way.

She was still very tense. He waited. Slowly, ever so slowly, he began to rock her back and forth. Time did a slow step. Then almost imperceptibly she began to relax, until she was leaning against him, trusting him.

"I think it's time we left here, don't you?"

"I guess so."

"What's your name?" he asked, as he slowly started to walk her down the trail.

"Candi."

"See, I knew you were sweet."

She laughed in spite of herself. She'd heard the line a thousand times before.

"What's your name?"

"Pete."

"What do you do, Pete?"

"I'm the local police chief around here."

He felt her body tense as her shoulders lifted a little.

"Am I in trouble?"

Pete smiled at her. "Not from me."

She looked into his kind face and nodded thoughtfully. They slowly continued down the trail.

The Meter Maid

HE JUST CAME around from the back of the shop where he had been for half an hour. Just in time to see her pull away and see the parking ticket on the windshield of a customer's car.

"Damn, damn and double damn."

He walked across the street and pulled the ticket out from under the wiper blade. Then he made his way down the block pulling another five tickets off the windshields of other customers' cars and finally the one off his own truck.

That b... The thought went unfinished. No sense getting mad at someone for doing their job, but it would sure be nice to know when she was coming down his street. As far as he could tell, it was a completely random schedule. He had seen her on just about every day of the week. The problem was it was sometimes a week apart, sometimes two weeks, and sometimes only once a month.

Fortunately, for him, he had gotten in the habit of looking for her chalk marks on the tires and had, on a lot of occasions, told his customers to move the cars before she came back to apply the tickets.

It had also come to his attention that she was blond and, having seen her out of her buggy, that she was quite attractive.

He would just have to be more observant.

THREE WEEKS LATER she got him again. This time there were seven tickets. He didn't even bother to swear. He had a small notebook on his desk that he had been using to keep track of the number of tickets and how much they were costing he and his customers. Twenty seven tickets to date totaling two hundred and seventy dollars, and it was only the middle of June. It was a good thing the tickets were only ten dollars apiece and not thirty or forty like San Francisco.

Another two weeks passed before he saw her again. He couldn't believe that every time he managed to see her, she was just finishing instead of being in the middle of her ticket writing so he could go and talk to her.

He thought, *Yeah that's brilliant. What the hell would you say to her anyway?*

Something wonderful like, 'It's not fair.' Oh yeah, that would impress her. He was sure that swearing at her would come to nothing but bad, and besides, he was sure she got a lot of that on a regular basis.

Maybe he would just ask her to let him know somehow when she came by. *Oh sure.* Her job was to write tickets, making revenue for the city and probably keeping her job. That would be a great thing to ask her.

Quit worrying about it, he told himself, *It is what it is; just get on with it.*

THEN, TO HIS amazement, it happened. He looked up from the bench, and there she was just putting a ticket on a customer's car. She moved to his truck at the same time he started across the street. What he was going to say he still had no clue.

He walked past her onto the sidewalk, turned around, folded his arms and just stared at her; he was tongue-tied.

She looked up at him a couple of times with, if not nervousness at least apprehension, but said nothing. She finished the ticket and put it under the wiper of the truck.

He found his voice. "It's not fair, you know."

He could see her shoulders sag in resignation for the harangue she knew was coming, "What's not fair?"

He smiled, "For a cop to have legs like yours."

He didn't wait for a reply; just walked back across the street and into his shop. He watched as she drove away.

He never spoke to her again. However, that being said, he smiled every time she came by. She always beeped her horn to let him know she was passing down the street.

The Key Bench

DESPONDENT. THAT'S WHAT her best friend Patty had told her she was, as if she needed anyone to tell her. What had happened to her world? A week ago everything had been wonderful. Life was a great big cake, and she had the biggest slice and now there was nothing, just…emptiness.

The man she loved had just told her that there was someone else, nothing more, not even how it had happened, nothing. Somehow she had managed to get through the week until this morning when she had been passed over for the promotion that she knew should be hers. Patty, her best friend and confidant, had taken her to a neighborhood bar, and they had a few drinks while they gave the wrongs in this world a good working over.

She felt a little better until she arrived home and saw his picture still sitting on the piano, and once again her world collapsed. She didn't even feel better when she threw the offending picture in the trash.

The Vicodin she took when she went to bed along with the drinks had let her sleep fitfully through the night until the light of the morning pulled her back to a reality she didn't want to face. She rolled her legs off the bed and sat with her face in her hands, not wanting to get on with the day and too tired to stay in bed. The nightstand at the side of the bed was covered with unfinished work that she just didn't care about anymore. She looked at the bottle of Vicodin sitting there. *Why not?* she thought, *there were enough pills to do the job. Her life was over anyway, wasn't it?*

The idea took hold and, by the time she finished her coffee, it seemed the only way out.

SHE WOULD HAVE to leave a note. She couldn't desert the people she loved without giving them a reason. The idea was gaining momentum in her mind. *What the hell! If you have nothing to live for, why live?*

Slowly she rose on unsteady feet and made her way into the living room that also served as her office. She sat at the computer to write her note of goodbye. In some strange way, the thought of it made her calm and almost relaxed, as though it were a perfectly natural thing to do. She had nearly finished the note when there was a knock on the door. She decided to ignore it. She wanted nothing to do with anyone or anything at all. The knock came again, louder. She sat still.

This time it wasn't a knock. Someone was banging on the door insistently like they were not going away.

"Oh, God." She pushed off the chair and moved to the door. Through the peephole she could see it was a deliveryman of some kind with a hand truck. Resenting the intrusion, she opened the door ready to blast him.

"Hi, I was beginning to think you weren't home, and I wasn't looking forward to lugging this thing around anymore. You tell me where you want it, and I'll put it there. It's kind of heavy."

She stared at him blankly, not really comprehending what he had said.

"Uh, ma'am, where would you like me to put this? Like I said, it's kind of heavy."

"Uh, uhm, what is it?"

"Ma'am, I haven't the faintest idea. I can tell you that it's from somewhere in Idaho."

Idaho broke through the storm in her brain. It was still her favorite place in the world.

"Just set it in the living room."

The deliveryman put the large box in the middle of the room

and pulled the hand truck out from under it, then handed her a clipboard to sign. She signed and returned it. He thanked her and started to leave, then he stopped and said, "Would you like me to help you open that? It would only take a minute."

She looked at him still with a blank expression, then said slowly, "No, no thanks, I can manage."

He gave her a funny smile, then turned and left. She sat on the couch and stared at the big box taking up a large part of her living room, and wondered absently what was in it.

What does it matter? she thought, *I won't be around to care.* The soft couch was making her sleepy again. She pushed herself to her feet and went back to the computer. She finished her note, then read it and decided it sounded okay. For reasons she didn't understand, she felt compelled to take a shower before she took the pills and went back to bed. She had a vision of how she would be found and what people would say, but she let it slide from her mind. It didn't matter; nothing mattered.

The shower refreshed her, making her thinking sharper, yet she still clung to the thought that there was nothing, nothing to live for. She put on her favorite nightgown and sat on the edge of the bed ready to take the bottle of pills. As she reached for the bottle, the big box in the living room caught her gaze. Her hand fell back to her side. She hadn't even looked to see who it was from. It could only be from a few people she knew in Idaho. She might as well see who sent it.

The name on the box was a name she had never seen before nor was the address familiar. She wanted to get on with what she had decided to do, and the box didn't matter. Instead, she found herself going to the kitchen for a knife to open the box. Curiosity is a terrible thing.

It took ten minutes of cutting, pulling and ripping to get the cardboard box open. Inside was a lumpy-looking thing, wrapped in styrofoam.

She hesitated for the smallest moment then pulled the styrofoam apart. *Oh, my God. It couldn't be. It just couldn't be. How? Why?*

She felt her knees buckle as she touched it and slowly sank onto the carpet. The tears that came unbidden from her eyes covered her cheeks. She could barely see. It was the key bench from her grandmother's front porch. This didn't make any sense. Her grandma had died two years ago. When grandma died, it left her feeling completely alone in the world. Desolate.

SHE WAS A young child when her parents were killed, so she was shipped off to her mother's sister, twenty years older than her mother. The aunt was, in reality, not able to care for her. Unfortunately, the aunt was the only family she had except for her grandmother who everyone thought was a little 'over the edge', not to mention a little strange. On top of that, her grandmother lived in, according to her aunt, 'God-awful Idaho.' But, to the little girl who felt abandoned by the whole world, that sounded wonderful.

Her aunt had never married and never wanted children. She tried for a year to take care of her niece. When she realized that she couldn't do it, she reached out to the vilified grandma to come get the little girl. It just wasn't working out, and it seemed to her that she and her niece just couldn't talk to each other. Grandma agreed.

On a cold day with a brisk wind and bright sun, she was put on a train in the care of a kind conductor, headed for Idaho. The train trip took two days. She knew the name of the town and, looking out the window, she saw it flash by on a signpost just as the train started to slow. The conductor walked her off the train, but her grandma was nowhere in sight. Instead, the conductor introduced her to a man named Earl, who said that her grandma was waiting for her, and he would take her to her house. That was how she found herself in Emmet, Idaho.

IT WAS A short drive to the house where her grandma lived; after all, it was a small town. They stopped in front of a rickety picket fence in need of paint, and no gate at the entrance. Without a word Earl handed over her small suitcase, then got in his car and drove away. Bewildered, she turned toward the house. On the porch an old woman stood waiting. The woman had a severe, unsmiling countenance. Slowly, now somewhat terrified, she walked up the path and up the stairs onto the porch. The old woman said nothing. Holding down the rising panic she felt, she stood still while the old woman looked her over.

THE SMILE THAT spread over the old woman's face made her look almost young. "My goodness, you are every bit your momma, but prettier." The old woman knelt down and embraced the tiny girl with a warmth that she could barely remember from her mother's arms. "Now, come over here with me, and we'll sit down and talk."

Her grandma led her to an old bench that sat in one corner of the large porch. Alongside it, a small table held a shimmering pitcher of lemonade and a huge red plate heaped with sugar-dusted cookies. She sat quietly on the bench waiting for her grandma to say something, her hands in her lap. When she was with Auntie, she had to wait to be told before she could have something off the plate.

"My goodness, girl, aren't you hungry or thirsty?" Grandma asked.

"Yes, ma'am."

"Well, then help yourself to the cookies, and I'll pour you some lemonade."

- - - - THE KEY BENCH - - - -

She reached out and took just one cookie off the plate as her grandma handed her a glass of lemonade. "Thank you, Grandma."

Grandma smiled at the little girl, understanding the reticence she showed in taking what she thought was too much.

"Now girl, you have to understand the rules here."

The girl solemnly shook her head. She had heard this before.

"There are no real rules here. I expect you to show me respect, and I will do the same for you. I have no secrets that I can think of to keep from you, and I would hope that you won't keep any from me. We are family, you and I, and that's important. You can call me Grandma or Granny or even Alice if you like. Now tell me about your train trip."

And she did.

IT WAS THE beginning of a time that made her whole again. All the fragments of her life were drawn back together with the simple, unqualified love of her grandma. She would more often than not come home to find her grandma sitting on the bench in the corner of the porch waiting for her, so she could tell her about her day.

After her first day of school when she joined her on the bench, Grandma showed her a little hook on the back of the bench from which hung a key. Someone had attached it to one of the slats that ran across the back of the bench just for the key to the house; a key to get in when grandma wasn't home. The girl thought that person was very clever.

NOW, AS SHE gazed at the bench, she forced herself off her knees, still in wonderment of how this could be happening. She slowly unwrapped the rest of the bench, gathered the cardboard and styrofoam and carried it out front to the garbage can.

Back inside the house, she willed her heart to stop beating so wildly. She walked gingerly over to the bench and sat down. Instantly, she was a little girl again just home from school, telling her grandma how good she did on the spelling test and feeling wonderful when she saw her grandma smile with pride.

She had been sitting rigidly on the front edge of the bench, then, as she relaxed, she slid back and rested against the cross rails. Caressingly she ran her hands over the bench, feeling the memories flow through a part of her that she thought was gone completely.

One particular memory popped into her consciousness; she smiled and then laughed out loud. She had come home from school one day to find her grandma waiting for her on the bench. She had asked, "Grandma, how come you like sitting on this old bench so much?"

"'Cause it fits my butt just right," Grandma had told her, smiling.

SHE SQUIRMED AROUND on the bench and found that it did indeed fit her butt just right.

Other memories began to bounce around in her head. Her first kiss from Billy Cramer had taken place on this bench. Then, the night she had graduated from high school and broken up with Todd, the man she was sure she was going to marry, Grandma had found her on the bench her head down, crying softly.

"What in the world are you crying about, girl? You just graduated from high school; the world's your oyster!"

She told her about Todd.

When she was through, Grandma said, "Wait here, I'll be right back."

She came back carrying a tray with a sandwich and two beers. They split the sandwich and each had a beer. It was her first. She had had sips before but never a full beer. When she handed her the can, Grandma said, "There are times when a beer is good for you, and this is one of those times. Now tell me about that fool crazy enough to let you go." Grandma had strange ideas.

By the time she finished both spilling out her heart and the beer, she felt better. She even slept very well that night.

SHE HAD TO see. Slowly, almost fearing what she would find, she leaned over the back of the bench. The tears again flowed freely when she found the key was still there. She would never be sure when the idea she had entertained so positively about ending her life faded away, and yet it was as gone as yesterday's sunrise. She just sat on the old bench with what she was sure was an idiotic smile, aware that somehow Grandma's old key bench and the providence which had arranged for it to arrive today had put her world squarely back on its feet.

Reminders

HE CLIMBED THE stairs into the attic with one purpose in mind. He was sure that was where he had left the old baseball glove that he wanted to show to his grandson. The air in the attic was stuffier than he remembered. He hadn't been there in a long time. It was just an attic. He once thought that he would convert it into an all-purpose room for the kids, but by the time he had the money, they were grown.

Now let's see where I put that glove. He glanced at the long clothes rack that he had installed at one end of the attic. It stretched from one side to the other. Diana said it was a good place to store the old clothes until she could sort them out and either keep them or give them to Goodwill.

He moved some boxes marked "Clothes" and then one marked "Dolls." The next three boxes he found weren't marked, so he started looking through them.

He was halfway through the second box when his grandson came up the stairs.

"Wow, this is cool. I didn't know this attic was here. What do you keep up here anyway?"

He smiled as he turned to his grandson. "Stuff. Lots and lots of stuff."

"Can I look around?"

"Sure. Just be careful of the dishes and glasses. Break any of those, and we'll both be in trouble with your grandma."

"I will."

He continued looking through the box and found nothing. He started on the third box.

"Hey Grandpa, what is this shirt from?" His grandson was

standing at the long clothes rack with a shirt in his hand.

"Bring it over here and let me take a look at it…Well, I'll be; I didn't think this shirt was still around."

The shirt was blue oxford cloth with a small patch over the pocket embroidered with a diver. It was obviously old and worn.

"Where's it from, Grandpa?"

"My partner and I had these made when we started a pool cleaning business; we were sixteen. It was quite an adventure."

"What happened to the business?"

"Oh, it came to an end; it wasn't that we didn't try. I guess it just wasn't meant to be."

They were quiet for a few minutes. He was remembering how it felt to be sixteen with the world at your feet. His grandson was wondering how you went about starting a business when you're only sixteen.

"There are a lot of shirts here with your name on them. Did you save them all?"

He got up from the box he was sitting on and walked to where his grandson was standing at the clothes rack, the shirt still in his hand.

On the occasions when he came up to the attic, he was always looking for something specific; so he had not really looked at what was stored here.

He was sure he had never looked at the clothes. Now he realized just how many coats, shirts, old jackets, and God knew what else were hanging on that long rack.

What else, he wondered, *would he find?*

HE RANDOMLY PULLED a shirt from the rack. He turned to his grandson and asked, "Do you have any idea what this shirt is?"

"Haven't a clue, Grandpa."

"No reason why you should, I guess. It's a bowling shirt; at least it was one of the shirts we wore when we were on that bowling team. I was working at a gas station. My boss decided to have a bowling team. He even had his mom custom fit our shirts. I don't think we had the greatest bowling team, but we sure looked good while we were doing it. Hmm, I wonder if it would still fit."

"Try it on, Grandpa."

"Maybe another time…"

"Come on, give it a try."

"OK… I'll be damned; a little snug but it still fits."

"Wow, that's a cool shirt. What's it made of?"

"I don't know. It looks kind of like silk, but it's something else. Your grandma would know."

He took the shirt off and hung it back on the rack. He randomly picked another shirt. It was badly stained; there was a rip down one side and it was filthy. The memory of the fire at their neighbors' house came flooding back, unbidden and wrenching. The neighbors had lost their little daughter in that fire. Everyone was out of the house and safe, so no one saw her run back in for her doll. When they found her, she was clutching it to her chest. *Why the hell did we keep this shirt?*

"Hey, grandpa, this shirt is cool."

He looked at the shirt his grandson held. "That's one of the shirts I had from a gas station where I worked."

"There are a lot of shirts like this here."

"I worked in a lot of gas stations."

He looked at the long rack and realized that just about everything on it belonged to him. It was a reminder in a very different way of who he had been and who he was now. How in the world had Diana managed to keep all of this stuff without him knowing about it until now?

"WOW!"

He turned and found his grandson at the other end of the

row of clothes.

"What now?" he asked, sure of another surprise.

His grandson lifted a hanger off the rack that held a plastic clothes bag. Inside the bag, he could see his Marine dress blues. His back stiffened slightly, and a smile lit his face.

"Wow," he said quietly.

The Coach

HE WAS TOO tall for his age and, as so often goes with that, he was gangly and awkward. His hair was a little too long. His face was rather narrow with the nose slightly more prominent than he would have liked, but his eyes were almost an iridescent blue, so vivid that people noticed little else.

He was pretty much an average boy. His grades in school were good, mostly As and Bs, with the occasional C. He got along well with the other kids and hadn't yet figured out why Molly hung around him so much.

He had a little sister two years his junior and a brother who was six. His mom and dad were a bit strict, but they taught their children that family was very important, and gave them a steady feeling of love.

Josh Williams was eleven years old, almost twelve. Passion is one of those things that we think of later in life, like when puberty takes hold, but there are other passions. In the case of Josh, it was baseball. It surely started with his father's love of the game. All the stories he would tell of the great players he had seen and more that he had heard about. He told Josh all about his days as a pretty good pitcher for his high school team, and how they had won their league championship.

JOSH LIVED FOR baseball more than any other thing in his life. If there was a game on television he watched it. It didn't matter if it was professional or college or the little league playoffs, he still watched it. He constantly asked his dad questions about the game; from how you turned a double play to how great was Babe Ruth, really. He read the sports section of the paper with the devotion of a fanatic. He had every magazine he could afford or that he could manage to talk other people out of.

When the World Series started, he got a regular score book and scored the game while he watched. His father kidded him that if ever there was a mistake made during the series, all they had to do was call him and he could straighten them out. The whole family thought that was pretty funny, and Josh did too. Still, he was far more knowledgeable about the game than anyone knew.

THEN, OF COURSE, there was playing the game. He wasn't terrible nor was he very good; he was average at best, no matter how hard he tried. And he did try and try, and try. His dad told him to be patient; that sooner or later he would grow into his lanky body, and all the awkwardness he exhibited now would go away. He believed his dad, but to Josh it seemed to be taking forever.

On Tuesday and Thursday the team had practice, which Josh looked forward to, and he was just about always the first one there. He had the bats and other equipment out of the locker when the coach got there, and the bases were all in place.

"Hi, Mister Vidler. How are you today?"

"Hi, Josh. Call me Coach, OK?"

"Sure, Coach."

The other coach, Mr. Davis, had quit, so Mr. Vidler was coaching by himself.

"Hey, Charlie. How ya doin'?"

"Hey yourself, Josh; want to play some catch until the others get here?"

"Sure."

Josh thought that Charlie was the best player on the team. He could field, hit and was their best pitcher, plus he had speed.

- - - - THE COACH - - - -

They played catch until the rest of the boys got there and then the coach yelled, "OK, bring it into the dugout."

They weren't quite into the middle of the season, having won two and lost two. They had eight more games to go.

"Boys, we're gonna have the usual practice with outfield first, then infield. But we won't have any batting practice. I have to be somewhere tonight, so we have to cut practice short. Mike, you catch for me. OK?"

Practice was over in an hour instead of the usual two hours, and some of the kids hung around after the coach had gone.

"Hey guys, why don't we do our own batting practice?" Josh asked. "I have the key to the locker."

Kenny, who they all called Snuffy, said, "I get first up."

The boys took their usual positions, and Josh took the mound to throw batting practice. Josh couldn't throw hard, but he got the ball over the plate all the time, which made him a perfect batting practice pitcher.

"Hey, you guys, let's play the hits like a game. OK?" Josh yelled. There were a few OK replies, and Josh settled on the mound to pitch.

Snuffy was a pretty good size for eleven years old and was squarely built. He should have been able to drive the ball; instead he seemed to pop up all the time.

Josh threw him the first pitch, and Snuffy promptly hit a pop up to second base. Next pitch, pop up to first. Next pitch, pop up to short. The frustration he felt was evident in his face which was turning red, and the fact that he tried to break his bat on the ground after every pop up.

Josh walked halfway to the plate. "Hey, Snuffy. How come you hold your bat so high above your shoulders?"

"'Cause that's the way it feels right."

"OK. But every time I throw you a pitch you either have to

bring the bat down so you can swing, or you have to loop your swing. I'll bet if you lowered your hands down even with your shoulders, you'd hit better.'

"Yeah, yeah, a lot you know. You don't hit worth a shit. Come on; just throw the ball."

Josh didn't say anything, just walked back to the mound, got himself ready and threw the ball. He did notice that Snuffy's hands were level with his shoulders and smiled when he heard the sweet sound of the bat making solid contact with the ball as it sailed over the shortstop's head.

The next batter hit a grounder to short. Davie the shortstop flipped the ball to Mike on second base, who threw over the head of the first baseman, then threw his glove in the dirt. Mike had trouble making the throw on the turn for a double play. Josh kept throwing 'til all the players had gotten to bat at least once, and then stopped the practice. "Hey guys, I gotta put the stuff away."

But he turned back to say, "Mike, you want to practice a little on the throw for the double play?"

"Aww, crap, Josh. I'll never get it right!"

"Hey Davie, hang around for a few minutes; you too, Eddie." Eddie was the first baseman.

Josh said, "Why don't we see if we can get Mike to quit throwing the ball over your head."

Eddie nodded and said, "That would make life easier."

The boys all took their positions with Josh at the plate, Davie at short, Mike at second and Eddie at first. "Ok, let's do this and this time, Mike, I want you to do it really slow. You know exaggerate it a little."

Josh hit a grounder to short, Davie fielded the ball, flipped it to Mike, and he stepped on the bag. Taking his time, he turned and threw the ball right to Eddie at first base.

"How about that, Mike?" Josh said, "Piece a cake."

"How come I can't do that when it counts?"

"You can."

Josh walked over to where the second baseman stood. "All you have to do is quit rushing to make the throw. That time, because you took your time, you planted your back foot, then stepped into the throw, and it was perfect. Quit trying to throw so fast and make sure your throw is good. If you work on that, you'll get faster and faster as time goes by.

"This time, Mike, make sure of the throw and not how fast you can make it."

They tried it ten more times and all the throws were good, not perfect maybe, but good, and by the tenth a little faster. The other boys said they had to go home, so Josh finished putting the gear away and headed home.

"HI JOSH, HOW was practice?" His mom knew how important baseball was to Josh so she always asked about his practices. The nice thing for his mom was he could talk to her about baseball. She was knowledgeable about the game, having had to listen to her husband, and also she just liked the game.

"It was fun, Mom. I wish that Dad had time to coach; he'd be great."

His mom smiled, "You know, Josh, I agree. He would be a good coach."

"Mom, you know Mister Vidler is coaching by himself, and I guess with his business and all that, it makes it tough for him to find the time."

"Is he a good coach, Josh?"

"Sure. He knows the game pretty well."

"That's good, hon; time for homework."

THE PRACTICE ON Thursday was again cut short because the

coach had to be at an appointment, and once again Josh ran the batting practice. He was happy to see that Snuffy was keeping his hands at his shoulders; he was hitting the ball really well.

Then there was Tony, also known as Red because of his flaming red hair, and sometimes he was called Shorty because he was the shortest kid on the team. But mostly he was called Red.

Red was the right fielder most of the time. There were only ten kids on the team, and Red didn't show up all that often. He was a pretty good player, but his dad, who was from Hungary, wanted him to be a soccer player and didn't care if he made it to baseball practice or to the games. No one on the team would say that Tony didn't try, no one. The problem was simple. He was afraid of the ball. When a fly ball was hit to Tony, he would close his eyes just before he was supposed to catch it. This is basically not a good idea. To compound the problem he did the same thing when he was hitting.

When practice was over Josh said, "Hey, Red, hang around a few minutes and help me put the gear away, OK?"

"Sure, Josh."

They put all the gear in the locker, but Josh kept the ball bag out. "Red, ah, look, I wanted to talk to you alone. I know better than anyone how hard you try; only there is one thing you have to quit doing."

"Yeah, what?"

"Closing your eyes. Why do you do that?"

"I'm afraid of getting hit with the ball," he said, with his head hanging down, not looking at Josh.

Josh started to laugh. "Red, think about what you just said. If you have your eyes closed, how can you not get hit by the ball?"

Red looked up at Josh with a kind of wrinkled smile on his face. "I guess you're right."

Josh was still laughing when he picked up a ball and threw it softly at Red. It hit him in the leg. "Did that hurt?"

"No."

"Not even a little?"

"Well, it kinda…No."

"Red, any ball that hits ya, you're gonna know about, but most don't hurt enough to count. Now I'm not saying that if you get hit in the arm with a fast ball that it isn't gonna hurt, but it sure isn't gonna kill ya.

"Tell ya what," Josh said, "Let's just play some flyout catches and this time, keep your eyes open."

They started out about ten feet apart. Josh threw the ball in an easy loft only about ten feet off the ground and watched his friend's eyes carefully. They threw half a dozen like that back and forth to each other. Red kept his eyes open.

"OK," Josh said, "let's move a little farther apart." They moved to about fifteen feet, and the throws got a little higher. Occasionally Josh threw the ball a little to one side or the other so Red had to go get it. Josh swore he could see Red relaxing as he caught each ball. When they finished, they were more than twenty yards apart, and Josh was throwing the ball as high as he could.

"Thanks, Josh, that was fun. Ya know, it's not as hard as I thought it was."

JOSH DIDN'T WANT to lie, but he felt like he had no choice; besides, the lie might come true.

"Ump, Coach Vidler said for me to start the game without him, and he would be along in just a little bit. He got hung up at work, so he's gonna be a little late."

"OK, kid, but if he isn't here by the end of the second inning, I'll have to call the game. The rules say that I have to have an adult supervising at all times. OK, let's play ball."

- - - - THE COACH - - - -

Josh let out a long-held breath, then walked to the dugout.

"Hey, Josh. Is Coach Vidler really gonna be here soon?"

Josh looked at Tony. "Boy, I sure hope so."

The team scored four runs in the first inning with the big hit coming from Snuffy, a two run double. Charlie was pitching and set the other side down in order. Josh was getting more and more nervous that Coach Vidler wouldn't show up. They scored two more runs in the second. Charlie went out to pitch just as Coach arrived. Josh took his first good breath since the game started.

"Coach."

"What, Josh?"

"I told the ump that you told me to start the game without you, and that you would be here by the second inning. Was that OK?"

The coach just looked at him for a minute then said, "Well, Josh, I don't know if that was the right thing to do, but we're ahead by six runs in the second inning…maybe I should let you start all the games without me. Nice job, Josh. Thanks for the help."

They won the game eight to nothing

WHEN JOSH WALKED in, he heard, "Hi, hon. How was the game?"

"It was great, Mom. I got to start the gam …uhm …..Coach Vidler said maybe he should let me…I got a hit and scored a run, it was great."

"That's nice, honey. Now it's time for homework."

Josh sighed. He would like to tell his mom about starting the game himself, but wasn't sure his mom would approve of the way he did it. He headed to his room still wishing he could tell his mom yet feeling that it had been a really good day.

- - - - THE COACH - - - -

THE PHONE RANG. "Josh, it's for you."

"OK, Mom. I got it. Hello."

"Hi, Josh. It's Coach Vidler. I was wondering if you could start practice for me today; I should be there by four."

"Sure, Coach. Anything you want us to work on?"

"Not really, Josh; some batting practice infield, whatever you want."

"OK, Coach. See you later."

"Thanks, Josh."

WHEN MOST OF the team arrived, Josh did what the coach said and held some batting practice. When it was Red's turn, Josh quietly reminded him to keep his eyes open. Red didn't set the world on fire, but at least he got a couple of grounders.

They finished batting practice, so Josh called the team into the infield and asked Eddie a question, "Where are you supposed to be when a relay is coming in from left field?"

"At first base, I guess."

Coach Vidler had gone over this play with the boys but only once, and most had forgotten where they were supposed to be. Josh pulled an old magazine from his back pocket. "Look, this has an article that shows us all where we're supposed to be on relays in from the outfield. Take a look."

Josh waited 'til all the guys had a chance to look at the article then said, "You guys think it's right?"

There were a few nodded heads and a few 'sures.'

"OK. Let's give it a try."

By the end of practice, everybody was pretty sure how the relays worked and where they were supposed to be. Josh smiled to himself as he put the gear away. This was a fun practice. Josh knew that the team was getting better. They were now five and two, having won their last three games. Two of them by only one

- - - - THE COACH - - - -

run, but they were still wins. Coach Vidler was having more and more trouble getting the time from work to be at the practices, and more and more Josh found himself running of the practices.

SATURDAY, 10 AM. It was game time, but Coach Vidler wasn't there. The ump walked over to Josh. "Where's the coach?"

"I don't know, Ump. He must have gotten held up."

"Well, we can't start without him"

"We started one game without him, and you let us have 'til the second inning for him to get here."

"I shouldn't have done it then, Josh, and I can't do it now." Mr. Jaeger, the umpire, lived right down the street from Josh. "I have to have at least one adult in charge of the team. We'll wait ten minutes, then I'll have to call a forfeit. I'm sorry, Josh."

To Josh and the rest of the team the ten minutes seemed to go by in thirty seconds. They saw the ump look at his watch, and then start toward their dugout.

"Josh, I'm afraid your team is going to have to forfeit."

Josh looked at the ground, "I guess we will."

"Ump, can I sit in for Coach Vidler?"

Josh turned in surprise on hearing his dad's voice; he hadn't noticed him walk up to the dugout.

The ump looked at him for a second then said, "Well, Bill, you have a boy on the team, so I don't see why not. I'll check with the other coach. If it's all right with him, we'll play."

Josh looked at his father, surprise and admiration in his eyes, "God, Dad, this is great."

"Don't swear, Josh."

"Sorry, Dad, but this is really great."

His dad took him aside. "Now listen, Josh, you're going to have to let me know what is going on with the players during the game. I don't know all the kids, so I'll have to rely on what you tell me."

"Sure, Dad. I'll help you all I can."

Josh then took his dad into the dugout and introduced him to all the guys on the team even the ones he already knew. That done they took the field

Coach Vidler got there at the beginning of the third inning. Josh's dad introduced himself and told the coach what was going on. They were ahead by three runs, five to two. In the fifth they scored two more runs. When the team was at bat, Josh's dad was amazed to see Josh in the coach's box at first base and more amazed to realize that he was giving the signals. They won the game seven to two.

Bill Williams walked over to Harry Vidler, "Coach, I'd like to congratulate you on the great job you're doing with this team and these kids; they play the game well."

Harry Vidler looked at Josh's father, "Bill, I'm the manager; the coach of this team is over there putting the gear away."

Bill looked to see that the coach was pointing at Josh.

"That's just my son."

"So you didn't have a hand in this?"

"In what?"

"The last three or four games the boys have been fielding better, hitting better and doing a lot of things that I should have shown them but didn't have time. They turned a double play in one game, ran an almost perfect relay from center field to get an out at the plate and, on top of that, they're all hitting better. I have missed practices and been late for the start of games, like today. So it isn't anything I've been doing that has made them improve. No, it hasn't been me.

"When I talk to the players, they all kept saying the same thing, Josh this, Josh that. I thought you might have a hand in this after all the great things Josh said about you when you were playing. Yet you just told me you didn't. That just leaves Josh."

Bill Williams looked over at his son, "Harry, that just…I mean, how could Josh…" He was looking at his son and remembering about how he scored the World Series, the magazines he read, his devotion to the sport pages and the conversations they had when Josh asked every detail about different moves the players should make on the field. "Well, I'll be damned."

He was quiet a moment; the pride was a knot in his chest that he couldn't wait to share with his wife.

"Harry, apparently you have one coach. Would you like another next year?"

The First Day Alone

HE SAT AT the bench in his garage working on a knife holder for the kitchen. It was pleasant in the garage with the propane heater blasting away, holding the cold of the January day outside the closed door. It was also quiet. He couldn't remember anytime in his life when it was this quiet; yet he was sure there had been some. Somehow this quiet was different; intense was the word that came to mind.

The knife holder was to go on the wall behind the stove to hold the carving knives. He had probably thought about making one for ten years. There had just never seemed to be enough time. He held it up and looked at it slowly. The rolled edges looked just right. When he had the stain and the finish on it, it would be just the way she would have wanted.

Two days ago that thought would have brought tears, but not today.

He laid the wood on the bench and picked up the cherry stain he had decided upon; it would go with the rest of the kitchen. His hand shook a little as he picked up an old brush, then started to apply the stain.

IT HAD BEEN three weeks since she had passed. The time since he had found her was almost a complete blur with the exception of some moments that were starkly clear. The expressions on the kids' faces when he told them their mom was gone. The church filled to overflowing at her service. The exact moment he turned away from her grave; his eyes awash with tears and yet able to see everything.

The rest didn't seem real. Watching the kids consoling each

other and soon talking about their mom as if she were the greatest mom ever. Friends, friends and more friends. She had touched so many lives.

He remembered all this; yet it was fuzzy as though he was an observer seeing it through some other eyes. In all those weeks he had never been alone, except when he went to bed and struggled with sleep. Out of concern for him one or the other of the kids or grandkids had found a reason to be with him.

He looked down at the bench amused to find that he had finished the staining. He set the piece aside looking at his watch as he did; two o'clock already, maybe time for a walk.

He walked briskly, feeling the beat of his heart as it picked up speed. She had always applauded his walks, knowing that it was good for him.

He walked for quite a while saying hello to those he passed. He watched people struggle to keep up with their dogs and wondering, as he had many times before, who was taking whom for a walk.

THE GARAGE WAS warm when he got back, so the piece of wood with its cherry stain was dry. He went into the house and poured himself some cola, and then went back to the garage and set about putting the finish coat on the knife holder. He worked with quiet efficiency; his trained hands doing automatically what needed to be done. With the last coat on and brushed down so he couldn't see any brush marks, he set the piece on the bench to dry. Once again he looked at his watch, a habit that she used to kid him about. It was time to go and watch the news, another habit.

As he walked through the kitchen, he grabbed a glass and started to make himself a cocktail to sip as he watched the news. He stopped. He looked at the glass in his hand wondering if it was a good idea. He had heard of people diving into the bottle for solace when they lost someone.

That's crazy, he thought, *I always have a drink when I watch the news*. He finished making the drink. After the national news, he watched the local news too. He rose from his chair and made his way again into the kitchen to prepare something to eat. He pulled a pork chop out and set it to cooking on the stove, then made himself a small salad and sliced a few pieces of French bread.

He was a little surprised to find that he was hungry. It wasn't surprising, though, he hadn't eaten since breakfast. At eight he watched the only show that he thought was worth watching on this night, *JAG*.

When the show ended, he watched the History Channel, then some politico that was sure he knew how to fix just about every problem the country had. The news came on, and he turned the TV off. There was no sense watching it again.

It took a little while for the water in the shower to get hot but, when it did, he let it run for quite a while on his back. He liked a long shower. He didn't turn the water on very hard; he just liked the warmth.

THE BED SEEMED much bigger with him in it alone. Knowing he probably wouldn't sleep again tonight, he thought about the TV, but never turned it on.

He sat up in bed as if he'd been shocked. "What?"

He knew he heard it. There was no mistaking that voice, not for him. His wife had just told him that he had had a good day, and that there would be more. He ran it through his mind again and again. She was right; he had had a good day. He felt that somehow she was still with him; then realized that no matter what happened in the future, she would always be with him. She had owned his heart for most of his life.

He started to chuckle when he looked in the mirror over the dresser and saw that he was still sitting up with a very strange expression on his face. He lay back down. Looking at the ceiling above, he could see her face just as it had looked on their first date. He knew he was grinning like an idiot, but he couldn't help it.

Still looking at her on the ceiling, he said, "Thank you, Babe."

He rolled over on his side and went to sleep.

The Letter Writer

A VOICE RANG out in the barracks. "Hey Gomez, what's the problem?"

"Screw you, Brown. If I had a problem, you'd be the last one I'd tell."

"Well, you may not have a problem, asshole, but this is the first time I've seen you lookin' this bad since your family didn't send you some goodies for your birthday."

Gomez looked up, "Up yours!"

Brown drifted away and Lopes hung his head over from the upper bunk and said, "Gome?"

"What?" he snapped back.

"Whoa, forget I asked."

"Hey, I'm sorry, man. I just got a letter from Elena, and it's all bad."

"She don't love ya anymore?"

"Not exactly. She says when I write her, all I talk about is the Marines and boot camp. What does she expect me to write about?"

"What she is telling you, stupid, is that she wants to know if you still love her, if you miss her, if you still need her. It's a womens' thing." Lopes nodded wisely.

"I can't write how I feel about her. I mean I try; I just don't know how. When I try it all sounds stupid! I say I love her in every letter."

"It ain't enough. I know; I got some of the same problem. I don't know what I'm supposed to write either."

"Maybe we should ask Kraft for help."

"Right. Nobody asks Kraft for anything; even the DIs don't

ask him for much."

"Well, he writes his girl a letter everyday. Grabowski read one he left out one night. He says they're really good. Ya know he graduated from college."

Kraft was Alfred Kraft. He was the oldest guy in the platoon at twenty-six. He also was, by far, the biggest. Six foot six, two hundred forty pounds with not ounce one of fat. He was formidable.

KRAFT SAT ON his footlocker cleaning the weapon. He picked up the trigger housing, giving it a close inspection. Satisfied, he slammed it back in place, flipped the M-1 up in the air and looked down the barrel, placing his thumb in the chamber to reflect light. It wouldn't get any cleaner.

He pulled the rifle down and closed the chamber keeping his thumb good and safe; he'd learned that lesson. He put the rifle by the head of his bunk. It was the third time he'd cleaned it that day.

He looked around the barracks. He had always been an observer of people; it was something he did without being aware of it. Even though he wasn't close to anyone in the platoon, he found that he liked some of his fellow recruits. They were just finishing their fourth week of boot camp.

There was Brown, at about six two probably the next biggest guy in the platoon. What he liked about him was that he was always up. *The man*, he thought, *must have been born happy.* He also liked the fact that he was quick-witted, good for a laugh anytime. He also liked Grabowski, or Grabass as everyone called him, who slept in the bunk above him. A guy who was nice to everyone. He spent another ten minutes just watching as men cleaned there rifles, wrote letters, told jokes, read, bullshitted and some already slept.

He picked up his tablet and decided to write her just a short note tonight. He wrote every night. It was something that he knew he had to do. It made him feel better without making him miss her any less. He had become more introspective in the last year. He would examine his motives for doing things that once he would have just done. Definitely her influence.

KRAFT ROUNDED A corner and heard, "Listen, ya little weasel, do what I tell you, or I'll make knots on your head."

Miller had Wilson by the collar up against the side of the quonset hut, pushing against his throat. Miller was six two or three while Wilson was well under six feet.

"When I tell you to do something, piss-ant, you do it, understand?" This said while he pushed harder against Wilson's throat. "Well, do ya?"

Wilson's answer was garbled.

"Let him go."

"Yeah, who says?" Miller asked without looking around.

Kraft grabbed him, lifted him off the ground and slammed him into the side of the hut.

"I did, and when I tell you to do something, *piss-ant*, you do it, understand?"

He didn't wait for an answer. He dropped him, turned and walked away. Miller sat on the ground with a blank look on his face, holding his neck and trying to catch his breath. He watched Wilson stagger off in the direction Kraft had taken. He'd get even.

"Hey, Kraft, wait up." Wilson said.

Kraft turned and waited.

"Hey thanks, man. I don't know what Miller has against me, but something sure bugs him."

Kraft stood there for a minute saying nothing, then nodded his head and walked into the barracks. Wilson just shook his head not understanding what the hell was going on, then went inside.

LATER THAT NIGHT, "It's after lights out, idiot. What the hell are you doing?"

Kraft snapped to his feet still holding the flashlight in his hand, rigid at attention. He hadn't heard the DI coming.

"Writing a letter, sir."

"To your MOMMIE?"

"No, sir."

"Right. Stow the gear and get your ass in that bunk, NOW."

"Yes, sir."

As he walked away, the DI Sgt. Alvin Stobbe realized he had forgotten how big Kraft was. *Shit*, he thought to himself, *I'm six feet and I feel like a friggin' midget.*

Kraft lay in his bunk knowing that he would not sleep. In the letter he had told her about Wilson, embarrassed that he had manhandled Miller, but he didn't like Miller because he was a bully for no reason. On top of that nobody messed with the men in Platoon 247. His platoon. Besides the man was a snake. It was not the first night he would lie awake, yet in the morning he didn't feel tired. He listened to the barracks; his senses finer-tuned because of the dark and the quiet. Eventually he drifted into sleep.

HE SAT ON his bunk; his pad across his lap, tonight's letter almost finished. The day had been busy. Shots first thing this morning, then classes in the morning and the parade ground 'til four. After that, policing the barracks 'til chow, then showers; now a little free time, it was all in the letter.

"Do you write her every night?"

Kraft looked up to find Gomez standing next to his bunk. He was inclined to say nothing, but Gomez had an almost pleading look on his face.

"Yeah. Yeah, I do."

"She's lucky."

Kraft said nothing.

"If I'm bothering, you just say so." Gomez said.

Kraft waited a moment. "Did you want something, Gome?"

"My girlfriend, I mean she doesn't sound the same in her letters as she did when I first got here. I don't know what to say to her, and Grabass says you write really good letters. I wasn't supposed to say that, and I was just wondering if I could get you to help me say something to her and…"

Kraft sat there staring hard at him. Gomez started to fidget, then said, "Hey, forget it. I just…never mind." He turned to go.

"Gomez."

He turned back. "Yeah."

"When was the last time you wrote her a letter?"

"Tonight, I wrote her tonight."

Kraft stood up. "I'm going to the head. Bring the letter over and leave it on my bunk. You don't care if I read it?"

"Hell no, man. I was hoping you would and tell me what I should say."

"I can't tell you what to say, but I'll look at it."

Kraft walked up to his bunk. Grabass was on top. He took hold of his arm and turned him so he could look in his face. "You reading my mail?"

"Hell no, man, why?"

"Gomez told me that you said I write good letters. Where did he get that from?"

"Oh. Uh, well, you left one of your letters on top of your locker box when you went to the head, and, uhm, I read it. Just the top page though. I thought it would really be cool if I could write that good. I guess I mentioned it to him." This was said fast and nervously.

Kraft stared at Grabass for a full minute then loosened his

grip. "OK." Then he sat on his own bunk and picked up Gomez's letter.

THE NEXT DAY they were on the parade ground almost the entire time. By evening chow they were all ready to hit the bunks. Gomez hadn't had time to even say hello to Kraft, and he was anxious to see what he had to say about his letter. Half the men in the barracks were so tired that they didn't clean their M-1s that night. A big mistake. Just before lights out the DIs held an inspection. All those who hadn't cleaned their rifles did a hundred push-ups, then cleaned their rifles in the dark. It had been a tough day.

Gomez found Kraft coming out of the head the next morning. He was waiting for him. "Hey Kraft, how's it going?"

Kraft was well aware of what Gomez wanted to talk about. "Gome, now ain't the time. Come see me tonight at free time."

Gomez nodded his head and walked away disappointed.

Kraft liked what Gomez had written in his letter; maybe not well expressed, but the soul of the letter was good. It was true.

GOMEZ WAS SITTING on his bunk waiting for Kraft when he heard him say, "Hey, Gome. How's things?"

"Good, Kraft, good. Is now a good time?"

"Sure, sit down."

Gomez sat on the locker box with Kraft. "Pretty bad, huh?"

"No."

"No. You mean it was OK?"

"Look, is this the girl that you want to marry, have kids, settle down, all that kind of thing?"

Gomez looked at him for a minute then very quietly said, "Yeah, she is."

"I thought so. The letter says a lot, and it says nothing. She does want to hear about what's going on here. But she also wants to hear about you and her, and how you feel about her. Putting 'I love you' at the end of a letter isn't enough. She needs to know that she is still the girl of your dreams, you know, number one in the world."

"So how do I do that? I can't think of anything to say."

"When you two are alone," Kraft asked. "You know, just the two of you, what language do you speak?"

"You mean when we're…"

"Yeah. When you're…"

"Spanish."

"Why do you write in English?"

"Elena thinks it's very important that I get my English better, you know."

"Very smart girl. Take this letter and at the very end tell her how much you miss her, need her and love her, but write it in Spanish."

"Why Spanish?"

"Look, just do it and when you get the next letter back from her, tell me about it, OK?"

THEY WERE NOW in the end of the fifth week of boot, gaining on halfway through and just starting to get confident that they were going to make it. In the Corps they called it getting a little salty; probably something left over from when the Navy really was their boss. Kraft, ever the observer, could see a lot of change in the boys who had come to boot camp. They were now becoming Marines.

Marine Boot Camp is an experience that few who go through the ordeal ever forget. When these men are in the last of their years, they will still have stories about boot. There are bonds made there that would never occur outside of that environment;

bonds that become and remain lifelong. It is a world unto itself that few that have not personally experienced it will ever understand. This was part of what the observant Kraft noted and put into his memory.

KRAFT WAS STILL thinking about the guys in his platoon when he heard a familiar voice.

"Man, how did you know?"

Kraft turned to find Gomez standing beside his bunk a letter in his hand. "What did she say?" he asked.

"She said she loved my letter, and that the last part told her for sure that I still loved her. Thanks, Kraft; I feel a lot better now, but how did you know?"

"Just a lucky guess." Kraft was somehow embarrassed by Gomez's thanks. "See you later, Gome. I gotta go to the head."

Kraft walked into the barracks where he was stopped by Lopes.

"Hey, Kraft. What you did for Gome was really cool; he says you're a genius."

Kraft smiled, nodded his head and started to his bunk.

"Uh, Kraft?"

He turned and looked at Lopes.

"Uhm, I was wondering if you would look at my letter for me. I got kinda the same problem."

Kraft shook his head, turned and walked to his bunk.

LOPES SAID, "SORRY I bothered you last night, Kraft."

"You didn't bother me last night. It's just that I don't understand why you guys think I'm better at writing to girls than you are. Especially your girls."

"Well, you sure figured out the trick for Gomez, and you write to your girl every night. On top of that you have a college education where most of us barely even graduated from high school."

Kraft shook his head. "This is nuts," he muttered then walked out to formation.

When Kraft got to his bunk after showers, there was a letter from Lopes to his girl sitting against his pillow.

He decided this was bullshit and shoved the letter aside. He rolled over on his bunk, then rolled back over picking up his tablet. *She'd get a kick out of this*, he thought.

Finished with his letter, he laid back down on his bunk and heard Lopes' letter crunch under his head. What the hell! He picked up the letter and started to read. The first word was "Lisa."

Kraft was already shaking his head. *No, it should be Dear Lisa, or, Sweet Lisa. What the hell did Lopes expect starting a letter like that.* He quickly read the rest of the letter. Kraft thought about what Lopes said about school. He had learned earlier that Lopes had a GED but hadn't graduated from high school.

He knew that going to school taught a person a great many things not related to education. Kraft remembered learning manners from some of his fellow students that he hadn't learned at home. And subtle things that came from just being around a mixed group of people, a mixture of cultures.

He had always been OK around girls and then he met her. She was so forthright and honest about herself that he had learned more about her and in the process, women, than he ever thought he would know in a lifetime.

THE NEXT MORNING in chow line Kraft snuck in behind Lopes and said, "Lisa." Lopes didn't react. Then he said, "Dear Sweet Lisa."

This time Lopes turned around. "Hey, that's my girls na…" he stopped when he saw Kraft.

Kraft handed Lopes his letter. "Is Lisa your girl?" he asked without preamble.

"Yeah, sure. What made you ask that you read the letter?"

"When I said Lisa, you didn't react at all. When I said dear sweet Lisa, you reacted. Get the idea?"

Lopes looked at Kraft the light of realization in his eyes. "I'm pretty stupid, huh?"

"Nope. It's just that most girls need to feel that you care; words like dear and sweetheart say all that."

"Thanks, Kraft, thanks."

"Oh, Lopes, if the next letter is better, let me know. OK?"

"You got it."

One week later. "Kraft, man, I got a letter from Lisa. It sounded like her. Ya know what I mean?"

"That's good, Lopes. That's good and, yeah, I know what you mean."

TIME WAS NOW going fast. The platoon had gone through rifle training at Camp Mathews without a hitch. They had just four more weeks to go and then graduation. Kraft had become a little more open with his fellow recruits to the point of helping a few more with letter problems. He was, however, still quiet and only just sociable. He was also now the platoon guide-on. Behind his back the rest of the platoon said it was only 'cause he was so tall nobody could miss him.

There was no doubt the boys were getting salty. They knew that they drilled better, stood taller and looked more like Marines. What the hell! It was what they had joined for.

Kraft rolled off his bunk, opened his footlocker and put away his pad. He wondered if he was a little weird for writing to her every single night; yet he knew that if you love someone, you let them know.

He sensed that someone was standing at the bottom of his bunk. He turned and found Miller looking at him; the look on his face could only be described as sheepish. Kraft waited.

Miller turned to leave.

"What the fuck do you want? Spit it out."

Miller's shoulders slumped. Whatever he wanted to say, it wasn't coming easy. He turned back to Kraft for a moment. He couldn't speak until he blurted out, "She wants a divorce." There were tears at the edge of his eyes.

"Who does?" Kraft asked quietly.

"Millie, my wife."

"I didn't know you were married, Miller."

"It's no big deal, you know."

"What do you mean it's no big deal? What kind of a fucking asshole are you?" This said as Kraft rose to his feet.

Miller drew back to the end of the bunk. "I mean it's just, you know, married. Fuck, I don't know what I mean. Forget it, just forget it."

Kraft's anger was in check. He realized that he had been close to taking a swing at Miller. He didn't like that reaction.

"Miller, sit down," he said. Miller stopped.

The raised voices had attracted attention especially since everyone knew about their attitudes towards each other.

Kraft looked around. "All you turkeys, bug off, NOW."

Everyone found something else to do.

"OK. What's going on?" Kraft asked.

Miller sat on Kraft's footlocker; Kraft on his bunk. He said nothing, just stared at the letter in his hand, then he extended it to Kraft. When he was done reading, Kraft asked, "How long you been married?"

Miller looked at the top bunk where Grabass was looking over the side.

"Hey, Grabass," Kraft said. "Find some other place to flake out for a while."

Grabowsky rolled off the bunk and walked away.

Kraft looked back at Miller, who said, "Five months."

"You've been here nine weeks. So you spent less than two months together after you were married?"

"Yeah, we got married kinda sudden like. I only knew her for two weeks before we ran off to Vegas and got married."

"Her letter sounds strange," Kraft said. "Like you didn't spend much time with her after you got married. Is there some kind of problem?"

"Nah, it's just that maybe it was too quick. I don't know…"

Again there were tears in his eyes.

"You love her, don't you?"

"Yeah, I do but…"

In a moment of pure insight, Kraft said, "You were a virgin when you got married weren't you?"

"Why the hell would you say something like that?"

Kraft's eyes bore into him, unwavering.

Miller put his head down in his hands. Kraft heard him mumble, "Yeah."

Kraft sat silently, letting Miller come to terms with what he had just told him. Miller who always played the big man braggart 'I been around' kinda guy was anything but, at least when it came to girls.

Kraft very quietly asked, "Did you consummate the marriage?"

"Huh?"

"Did you have sex?"

"Oh yeah, sure."

"How did it go?"

"It was great, super."

Again Kraft let his eyes bore into Miller.

"OK. Bad."

"Miller, you're not the only guy who's had a bad wedding night."

"It got worse. We cut the honeymoon short and came home from Vegas the next day. I made up some stupid reason why we had to, and then we were staying with her mom that made it even worse somehow. I started staying at work late and going with the guys after to have some drinks, coming home half loaded. Hell, I was afraid to even look her in the eye let alone touch her. I was glad when I had to leave for boot."

"Are you writing to her?"

"Yeah, once a week."

Kraft couldn't help himself. "Jesus Christ, once a week; what the hell is the matter with you? Once a fucking week!"

"I don't know what to say to her." This was said pleadingly.

Kraft said, "So you came to me 'cause you think I do?"

"Everybody says that you can write to anybody."

Kraft was at a loss for what to say. He stood up and looked at the rounded ceiling of the quonset hut. *Now what?* he thought, *now what?*

"Miller, didn't anyone ever talk to you about sex?"

"I didn't have a dad, and my mom acted like sex was something dirty."

Kraft still didn't like Miller, but he knew what it had cost him to ask for help. Worse, Kraft had no idea what to tell Miller to do.

"Look, I need to use the head." Kraft said. "I'll talk to you about this in the morning at chow."

With that he walked away still wondering. *What do you know?* he thought. *Who would have thought the tough guy couldn't deal with women, and apparently was afraid when it came to sex, and apparently clueless.*

Kraft spent a restless night wondering, hell, agonizing over what he should tell Miller. He was dressed and sitting on his bunk an hour before reveille with his flashlight looking at the letter that Miller's wife had written.

How the hell did I become the company shrink? He had written his own letter last night telling her about Miller and hoping for a little mental feedback. He glanced at the letter again and suddenly there it was; how could he have missed it?

MILLER FELL IN behind Kraft in the chow line; he said nothing. Kraft turned around and looked at him. From the way he looked, he'd slept less than Kraft.

"Free time tonight, come and see me." Kraft said. "By the way, she doesn't want a divorce."

"How can you say that? It said right in the…"

Kraft cut him off. Tersely, he said, "Tonight."

WHEN MILLER APPEARED at Kraft's bunk, he had a 'You don't know what you're talking about' look on his face.

Kraft held up his hand before Miller could speak.

"Miller, what she says in the letter is 'MAYBE we should think about a divorce', not 'I want a divorce.' There is a BIG difference."

"What do you mean?" Miller asked.

"Let me see her picture."

"Uhm, I don't have a picture."

Slowly Kraft turned and looked Miller in the eyes. He said nothing. Finally Miller looked away.

"You are without a doubt the biggest, fucking, no-brained asshole I have ever had the displeasure to meet. You married this girl, and now you don't even have a picture of her. What was it?

Just a convenient piece of ass, something to pass the time, somebody you could dump when something better came along?"

Kraft missed the first sign and got nailed good as Miller hit him. He went down more surprised than hurt, and Miller landed on top of him, still swinging. "I love her, God damn you, I love her."

Kraft grabbed both his wrists and rolled him to the floor.

"Don't tell me that, asshole. Tell her!"

Miller still lay on the floor, tears at the corners of his eyes. "I don't know how," he whispered.

"Yeah, I got that." Kraft said. He looked around at the crowd that was gathered. "Beat it," he said softly. The men melted away.

Kraft leaned down and lifted Miller by the arm, setting him on his bunk.

"I believe you. Now you have to make that girl know that what you told me is true. You have to tell her the truth about why you haven't touched her since the wedding night. You can't sweet-talk her, and you can't bullshit her; it has to be the truth. She'll see through anything else. Now go write your wife a letter."

That night Kraft wrote her the longest letter since he had been in boot camp. He put the letter away and lay down on his bunk, not sure if he had done a bad thing or a good thing. He slept well.

A WEEK LATER Kraft was walking back from chow on Sunday evening, the only real free time they had during the entire week. He felt someone approach from behind. Soon Miller fell in step with him. Miller handed Kraft a laminated card; it was a picture of a cute brunette with wide spaced eyes and a turned-up nose. The expression on her face was serene, yet in it was the sense that she would laugh easily.

Kraft handed the picture back. "I'd say you got lucky."

"Yeah. Yeah, I think you're right."

"You gonna be able to work things out?"

"I think so. I told her the truth."

"I'm glad to hear that."

"Hey listen, Kraft. I..."

"Forget it."

"No, really. I..."

"I said forget it." Kraft growled. "You just take care of that girl." He turned his back and walked up the company street and into his barracks.

Miller watched in dismay, then walked to his own barracks totally bewildered by Kraft.

THE FOLLOWING WEEK, their second to last, Kraft talked to no one unless he had to. Everybody had thought he was loosening up, getting more relaxed with the rest of the men in his platoon. Instead he was biting people's heads off at the least provocation or none at all. He did what he had to and nothing more. Grabass mentioned that his letters at night were even longer than usual. He also said that he didn't think Kraft slept at all. Being the intelligent types they all were, they stayed the hell out of his way.

Grabass also noticed that he'd seen the Senior Drill Instructor, Sergeant Gagnon, talking to Kraft a lot during the week.

By Monday of their last week, Kraft seemed a little more relaxed; not the welcome wagon but not barking at everybody either.

They had been on the parade ground for an hour and the men in the platoon knew they were getting good at drill. The famous shout from the DI 'One heel' was becoming a reality. Stobbe marched them down the parade ground, gave a sharp 'Column left' and headed them for the company street. When they turned they saw the commotion.

A recruit named Ralston from the 248 Platoon was holding a length of 2x4 and swinging at anyone who came close. He was muttering and then yelling at the top of his voice; none of what he yelled made sense. Gunny Gagnon called the platoon to a halt, then went to see what the hell was going on. As he approached Ralston, he made the mistake of turning his head to say something to the men gathered round.

Ralston shouted something that sounded like "You're to blame," and swung. The 2x4 hit Gagnon on the side of his chest and he went down, hitting his side and smacking his head against the ground. Ralston was over him in an instant; the 2x4 raised to strike.

Later when they talked it over, nobody in the platoon could remember seeing Kraft move. Somehow he covered the distance between where Gagnon lay on the ground and Ralston who was raising the 2x4 to hit Gagnon again. The blow struck Kraft on his left shoulder after glancing off his head. He staggered but somehow was still able to snatch the 2x4 from Ralston with his right hand and bring it across Ralston's face, knocking him to the ground.

He collapsed with what almost sounded like a sigh. One of the guys standing by Ralston grabbed him and kept him from falling hard. There was blood coming from the side of Kraft's head; it looked like from his ear. He was now unconscious.

There were two men sitting on Ralston who also was unconscious. Sergeant Gagnon was helped to his feet by two of the men in the platoon. He was holding his broken ribs with his left hand.

"Davis, move your ass to the duty hut and tell Sergeant Stobbe that we need the medics and an ambulance here NOW. Quist and Plummer, get Ralston over on that bench. The rest of you get the hell back and give Kraft some room to breath. Somebody give me their T-shirt." Grabass had his off in an instant and handed it to the sergeant.

Gagnon pressed the T-shirt to the side of Kraft's head.

"Grabowsky, get over here and hold this shirt. Keep it firm against his head, that's good."

The sergeant stood up. "All right, fall in! You men from 248, get back to your area; find Sergeant Fullbright and tell him what happened."

At that point Sergeant Stobbe came running around the corner with Davis.

"Al," Gagnon said, "You want to take them back to the barracks?"

"What the hell happened? You OK? Davis said you got smacked good."

"I'll live. I'll tell you about it later."

"OK. Men, let's move"

At that moment the medics and ambulance arrived.

FOUR HOURS LATER, Senior DI Mike Gagnon returned to the duty hut. He was taped around his ribs, and the doc had told him from the size of the bruise he was lucky to have only two broken ribs.

Stobbe watched Gagnon walk gingerly through the door of the duty hut. "You OK?"

"Yeah, the doc says in a few weeks or maybe a month, I'll be as good as new. Everything all right here?"

"Yeah. Everybody is talking about Kraft. Are you gonna tell me what happened out there?"

In as few words as possible Gagnon told him what had happened. "I think that if it weren't for Kraft, I might be dead," he added.

"How is Kraft?

"He was still unconscious when I left."

THE FOLLOWING MORNING at formation Sergeant Stobbe filled in the troops. "I know you all want to know about Kraft and Gunny Gagnon, so listen up. The gunny went home last night with two broken ribs and a whole lot of hurt, but he'll be OK. Kraft regained consciousness early this morning. He has stitches in his head and his ear, and a broken collarbone plus a concussion. The doc says he will be in the hospital for at least a week or more. We need to bring his footlocker and put his gear in the duty hut. How long he stays in the hospital will determine whether he graduates with the rest of the platoon. Grabowsky, get up here!"

"Yes, sir."

"You, Gomez and Lopes, go get Kraft's footlocker. Bring it to the duty hut and give it to Sergeant Snow."

"Yes, sir."

"The rest of you girls fall in. Right face, forrrward MARCH."

GRABOWSKY SAID, "MAN, this is weird. Who would have figured Kraft would get screwed up? This is weird."

"Hey," Gomez said. "The lock isn't closed. Maybe we should lock it."

"Fuck that, let's look inside." This from Lopes.

They raised the lid of the footlocker with a certain apprehension.

"What the hell?" Grabowsky said.

On the right side of the footlocker was a neatly stacked bundle of letters. At first they thought they were from his girl. But then they realized that the letters were the ones that Kraft wrote every night and apparently never mailed.

"Why would you write letters if you weren't going to mail

them?" Gomez asked.

"Gentlemen, you were told to bring that footlocker to Sergeant Snow."

The three men snapped to attention at the sound of Gunny Gagnon's voice. Standing at attention the three of them said nothing. The DI walked to where they were standing, then bent down and lifted a few of the letters out of the footlocker. Silently he looked at them before putting them back and grabbing his ribs.

Grabass, the bolder of the three said, "Sir, do you know why someone would do that?"

Gagnon looked at the three men; he knew they were all friends of Kraft. "Any of you ever talk to Kraft about his girl?"

"Well sir, if you asked Kraft about her he would look at you, but he never said anything. It didn't take a genius to figure out that he didn't want to talk about it."

Gagnon remained silent looking at each of the three, then spoke, "Those aren't for his girl, they're for his wife. She died a year ago last week while giving birth to their son. He also didn't make it. After her funeral Kraft went off the deep end and finally ended in court where he had two choices. One of his choices was the service; he chose the Corps. A court appointed psychiatrist suggested that he write her letters as a way of easing the pain."

The three men were silent for a moment, then bowed their heads in recognition of Kraft's loss. They carefully closed his footlocker and picked it up to take it to the duty hut; each one now well aware of the meaning of strength and honor.

Road 18

IN HIS WORK he drives through Northern and Southern California, through the Central Valley from Bakersfield in the south to Redding in the north. There is one thing in that routine drive that has remained a curiosity to him, and that is, Road 18.

As innocuous as this may seem, the exit sign created unanswered questions in his mind. *Why doesn't that road have a name? Is the road too short? Does it just end in the middle of a cotton field or does it go to Fred's farm?*

He promised himself that sometime, when he had the time, he would drive down that road just to see where it might lead. It could lead to Road 19, or Road 14 or even Road 29A! It really doesn't matter because at some point he has to drive down that road to see where it goes. Perhaps he'll find out why it has no name.

There are probably a thousand roads in this country that are designated by nothing more than a number; yet they all take us somewhere, and to many people that 'somewhere' is important. So today, which happens to be a Saturday, he's going to drive down Road 18 and see where it takes him.

HE TURNS OFF the highway onto Road 18 and, with the curiosity of an explorer, sets out on this adventure that is this 'road without a name'. He finds fields that stretch as far as the eye can see. He notices that the crops on both sides of the road change from green to yellow to green with red (which are probably tomatoes) and then to barren soil, which perhaps is a field just harvested and turned under.

By this time he is some miles off the highway and has yet

to see another car or any sign of life at all except the consistent fields. Ah! There is something ahead! A bridge. A large sign says that caution is due as this is a one lane bridge. The sign warns drivers to 'be sure and stop and make sure the bridge is clear before crossing'. He stops. He looks and finds the right of way clear. He drives slowly, crossing the bridge and looks down stream. He can see two young boys fishing in the clear water of a perfectly beautiful creek, a great way to spend a Saturday afternoon.

He is soon off the bridge. The road stretches in front of him once again, and he is surrounded by the ever-present fields of crops, burgeoning with promise. At a crossroad, the sign says 'Smith Ranch Road'. On one corner is a very small store with a single gas pump and a very faded sign that reads, 'Diana's Fresh Baked Pies'. He can't resist. He pulls into the small dusty parking lot and walks into the store.

THERE'S NO ONE there. There is a bell on the counter with a note attached that says 'Ring for service'. He rings the bell. Nobody comes. He rings it again; still nobody. He is about to leave when he hears laughter through an open door leading out to the back of the building. Of course he can't leave without taking a look. There, at a picnic table, are three people enjoying lunch and obviously each other's company. Not wanting to disturb them, he turns to leave.

"Hey, I'm really sorry we didn't hear you. Did you need something?" a woman calls out.

When he turns around, caught in the act of being nosey, he can't think of anything to say, so he says the first thing that comes to mind. "I was just wondering about one of those pies," he stammers.

By this time the woman, who is now coming toward him, says, "I really am sorry. If you rang the bell, I'm afraid I didn't hear it. We don't get too many people passing by on Saturdays; it being so far off the highway. I only have apple and apricot pies today. I made cherry pies, but only a couple, and they're gone."

He replies, "Umm, I'll have an apple pie. That sounds good."

"Well, before you buy one, you should taste it to make sure it's what you want." Without waiting for a reply, she walks behind the counter and opens the cold box, pulls out a pie, cuts a small slice, plunks it down in front of him and shoves a fork in his hand. "Enjoy!" she says.

Tentatively he takes a bite. *Oh. Oh my goodness, it's heaven!* Apples still just a bit crisp, a cinnamon sauce that can't be described, and a crust that if you threw it in the air would float there forever.

"OK?" she asks.

Without hesitation, he says, "Do you have two?" The woman just smiles and wraps up two pies for him.

He thanks her and starts to leave, but turns back to say, "Excuse me, just where does this road lead?"

She smiled again. "Oh, it just wanders on for another couple of miles through the farms and ends when it hits Walden Road. You know, just another farm road."

With that he says, "Thank you, and thanks again for the pies."

She says, "Anytime!"

He starts the car and pulls out of the parking lot onto Road 18 again and heads back for the highway. He didn't find out why this road has no name, and he was suddenly aware that it doesn't matter. Road 18 led him nowhere really, and yet he had the feeling that next time he has the chance, he just might go see what's down Road 29A.

To Find Love

THE FIRST SUMMER

He entered the dance hall for the first time in a week. He walked to the snack bar and bought a coke, then he walked to the benches at the far wall and sat down. The week on the beach had been hectic. It was the busiest time of the summer, mid July. Everybody thinks that being a lifeguard is a walk in the park, not on this beach.

He looked around the dance hall and saw his buddy Mike dancing with the same girl he had seen him with at the beach. If they were any closer together, he would be carrying her.

"Hey, big guy. What's happening?"

It was his friend Larry, also a lifeguard, who slid onto the bench beside him.

"You know, thought I'd come by and do a little dancing. See if there was anything that I had missed."

"You mean *anyone* that you had missed."

"Yeah, that too."

They sat in companionable silence for a while, just people-watching.

Larry said, "There's Dina."

Dina was one of the girls that he really liked to dance with. He could make any dance move he wanted to, and she always followed easily. She was not too good looking and wore much more makeup than she needed, but she was really nice.

He tapped her on the shoulder and, as she turned around, he opened his arms, and they were dancing. The song ended, and he thanked Dina for the dance. She headed for the snack bar, and he found his seat on the bench.

"She is really nice, you know that?"

"Sure" Larry answered.

Again they sat and people-watched.

"Wow!"

He turned to Larry, "Wow what?"

"Over there in the green dress."

He looked at where his friend was pointing. He didn't see a girl in a green dress. "I don't see anything."

"She is behind that big guy with the belly."

He focused on the big guy just as she emerged in front of him. "Wow."

"That's what I said."

"Have you seen her before, Larry?"

"Nope."

They watched as she went to the snack bar and got a drink. On the way she was asked by three or four guys to dance; she apparently turned them all down. She walked across the floor and sat down not far from where they were sitting.

"OK, who's first?" Larry asked.

"The usual?" he replied.

He won the rock/paper/scissors game they played, and stood up to go ask the girl to dance. Just then the band finished the song they were playing and announced that they were taking a short break. He stood a few feet from the girl not knowing what to do until the band came back.

He turned around and sat back down. The ten minute break seemed to last for at least an hour. When he was sure the band was about to start playing, he walked over to where the girl was sitting.

"Hi, would you like to dance?"

"Hi," was all she said as she rose and held out her arms. She was perfect in his arms, just the right height. She was slender but not skinny, and her body seemed to conform to his.

She whispered something.

"What?"

She said louder, "I love this song."

The band was playing *Harlem Nocturne*. It was his favorite song by this band. The song was played with a quiet background to a very good tenor sax. He didn't look down at her, but he said in her ear, "Me, too." They didn't speak for the rest of the dance. When the song ended, she stood close to him without moving; it felt good.

"May I have the next dance?"

She stepped back from him then and smiled. "I thought you'd never ask. Dina said you would ask me to dance."

"Dina's a friend of yours?"

"I met her on the beach today. She asked if I was coming to the dance, and I said I didn't know. She said there were some good dancers here. She mentioned you; I think she has a crush on you."

"I like Dina, she's sweet and a good dancer, but I, uhm…"

"It's OK, she knows that."

The music started and they moved out onto the floor. They spoke little as they danced. He was amazed at how easily she followed, and the way her body moved with his as if they were joined somehow together. He couldn't believe it when the band started playing, *Goodnight, Sweetheart*.

"It can't be midnight," he mumbled.

"It is."

"Can I walk you home?"

"I'm walking home with Dina. It seems we're staying right next door to each other."

"Uhm…OK. Will I see you on the beach tomorrow?"

She stood back from him a little and looked into his face; her smile was dazzling. "Without a doubt."

Now he smiled. She walked toward the door.

"Hey, wait a minute."

She turned with a laugh and said, "Lorraine."

"Oh… I'm Chris."

"I know."

THE EARLY MORNING dragged as they got ready for the day. He kept looking for her to cross the bridge to the beach. Noontime came and went. Two o'clock came and went. By three he realized that she wasn't coming. It left him confused and incredibly disappointed, which left him more confused since he had only met her last night.

He didn't see her come onto the beach because he was working in the snack bar. He went back to the lifeguard stand at four thirty to give Eddie a break, and she was there. He wanted to be cool.

"Hey, I was beginning to think you wouldn't make it."

"Miss me?"

"Maybe."

Man, he loved her smile.

"I have such light skin that I can't be on the beach until late in the day. Besides I thought I'd come late in the day; that way you could walk me home."

"What makes you think I want to walk you home?"

She smiled at him without saying a word.

"OK, I'll walk you home." Really, really cool.

THAT EVENING, HIS mom said, "Going to the dance early tonight and with your favorite shirt on? Who's the new girl?"

"New girl?"

"Yes, new girl."

"Lorraine."

"Lorraine what?"

"Wow, I don't know."

"Boy, this must be some girl. Might be a good idea to find out and tell me tomorrow." How did his mom know?

HE LOOKED AROUND the hall, but she wasn't there. Oh well, he was early. He turned back to the door just as she entered. He held out his arms, and she walked into them just as the band started to play *Harlem Nocturne*.

She smiled up at him, "Is this our song?"

"I think it must be."

"Good."

The rest of the night flew by; they danced and danced, and danced. It amazed him that she didn't need to talk a lot, although he did find out that her last name was Richards. She was from Seattle and came to the river to visit her uncle. She found out that his last name was Ryan, and that he was here with his mom and his dad, who only came up on the weekends. He told her that the house they stayed in belonged to his grandfather. He also found out that she was staying until a week from Saturday, which was tomorrow.

A WEEK FROM Saturday came the next day, or so it seemed. The last night she was here, they couldn't see each other because her aunt and uncle were taking her out to dinner. She was leaving the next morning at six to go to San Francisco and fly home.

Thursday night they left the dance early and took a walk on the beach. The night was warm with almost a full moon shining off the river.

He turned to say something and she was in his arms, and they were kissing. He felt as if time had stopped and he was swooning. He couldn't believe how fast his heart was beating.

They parted, and he started to say something. She smiled and said, "Will you please be quiet and kiss me again?"

They walked the beach and kissed. They walked in the water and kissed. They held hands and kissed.

He turned her around to face him, dropped his hands to her waist and rested them on her hips. "I know that this is cliché, but I have never ever felt the way that I feel right now."

She laid her head against his chest and whispered, "I know."

He walked her home. He kissed her so very gently when he said goodbye that she wanted to cry.

They were sixteen.

THE SECOND SUMMER

They had decided not to write during the year to see if, when they met the next summer, it would be the same. The only exception had been by her when he received a Christmas card that spoke of missing someone and love, but was unsigned. The Seattle postmark gave her away.

He had no idea when she would get there, but he had to assume that it would be about the same time as last year. June passed quickly enough, and then July crept along ever day seeming to never end. He counted the days 'til he would see her walk across the bridge.

He knew his feelings had not changed, but had hers?

SHE THOUGHT THE drive to the river had taken at least twice as long this year as it ever had before. She wondered if he had gotten taller. Would he be looking for her when she came to the beach? Would he be looking for her at all? She knew her feelings had not changed, but had his?

They arrived at the river at three, and she helped unload all the stuff from the car. By the time everything was done it was four-thirty. She fiddled around the house not knowing if it was rude to go to the beach right away.

"Hey girl, you gonna try to get to the beach this afternoon?"

"Is it all right, Uncle Tom?"

"Sure, we have everything under control here; besides there might be a lifeguard looking for you."

"But how did…I mean…"

"Lorraine, I'm not a teenager any more, but I do remember and I'm not blind. Go, go see the guy."

"Thank you."

She put on her new suit, just a little lipstick and started for the beach. It was already after five.

WELL, NOT TODAY, he thought. It was the suit that caught his eye, white with two black stripes that went from the right shoulder and ended at the left hip; *nice*, he thought.

Then his heart slammed into his throat. He didn't know what to do. He started to climb down from the stand, changed his mind and sat down, then stood up. *Slow down, stupid. You don't know what's happening yet.* He sat down and turned his eyes to the river. The beach was beginning to empty so there weren't that many people in the water. He relaxed, sort of. He didn't want to be obvious and let her know that he was anxious to see her. Then he thought, *the hell with it*, and turned to look. She was right next to the lifeguard stand, looking up.

She smiled. "Hey."

When she saw the smile that lit up his face, she relaxed.

"Hey, yourself. I'm done at six."

"Maybe you could walk me home?"

"What makes you think I want to walk you home?"

She looked at him without saying a word.

"OK, I'll walk you home." They both smiled. This time it was cool.

He had often been a little skeptical about the true love thing, about love at first sight, about how two people could forge a bond that would last a lifetime. Now he was pretty sure it was true.

ALL HER LIFE she had wanted to have the kind of love with one man that had never existed at home between her mom and dad. Her dad was kind of mean. He treated her mother with little respect and her with even less. She had always thought he must have wanted a boy. She wanted to be sure that she was loved by the man she chose to spend her life with. She was sure that Chris was the one, without a doubt.

HE WAITED WITH his back to the door watching the band; he still didn't want to seem over anxious.

"Hi."

He turned, starting to say something, and his voice stuck in his throat. "My God, you are beautiful."

She was seventeen. She realized this spring that she had probably quit growing. She was five seven, which was, she decided, a good height for a woman. When she tried on her new swimsuit at a little boutique, she realized that she had a really good figure.

There was a beautiful black girl there that waited on her and when she came out of the fitting room and stood in front of the mirror, the black girl was standing behind her.

"Girl, there are Hollywood stars that would kill for a body like yours."

"What!"

"Come on now, girl. Don't tell me you don't know how put together you are."

She had never thought of herself as being put together, but

she smiled now when she considered it. Right now she knew it was true by the look on Chris' face. It was the first time she had really dressed up for him. She had on high heels, a green sheath, very form fitting, a string of pearls and her hair down around her shoulders, with just enough make-up.

"Are you going to stand there gawking or are we going to dance?"

"Uhm…yeah sure…WOW!"

He pulled her into his arms. She loved the way he held her tightly, but gently. "Thank you for the WOW."

"Lorraine, trust me; you'll hear it again."

She looked up at him. He was about six two, fair skinned with almost black eyes and dark hair. He had a good build with enough muscle to be impressive, but didn't look like he lived at the gym. He was seventeen, but seemed all grown up.

AT THE END of the dance they decided to take a walk on the beach. They talked little as they crossed the footbridge over the water to the beach. He climbed up on the lifeguard stand and helped her up beside him. He kissed her lightly and said, "I was afraid that maybe things had changed; you know, about how you would feel."

"Nothing has changed. This whole year I worried about the same thing; that you had found someone else."

"No. No, I never could get over last summer and you. This whole last year I have thought about everything, about the little I knew of you, who you were. I mean I didn't know shit. Sorry. But I mean, oh hell, you know. I didn't know your birthday, what your favorite color was, what singers you really like, what your favorite food is, what you hate. Nothing. How could I be in love with someone I know nothing about?"

"What?"

"What what?"

"Did you say you're in love with me?"

"Did I? Yes, I did. Why?"

He couldn't believe when she started to cry.

"Are you OK?"

"Yes…I thought it was just me."

He pulled her very close. "No, it's not just you. I hope that means that you love me too?"

"With all my heart."

They sat and talked. They kissed a little, but mostly they just talked. They needed to know about each other. He told her things that he had never told anyone, and she told him of her dreams. They asked each other timid questions as though they had just met this night. And they talked about other things as though they had known each other forever.

He told her about his mom and dad. She could tell by the way he spoke of them that they were nice people. She said that she would like to meet them. She told him that her mom had died three years ago; that it was just her and her dad. About her dad she said little.

"Oh, boy."

"What?"

"The time, it's quarter to three."

"I've got to get home. My uncle will be worried to death."

He helped her down from the lifeguard stand and gave her a kiss that said a lot. "I have a feeling that I'm not gonna be your uncle's favorite person."

"Do you want me to go home alone?"

"Nope. My dad would kill me if I did that. And besides we wouldn't be in this mess if I had paid attention to the time."

"I love you."

He stopped walking. Gently he took her by the shoulders

and turned her until they were face to face.

"Look at me." She did. He loved her eyes. "Tell me that again."

"I love you, Chris Ryan."

"I love you, Lorraine Richards. I always will."

They got to her uncle's place and found the lights on; so they knew right away that this was not going to be easy. As they walked up the steps, the front door opened, and her uncle stepped out on the porch.

Before he could speak, Chris said, "I'm sorry, sir. After the dance we went for a walk on the beach, and we sat and talked. I didn't pay attention to the time and…well, I'm sorry. It won't happen again."

Her uncle said nothing, then, "I see. Lorraine, it's time you were in bed. Good night, young man."

He turned and followed Lorraine into the house.

AS HE WALKED home, he said, *Damn, damn, damn* to himself, over and over again, cursing himself for being such an ass.

He was not surprised to see the light on in his house as he walked up the stairs. He was a little surprised to have his dad open the door.

"Little late isn't it?"

"I know, Dad. It wasn't on purpose. We just were at the beach talking, and I didn't pay any attention to the time."

"Did you get the girl home OK?"

"Yeah. I apologized to her uncle, but he didn't say much. Boy, I hope I didn't screw this up."

"This the new girl that Mom told me about?"

"Yeah, I really li…No, I really love this girl."

"A little young to be in love, don't you think?"

"Dad, a couple of weeks ago I probably would have said yes,

but not now. I really love this girl."

His dad looked at him for a moment, then said, "Maybe you do, Chris, maybe you do. Let's go to bed; you have to work tomorrow."

Tomorrow came too soon.

HE GOT TO the beach early; more because he couldn't sleep than because he was anxious to work. The morning was busy what with umbrella rentals and boat rentals plus stocking the snack bar.

When Larry showed up, he left the snack bar and went to the lifeguard stand. It was shaping up to be a long day.

He didn't know why but he was sure that he would not see her today. On top of that he didn't know what to do to make things better.

Stupid. That was what the whole thing was, stupid. *OK*, he thought, *who's stupid?* The more he thought about it, it all came to rest with him. Now the question was what to do about it. The end of the day finally came. He had made up his mind to go to her house and try to explain to her uncle what had happened.

It was with some trepidation that he had talked himself into this solution, but he could see no other way. He walked slowly telling himself how he would explain. He was half surprised to realize that he had arrived at her house.

He took a deep breath then walked up the stairs and knocked at the door. Nobody answered. He knocked again. Still no answer. He didn't know if he was relieved or disappointed. He walked home slowly, still rehearsing what he would say when the time came.

He got to the dance hall early that night, found a place on the bench and waited. When it got to be eleven, he knew he would not see her tonight but stayed till midnight, not being able to leave, just in case.

SHE DIDN'T KNOW what to say to her uncle. The following morning it was hard to know what to say when you feel like a fool. Fortunately her uncle solved the problem for her.

"Hi Lorraine, it is another beautiful morning. You OK?"

"I'm fine, Uncle Tom."

"Lorraine, nothing happened last night that I should worry about, right?"

"No, nothing happened last night. Chris told you the truth."

He watched her for a moment, then said, "That's good. By the way I think I like that young man of yours. He made sure you got home, and he stood there ready to take anything I might dish out. That is not an easy thing to do."

"Uncle Tom, I think you'll like him a lot."

"We'll see, honey. Did you remember that we are going out to the ocean for the day, and then dinner with the Haggertys?"

"Oh, I forgot completely…that should be fun."

HE WAS SURE that she had been forbidden to see him, or she would have been at the dance last night. Boy, he couldn't believe that he had screwed things up this bad. He had to see her. He just had to see the girl that he was in love with. The last day without her had erased all doubt about how he felt. Not seeing her was almost physically painful.

He was at the beach early again and had things pretty well set up before anyone else even got there. He kept his eyes on the river and the bridge waiting for her to arrive by four o'clock. He was sure that she wasn't coming. He was sure that she had been told not to see him again.

THE WAIT UNTIL four o'clock was the slowest hours she could

ever remember. Since her uncle had said that everything was fine and that he even thought that he liked Chris, the weight that had been crushing her had lifted in an instant. Now the only thing she could think about was getting to the beach and seeing Chris.

She ran all the way to the beach then made herself slow down and catch her breath before she crossed the bridge to the beach. Her heart raced a hundred miles an hour.

IT WAS THE suit that caught his eye just as it had done the first day. His heart jumped just as it had the first day. He watched to see how she was walking. Her head was down as though she had something to do that she didn't want to do. *So*, he thought, *it is still bad news.*

He turned his attention to the river and carefully surveyed the swimmers. Everything looked all right.

"Hey."

He looked down at her smiling face and felt for the first time that maybe…"Hey."

"I thought that maybe you'd like to walk me home."

"Maybe; will I get shot?"

"Oh, I hope not; I'd miss you."

"We're OK?"

"Yes, though my uncle would like to talk to you."

"Just so you know, my dad told me that talking to your uncle was something I had to do."

HE HAD NEVER been what most people would call a pleasant person. In actuality most people thought he was that kind of person you could well do without. His only saving grace had been the girl he married. The only real friends that he had ever known were her friends that put up with him for her sake. They called him Big John because he was. At six four and two hundred and twenty pounds, he was an imposing man. What made him more imposing was that there wasn't an ounce of fat on him. She, Della, on the other hand was a slight five foot four and a trim one hundred and ten pounds, with sandy hair and blue eyes that sparkled, and the most infectious laugh you ever heard.

She died, without warning, of a brain aneurism at the age of forty-two. He and his daughter Lorraine buried her three years ago. Many thought that her death might change him. It did; it made everything worse. He became more morose and angrier. The few people that had been in his life saw little of him anymore. The worse thing was that he became a complete stranger to his daughter.

She loved her father. She asked her mother many times why her dad seemed distant from her. Her mom would laugh and say that he just didn't relate to women, but that he loved her for sure.

The first year after her mom's death Lorraine cooked dinner for him when she came home from school. After the first six months they were speaking only when necessary. She had given up trying to have conversations. He provided money for the house and the groceries, and made sure she was staying up in school. There were some nights when he didn't come home; he never explained why.

He wasn't mean to her nor did he treat her anyway other than what she thought of as neutral, as if she were someone else's daughter. She finally conceded to the idea that he just didn't care. But she still loved him, though she was sure that she would never understand why.

He looked at his daughter one night when he walked in from work, recognizing for the first time that she was growing up. He also recognized that she annoyed him because she was always cheerful and seemed to get along with everyone, like her mother. He was not sure if he even cared about her. In a few more years she would graduate and no longer be his problem.

THEY WATCHED THEIR son as he sped down the floor of the basketball court, stopped short and drilled a jumper from the top of the key. He was a good athlete. He was also a good student with a high grade point average and plans to go on to college.

They went to a burger place after the game, where Chris and his parents enjoyed the meal and the company. With the respect and love that they showed each other, it was easy to see he thought his parents were great and they thought he was a marvelous kid.

Chris and Lorraine could not have come from more different backgrounds in terms of their parents.

CHRIS DECIDED THAT he liked Lorraine's uncle after their talk. He didn't belittle him or talk down to him. However he made it abundantly clear what was acceptable and what wasn't.

He and Lorraine spent the next four days together every waking moment. What surprised Lorraine and Chris, though they came to the conclusion in different ways, was how much they liked each other. It was different than the love and the passion they felt. It was that if they had not been in love, they would have been the best of friends.

THEN IT WAS time for her to go home. They spent the last night dancing; they talked little. She knew her heart was going to break that night when he said goodbye. How could she not see him for another year? How could she bear it?

Chris asked her uncle if he could bring her home at one o'clock instead of right after the dance. He smiled and said yes.

When they finished dancing to the strains of *Good Night, Irene*, they decided to go for a walk on the beach. Once again they ended up on the lifeguard stand. They kissed, and they talked. Her head felt just right on his shoulder as did his arm around hers.

"Lorraine?"

"What?"

"You know that I want to make love to you."

"Yes," she hesitated. "I want to make love to you, too."

He pulled her very tight and just held her. He could feel how tense she was. With her head on his chest, she could hear his heart racing.

"More than anything else that is what I want, but not until I know that it will mean the start of our lives together."

She pulled back from him and looked into his eyes. Slowly she took his hand and put it on her breast. "I want you right now more than I have ever wanted anyone or anything. Yet I am happy that you want to wait. I'm glad you said it. I don't think I would have been able to."

He smiled and then laughed, then shook his head. Reluctantly, he took his hand from her breast.

"What's so funny?"

He felt the tension drain from both of them. "You and I. We are a little weird, aren't we? I mean here we are totally in love with each other, and we only spend two weeks of the year together. That is a little screwy."

"Speaking of which, are we going to write or talk to each other this year?"

"By the way, thank you for the card at Christmas. Wasn't too hard to figure out who it was from. I think the postmark gave it away."

"Oh, you are a clever devil."

"I liked knowing that you were hopefully waiting for the summer just as I was. How about we send something to each other once a month?"

"Thank you. I didn't want to go another whole year and hear nothing from you."

He turned to her and drew her into his arms, then kissed her with all the pent up desire that they both felt. They parted and looked at each other; the love was complete and unspoken.

"And now, you absolutely beautiful woman, I have to get you home or I will be shot."

WAITING FOR SUMMER

His senior year was supposed to be special and it was. The only thing that was missing was the fact that the girl he loved was living in Seattle. The football team almost made the championship, losing only the final game of the season. The swim team did win the championship; it was their third in a row. He dated some, but didn't take out the same girl twice. It was all in all a good year.

HER SENIOR YEAR was good at school and with her friends. But she and her dad seemed to drift even further apart. The loneliness she felt with Chris being so far away was made worse by her relationship with her father. It was rapidly deteriorating to the point where, for the first time, he seemed angry with her. She had no way of knowing that, for her father, everything including work was going downhill.

Everything he did turned out wrong. As for his daughter, everything she did seemed to turn out right, and he got angrier.

HE DIDN'T HATE his daughter, at least he didn't think he did. Yet his anger kept getting greater. He noticed the cards that came for her from California and wondered if it was some new girlfriend that she had met when she spent her two weeks with her uncle.

Finally after a bad day at work, he read one of the cards. It definitely wasn't a girlfriend.

It was some horse's ass that probably wasn't good enough for her, someone she had met on some beach. He thought he would just put an end to it. He picked up the paper he had read that morning and reread the story of a terrible accident that had killed a seventeen-year-old girl. He read the article carefully and found no mention of name or any relevant facts. He cut the article out of the paper, put it in an envelope and sent it to the little prick. *That should end it*, he thought. He took the post card that he had read and shoved it in the garbage.

He told himself that she wouldn't care one way or the other.

THE THIRD SUMMER

Summer. Lots and lots of people looked forward to summer. In the case of Chris Ryan, it wasn't just wanting summer to be there. It was a longing for summer, and a greater longing for the week after the fourth of July when she would be there.

He would graduate on this coming Saturday, and Monday he would be at the river; five more days, that's all he had to wait.

He looked at the mail, thinking that they would hear from each other one more time before July and there it was, a letter with a Seattle postmark. But it wasn't her writing. *What in the world is this?* he thought. *She's playing some kind of joke, maybe?*

He opened the envelope and pulled out the folded newspaper. As he read he slowly sat down on the bench in the garage. *It couldn't be true; it just couldn't be true.* He didn't know when the tears started; he didn't care. When he heard the sound of someone choking back a sob, he knew it was him.

How long he sat paralyzed on that bench he didn't know. He did know that there was absolutely nothing he wanted to do or anyone he wanted to see. He just wanted to sit there until he found out that this couldn't be true.

EVERY DAY NOW that school was out, he watched his daughter run out to get the mail. *She's waiting for a letter from that beach bum*, he thought, *stupid*. Being in love, what does that get you; nothing but heartache. He should know. He walked into the kitchen. She was sitting at the table writing a letter, probably to that jerk.

"Lorraine, some kid called yesterday and asked to talk to you. When I told him you weren't here, he said to tell you that there was someone else, and then he hung up. You know who that was?"

She was shocked by what he had said and wondered if it were true. It could only have been Chris.

"Haven't a clue. What did he sound like?"

"Young, probably your age. Listen, I'm going to walk down the street." That meant that he was going to the bar.

"OK, see you when you get back." That was a joke. When he came home, she was always fast asleep.

To try to reason with yourself that something is not true because you don't want it to be is a fool's mission. Even though you know that it is, still, that's what you do, over and over. She finally went to bed deciding that she would work it out in the morning simply because she knew it wasn't true. It couldn't be.

Sleep was denied her all night long. She finally gave in and got out of bed. It was five-thirty in the morning, and coffee sounded good. She watched the sun come up and wondered if he were watching it too. She knew what she had to do. She would wait 'til this summer at the beach and find out the truth. At seven the phone rang. It was her favorite uncle, Tom. She felt a lift in her spirits; she loved her uncle.

"Hi, Lorraine. How are you, girl?"

"I'm fine, Uncle Tom. How are you?"

"Never better. However that being said, I have bad news. Your aunt fell down some stairs at work…"

"Is she OK?"

"Well, yes and no. She broke her right ankle and her left wrist, and, on top of that, she messed up her shoulder. Now according to the doctors, she is out of commission for at least two to three months. Sooooo, we are going to have to call off our summer vacation this year. I'm sorry, honey, but we just don't have any choice."

She felt her heart fall out of her chest; now it was impossible.

"Oh Uncle Tom, I understand completely. Would it help if I came down and took care of Aunt Janet?"

"That's sweet of you to offer. I'm sure that we have it covered, but thank you, I'll keep in touch and let you know how Janet is doing. Bye, sweetheart."

"Bye, Uncle Tom."

Now she wouldn't even be going to the beach.

For the first time since her father had told her about the phone call, she was lost as to what to do. She still consoled herself that it wasn't true and then came the tears. She had always known that something could happen like this, but she had never really believed it would. Now it had; so somehow or other she would deal with it. Her heart knew it would take a long time. A very long time.

HIS MOM SAT down beside him. "Do you want to talk?"

He looked at her and wondered if he could tell her about what had happened. "It's about Lorraine. She…" Finally he held up the newspaper clipping, and his mom carefully took it from his hand.

"Oh, honey, how did you get this?"

"It came in the mail. I don't know who sent it. It just can't be true."

The tears were streaming down his cheeks. He sat on the bench as though he was frozen; the only thing moving were the tears.

She pulled her son close. "I wish there were something that I could say. I wish desperately for that, but nothing I could possibly say will make any difference. The only thing I can say is that I am so sorry. I know that you loved that girl."

"Mom, I don't know if I will ever find another girl that I could love as much as I loved her. We met at the dance at the river, and the first time I held her in my arms, as crazy and foolish and childish as it may sound, I knew. When we talked about the night we met, she said that it was the same for her. I just don't know if I'll ever find that again."

TWO DAYS LATER Chris came into the house; it was the day after his graduation. He called a hello to his mother.

When she called back to him from the kitchen, he went in and said, "I got a job down at Twentieth Century Market for the summer. It's full time and it pays better than lifeguarding. I hope you're not mad, Mom. I just couldn't go back there this summer. OK?"

"I understand, honey. You will come up and visit a few times during the summer though, won't you?"

"Oh, sure."

BY MID JULY she couldn't stand the thought of it anymore. She had to hear from him directly that it was over. She had some money, so she decided to go down to California and get a friend to take her to the river and find out if it was true. It took her two days to get to the river, arriving on a Thursday afternoon. She got down to the beach at four o'clock and ran into a lifeguard that she had met the year before.

"It's Larry, isn't it?"

"Uh, yeah. Do I know you?"

"We met last year. I was wondering if you could tell me where I could find Chris Ryan?"

"Oh, Chris. Yeah, well, he isn't working here this year. I heard he got a gig down in the Bay Area, changed his whole scheme. Probably got a new girlfriend or something; can't see any other reason you wouldn't want to work here."

She didn't even remember thanking him as she made her way off the beach and up the hill to the road. When she arrived here, she was fearful that it would all be true. Now she felt devastated that it obviously was. She slowly climbed into her friend's car, and they set off for Santa Rosa.

CHRIS' MOM TURNED to get a better look at the girl getting into the car across the road. But the girl disappeared and the car drove away before she got another look. She shook her head. That couldn't have been Lorraine; she's gone. She decided not to mention it to Chris; obviously, she was wrong.

THE END OF SUMMER

Fall came; time for college. Chris had decided to stay close to home for his first two years. He had checked into the local community school and, to his surprise, found it had a great reputation. Also all its credited course grades could be transferred to four-year schools.

He thought of Lorraine all the time; still in his heart wanting to believe that somehow it was a mistake or a bad dream. He flew through school with good grades, but it seemed it was all by rote. He still worked at the grocery store where he eventually was promoted to clerk. By living at home, he was able to put almost all the money away for his last two years of school.

Graduating, what a concept. It really didn't seem as though he had started at Cal and suddenly, it was over. So here he was, a gentleman graduate of the University of California.

THE UNIVERSITY OF Washington was a huge surprise to her. Here she would get a good education, thanks to her mother's foresight. She would never know what possessed her mother to buy a one hundred thousand dollar insurance policy in her name for her education. Could she somehow have had a premonition that something was going to happen to her? That she was going to die? Lorraine knew that trying to understand or rationalize her mother's reasons was futile and instead just accepted it as a mother's love for her daughter.

The four years at the university would go by far too quickly, according to her Uncle Tom and Aunt Janet, but she thought it would be a drawn out process. They were right. The four years were gone in the time it took to take a deep breath. She dated and yet she still thought of Chris, never quite letting go. The memory of what could have been was as alive as that night on the lifeguard stand.

LIFE MOVES ON

Chris called out as the man walked toward him. "Hey, Phil. How's the world treating you?"

"It isn't. I have to buy most of my own. How about you?"

"Can't complain. Want to go to Shorty's for lunch?"

"Sure, you buyin'?"

"We'll see. It's a possibility; though not likely, it is a possibility."

He had been working with the small airport as one of his clients for three years. He was hired to work out a new business plan and fell in love with the place. He had finished college in three and a half years and gotten his master's in business in one and a half. He spent one year working for a small accounting firm until he was sure that it wasn't what he wanted to do. He wanted something that challenged him.

On Sunday mornings he started looking through the classifieds. With his coffee and pastries satisfying his sweet tooth, he browsed. He had seen an ad for a manager wanted for a small firm with the proviso that he set up a new business plan. He applied for the job. He found that he had vision and a knack for getting down to the nuts and bolts of what needed to be done. It was also noted by his clients that he had the ability to listen.

He now had more than a dozen clients that he had helped set up business plans, and who still used him as a consultant. The airport was, however, his favorite; for with the job came an offer to learn how to fly. One flight with an instructor and he was hooked.

Hooked might not describe the depths of his enchantment of flying. He found it an ethereal world without limit. The complete freedom that he felt the minute the wheels left the ground was both calming and exciting.

One of the mechanics had an old bi-plane that he let him use on the cheap and, brother did he use it. Every minute that he could spare he was flying. Within one year he had his instrument license. He was out at the field getting ready to fly down the coast to Santa Barbara when Jed the mechanic, who owned the plane, stopped to talk.

"Hey, Chris. How goes it?"

"Great, Jed. How about you?"

"Can't complain. Listen I've been meaning to talk to you. Since I never get to use my own plane anymore, why don't you just buy it from me?"

"Great idea; it's a great plane."

They settled on a price and Chris found himself the proud owner of a Stearman bi-plane. He flew all over the state of California to little airfields that nobody had ever heard of, some even private fields. As he flew, his skills as a pilot improved, until he knew that he was a very capable pilot.

SHE HAD JUST finished working five hours in the operating room when she heard, "Ahh, you look marvelous darling, just marvelous."

She knew that she looked like shit. She had no makeup on, her hair has bedraggled from sweating under the hot lamps, and she needed sleep.

"You, kind sir, are an idiot."

Malcolm Green was a friend and also a nurse. He was a tall blond with a perpetual smile. They dated for a while. When they realized that it wasn't going anywhere, despite his wanting otherwise, they became fast friends. He had since found a girlfriend, but they still did things together quite often.

She and Malcolm walked down the hall together, chatting about how their days had been.

WHEN SHE GOT back to her locker, Lorraine flashed back to how she had come to this point. She had finished at Washington with a degree in business administration with a minor in language. She had gone to work in a large company's tax department that she found was OK but left her wanting something else. What that was exactly she had no idea.

She had not spoken to her dad in a year, which she gathered was all right with him. She still felt a certain love for him at times and, in the next instant, a deep sorrow and loneliness for the love of a father. Loneliness for the arms of a father to give her comfort and tell her that everything was going to be OK. She had needed that more than once.

The neighbor who had lived next door to them for years called her at the office and told her that her dad was seriously ill, and that she should probably come home.

When she got there, she found a hospice nurse at the house.

"Hi. I'm Lorraine."

"Oh, hello. I'm a nurse with hospice; just call me Billy. Are you a relation?"

The rueful smile on Lorraine's face made Billy a little sad.

"Yes. I'm his daughter, Lorraine."

"Oh, uhm, your dad never mentioned a daughter."

"Billy, I'm not surprised. We were never close. I don't really know what is going on here. I just received a call from Katy next door saying he is very ill, so I came home. Could you please tell me what is wrong with him?"

"Since you're his daughter, I'm sure it's OK. He's in the last stages of cancer of the lungs. He didn't let you know that he was sick?"

"We don't, uhm, talk much. Is he awake?"

"It is hard to tell if he is awake. He is pretty doped up so he may or may not recognize you. He may only have a few days left; I'm sorry." Billy said.

"Thank you. I have the feeling that he is being well taken care of."

SHE SLOWLY WALKED into the bedroom noting that it had not changed since she was a kid. He was lying propped up on pillows; his eyes were closed, and his breathing labored. His face was sallow, showing how much weight he had lost and had a poor, pasty color. She walked to the bed and gently took his hand. It was almost cold.

She stood that way for a few minutes, then said, "Hi, Dad. It's Lorraine. I don't know if you can hear me but I came as soon as I found out you were sick." She hoped that she would see his eyes flutter or something, so that she knew that he was aware of her presence. But nothing.

She stood for a few minutes more, intending to leave, then from some hidden place within her it came.

"Dad, did you ever love me? You never said so that I can remember. When I was small you never seemed to have time for me. I don't remember you even hugging me. Then when Mom died, it got even worse. I lived in a house with a stranger; someone I didn't know at all. And yet you made sure we had food, that I had clothes and that I was doing all right in school."

There were tears rolling down her cheeks but she kept on. "Why? I just don't understand why."

She didn't know how much longer she talked, but it all came out. All the hurt, the disappointment, the unending frustration, the feeling that somehow she had done something wrong. When it was all said, she quietly left the room. It felt as though she had been rung out like a dishtowel and thrown on the floor. She had never felt so tired in her life.

Billy was in the kitchen. "Are you all right, sweetheart?"

"Oh...yeah, I'm all right. Thank you, Billy."

"Well, sit down and have some tea."

"No, that's OK. I just..."

"Lorraine, just sit down and have some tea before, from the look of you, you fall down. Now I'm just going to go check on your father."

When Billy came back, they started to talk and, before she knew it, she was telling Billy her whole life story, even about Chris, something she never told anyone.

The next three days Lorraine stayed at the house and helped

in whatever way she could. The night nurse along with Billy did a remarkable job of caring for her father. She wasn't surprised that no one came to visit. She was not aware of her father having any friends. She thought that was a lonely and awful way to go through life.

On the morning of the fourth day, he quietly passed. He had never regained consciousness, leaving her with what he had always given her, pretty much nothing. She was surprised to find herself quietly crying when the funeral home came for him.

HER FATHER LEFT a letter of instructions for her that was concise, without fanfare. The following day she met with the lawyer mentioned in the letter.

"Lorraine, it's a pleasure to finally meet you."

"Thank you, Mister Bellows."

"I've known your father for quite a few years. We met at Clancy's Bar and Grill. Your father was a very different sort of person. From what I can gather, he had few friends. But for whatever reason, he and I hit it off and remained friends since we met. He did not speak of you often and yet, in his own taciturn way, I had the feeling that he was very proud of you."

"Thank you for that, Mister Bellows. My father and I just couldn't talk to each other. I never knew if he liked me, hated me or just didn't care.'

"I see. Well, that is sad, very sad. But to business, the will your father left is very straightforward. He left everything to you. Your dad was a man with simple needs that precluded him spending a lot of money. On top of that he was thrifty. To briefly sum up the contents of the will, he had the house, which, by the way, is paid for, a Buick that is also paid for and cash amounting to about sixty thousand dollars. Other than that are the personal things and, of course, all the household items."

"Wow…that's more than I thought, I mean…uhm…"

"Lorraine, I understand."

She and Mr. Bellows finished up their business, and she left his office enjoying the thought that she was somewhat independent now. She could now afford to become a nurse. This was something she had decided to do after seeing her father pass and watching Billy, who she had come to admire greatly.

She went back to the University of Washington, but this time for an accelerated program which gave her a BS in Nursing in two years. Now she felt ready to tackle the rest of her life.

THE FINAL SUMMER

Chris was standing next to his plane when he heard, "Hey, Chris. What are you doing here?"

"Oh hi, Mickey," he said to the owner of the airport. "Just thought I'd take a little fly out over the coast; should be a beautiful sunset."

"Yeah, just enough clouds to make it really beautiful. How many hours you have on that new engine?"

"About two hundred, they did a beautiful job." In the year that he had owned the plane, he had had almost every inch of it rebuilt. Its teal and white paint job made it stand out from the rest of the planes on the field. He had even named it.

"Chris, I was wondering if you could do me a favor. Edgar is sick, and I have a request for a patient flight from Boise. Would you have time to do it?"

"When?"

"Tomorrow."

Chris went through his calendar in his head. "Sure, as long as it's early."

"You can leave at six in the Cessna, and you should be back by four."

"Works for me." Chris said.

The Cessna was set up to carry hospital patients. Originally a four-seater, it had been reconfigured to fly patients from state to state or from one city to another. Chris had flown it half a dozen times but always with Edgar. It made him feel good to know that Mickey had enough confidence to let him make a flight on his own.

THE EMERGENCY NURSES was a small organization in Seattle that provided emergency care in rural areas that had little in the way of hospitals. They mostly worked in Washington State but on occasion had gone to Idaho and Oregon, and one or two times into British Columbia.

Lorraine's friends, Lotty and Billy, had been in on the founding of the group, and she had joined not too much later. This was her fourth time out. She smiled when she realized that she did not feel nervous this time.

When they arrived in Linden, Idaho, she, Dr. Landon, also a volunteer, and another nurse Shirley, were driven to the site of the gas explosion. They realized just how isolated the town was. The drive had been three hours over what could barely be described as a road. Flying in would have been faster, but the weather had made that impossible. Fortunately it was supposed to clear the next afternoon.

The only person in town with any medical knowledge was a retired Navy corpsman in his seventies. After they had examined the five injured people, they acknowledged that he had done a remarkable job.

They administered pain medication and cleaned the wounds. Two of the patients required hospitalization as fast it was possible to get them there. They prepared the patients for transfer and hoped the weather would clear early the next day.

HE WAS AT the airfield at five-thirty the next morning. He walked around the plane doing a visual check even though he knew it had been checked and rechecked.

"Hi, Chris. Ready to go?" It was Mickey.

"Ready as I'll ever be. OK to get going now?"

"No reason not to. There has been one small change though. They want you to fly into the town of Linden. They have a small airfield which they assured me is good enough for our size plane, but the town itself is tiny, only a little over a hundred people. The reason they gave me was that they didn't think the patient would survive the trip out by road. You all right with that?"

"Sure. Let's go look at the map and you can show me where Linden is located. I wouldn't want to fly by it."

"That will be the day. You know every small nowhere field in California. Why not in Idaho? Oh, one other thing, there is no ground communication with the field, so when you find it, just go ahead and land."

SHE LOOKED UP in frustration. "Shirley, is there any word on when that plane will be here? This poor man really, really needs a hospital."

"Doctor Landon said that the plane is already in the air on its way here."

"Thank God." Lorraine looked at the other man's chart. "I think Mister Simon can hold out 'til another plane can get here. This stinks!"

Shirley looked at her. "What stinks?"

"Not being able to do anything; that's what stinks. It's frustrating as hell."

HE LEVELED OFF and set his course for the little town of Linden. His adrenaline level was high as he felt the thrill of going to help someone by himself for the first time. He settled in for the nearly four-hour flight.

He was glad that he had spent so many trips flying to small, short airfields. All that practice would serve him well from what he was able to find out about the runway in Linden. It was gravel, not very wide and not very long, and apparently ran slightly uphill.

He was flying northeast across Nevada, then he would turn up into Idaho flying north until he reached Linden. He turned the radio on and found a station out of Elko that played a nice mix of music, some new and some old. It was just as he turned north that he heard the familiar strains of *Harlem Nocturne* float from the radio. He reached over to turn it off, but instead just relaxed and listened to a song he loved. He normally would turn the song off rather than let it make him remember the memories as clear and sweet as ever. Today he listened…it was still hard to believe she was gone.

ONE OF THE nurses would fly with the patient to the hospital in Boise. They decided that Shirley would go while Lorraine stayed with the other patients. In the meantime, they could do nothing except make them as comfortable as possible and wait.

Lorraine turned on the radio. The only station the town received was one from Elko. The first song that played was *Harlem Nocturne*. She wanted to turn it off but didn't because the memories stirred as vividly as if it were all yesterday. She wondered if he was happy, or if he were married, or if he had kids. She felt tears in her eyes. *This is crap*, she thought and walked away from the radio. Funny though, she still loved the song.

HE HAD A few landmarks that he had been given to help find Linden. It was with some surprise that he found it easily. When he saw the small water tower with the town name on it, he knew he was where he wanted to be.

He over flew the runway to take a look. It was longer than he had been told, and it looked to be in decent shape. There were a few people watching the plane from the upper end of the field by the only building, a small hangar. One woman waved.

He put the plane down smoothly, then taxied to the hanger; it was quarter to ten. He swung the plane around facing down the runway in preparation for takeoff and shut down the engine. He pushed the cabin door open and could feel that the heat of the day was already building.

"Good to see you. Glad you could make it so early. I'm Dill Monahan."

"Hey, nice to meet you. I'm Chris Ryan."

"It's a pleasure, Chris. I'm sure they heard the plane come in. They should be bringing the patient down very soon."

SHIRLEY, WITH THE help of two of the people from town and Dr. Landon, rolled the gurney to the door. From there it would have to be carried to the plane. She stepped out the door onto a rock the size of a fist, then tumbled into the street. She got up and immediately fell down again. "Doctor Landon, I think I screwed up my ankle."

He knelt beside her. "Let me see."

He did a quick examination. "Shirley, I don't think anything is broken, but we should get you off your feet 'til we can be sure. I'll have Lorraine go along with this patient, and we'll have time to see how you are."

All Shirley said was, "Shit."

HE BRIEFLY WATCHED as they approached the plane. He had done his visual and refueled, ready to take off for Boise. He heard the commotion as the patient was being brought down to the plane though he was occupied with checking the weather forecast for the flight to Boise.

"Be very careful when we put him in the plane. He is in a lot of pain."

The woman's voice was eerily familiar; he turned in his seat to see who she might be.

He knew that it is impossible for the human heart to stop and the lungs to quit breathing and not be dead, yet he was sure that was happening now. The shock was overwhelming. She was dead. Though he knew without reservation that he was looking at her now, how could this be? She was back from the dead? He was frozen in his seat not able to move or think or understand. Somehow he roused himself and got back to the bay door to help load the patient.

SHE LOOKED UP to the bay door and broke out in an immediate, 'Oh my God' set of nerves. *This can't be true; it can't be true.* Only a short time before, thanks to a song, she had been thinking of him and wondering about him. She felt her heart beating against her ribs so hard she thought they might break. And sweat, she was sweating like it was three hundred degrees.

STOP IT, STUPID! she thought; *it is not eight years ago. Do what you are here to do, take care of your patient, but my God, he looks wonderful. Stop it, you dumb broad; that is probably what his wife thinks.*

"You ready to load the patient?" Surprisingly her voice was steady.

"Uh…yep. I'll, uh…need one of you to get in the plane for, uh…when we swing the gurney and set it in place." *That's funny; why am I having a tough time talking?* One of the guys jumped up into the plane, and they strapped the gurney in place.

He looked down and for the first time their eyes met, and he knew that it was just like the first time he asked her to dance.

"Are you flying with me?"

"Uhm…yes, I am."

"Good. I mean, come on; let's get going."

He reached for her hand as she came up the stairs; his touch was so overwhelming she thought she would faint.

At the touch of her hand, he knew. What? He hadn't a clue but he knew. With that, he relaxed. He knew somehow things were going to work out. He was going to find out how this was possible. He also found that his tongue was in working order again.

She checked the patient who was sleeping from the strong sedative that he had been given, then climbed into the right hand seat.

"You need to put on the headphones so that we can talk when we are in the air."

She put on the headphones.

"Can you hear me all right?"

She nodded. He was looking at her as she stared straight ahead.

He started the engine, did his checks, and released the brakes, letting the plane start down the runway. He gave it more power and shortly it lifted gently into the air. Once high enough he checked in with the Boise tower; they were only half an hour away.

"How long 'til we get to Boise?" she asked.

"Half an hour…Lorraine, uh, you look wonderful…for a dead person."

"What!" She turned to look at him, confusion framing her face.

"I thought you were dead."

"What…why?"

"Just before summer, our summer, and two days before graduation, I received a letter postmarked Seattle. There was no note or explanation just a clipping with the details of a car accident telling of the death of a seventeen-year-old girl. The description fit you perfectly. The only thing that I could figure out was that your dad must have sent it to me, just to let me know. I almost came to Seattle to see if it was true…but I just couldn't do it. Why would anyone send me something like that if it weren't true?"

He was silent for a few minutes while her head went round and round in a maelstrom of thoughts, trying to make some sense of something that made no sense at all.

"I knew that I couldn't be on that beach that summer. It would be too…anyway, I knew that I couldn't, so I took another job. I haven't been back there since."

THERE WAS ONLY one explanation. With every passing moment she was sure that what she was thinking was true; it was her dad. He hated that she had a boyfriend. She hadn't mentioned Chris, but somehow he had known, probably from Uncle Tom. With complete clarity she remembered him telling her about a boy who had called saying there was someone else. She remembered her heart jumping into her throat and then dismissing it because she knew it couldn't be Chris. She closed her eyes as tears formed. *Why*, she thought, *had her father hated her so much?*

"Did you ever call my house?"

"No, Lorraine, I didn't. Why?"

"I came down to the river to find you, but you weren't there. Your friend Larry said you didn't take the job that summer; he thought you had a new girlfriend. My dad had told me that some boy called me and when he learned I wasn't home, the boy said that he had found someone new. I put the two together and just turned around and went home."

At the same moment, they both glanced at the other's hands; no rings.

"You're not married?" he asked, very tentatively.

"No." A pause. "You?" she said, very softly.

"No."

Their thoughts raced as each tried to come to grips with this extraordinary turn in their lives. The moment he saw her, after getting over the shock, the love that had lived within him rose up as strong as the day it began.

She glanced at him from the corner of her eye, feeling her heart beat faster every time she looked at him. She knew the swelling she felt in her heart was the total love for him that had never changed and never died.

"Lorraine, we are getting close to landing. Make sure your seat belt is tight."

She nodded, not daring to speak and checked the belt. For the next few minutes, she watched him, talking to the tower and preparing to land. *What*, she wondered, *is going to happen now? Does he feel the same way?*

"Lorraine."

She turned to look at him.

"Just so you know, I love you as much today as I did that night on the beach, perhaps even more."

She said nothing, but her tears flowed unchecked and that same dazzling smile lit her face.

The Dice Players

THE BAR WAS very quiet, then they heard, "Excuse me."

Tom turned and looked at the guy who had just spoken. He was average height, hair cut short, a little bit stocky with a smile, that you could tell by the lines around his mouth, was often and easily given.

"Yes?"

"I don't mean to intrude, but I was wondering if I could join your dice game? My name is Paul Gardner."

Tom turned to his friend Eddie. "You care?"

Eddie leaned around and looked at the stranger. "You play liars dice?"

"One of my favorite games."

"Yeah, then it's fine with me."

Tom held out his hand. "I'm Tom, and this is Eddie." They shook hands, and Eddie handed Paul a dice cup.

Three hands of dice and one more beer, and it was time for everybody to head home.

"Nice to meet you, Tom and Eddie. I hope to see you here again."

"Nice to meet you too, Paul. If you stop by here after work, I'm sure we'll see you again. Good night," Tom said.

SOMEWHERE IT'S WRITTEN that some people are just meant to be friends. Tom, Eddie and Paul just happened to be three of those. The meetings at the bar after work became a regular affair for the three. Turns out that Paul was the equal of the other two at dice and around that, a friendship was born. Let's face it; friendships have been formed around lesser things.

It was close to a year later when they were sitting at a table, the bar being too crowded, and Tom said, "Ya know, Paul, I still don't know what it is that you do for a living."

"Hmmm, I believe you're right, Tom." Eddie chimed in. "Now that I think about it, every time the subject comes up, Paul, you seem to take the conversation in a different direction."

"Oh, it's no big deal. I work for the Smith Lock Company." Paul had had just enough to drink and was relaxed, or he probably would have tried to change the subject.

"Like it?" Eddie asked.

"Yeah, it's a good job. The pay is decent and the benefits are good, so you can't ask for much more than that. Now I believe that you have the honor of starting this game, Edward."

"It's Eddie, remember. Only my mother calls me Edward."

IT WAS TOWARD the end of summer when Tom and Eddie walked into the bar. At the far end they saw Paul sitting with the two stools next to him empty, and three dice cups set out.

"Well, looks like you're waiting for someone." Eddie said. "Mind if we sit here 'til they show up?"

"Nah, that will be fine. They're late already, probably won't show anyway. You know, not real dependable types."

Tom said, "I know a few like that. While we wait, want to play some dice?"

"Sure."

They played three games, then let the cups rest while they enjoyed their beers.

"Paul, how did you get into working for a safe company? What do you actually do for them?" Eddie asked.

Paul, as the other two had already noticed, had had a few beers before they got there and was in a rare talkative mood.

"It's a crazy story. You guys probably wouldn't believe me if

I told you."

"Try us," they said in unison.

"It's no big deal. Let's play another round, and I'll think about it."

The three men finished the round of dice and their beers, and ordered one for the road.

Tom said, "Listen, Paul, if telling us is going to embarrass you or something, forget about it. It's no big deal."

"I don't know if you realize this, but I consider you guys as two of my best friends. It's just that I feel if I tell my story, you might think less of me. Does that make any sense?"

"Hell, yes," Eddie answered. "Nobody likes to think that people, especially friends, would think less of them because of something in their past. It is in your past, isn't it? We all hope people will judge us on who we are now and on the friendship they feel."

"Uhm…the thing is I did some time. You know, prison."

The answer hung in the air for a moment. "You kill somebody?" Tom asked quietly.

"No, no, nothing like that" Paul said.

Eddie looked at Paul. "Maybe I'm missing something but how does this relate to how you came to work for a safe company?"

"On that note," Tom said, "I think I'll have another beer."

Paul looked at his two friends, shook his head and said, "I guess the best thing is to start at the beginning."

Eddie and Tom nodded their heads in agreement.

SO PAUL BEGAN, "I grew up in a city in New Jersey. My dad was an immigrant from Germany who, I believe, thought that this country should be run more like his memories of growing up there. He wasn't an unkind man at all, and, in his way, he showed me that he loved me. However that being said he was strict, and I do mean strict.

"When I was four, he had me spending time in his shop. He was a locksmith, a very good locksmith. What made the whole thing work and kept me from hating my father 'cause I couldn't go out and play with the other kids was that the tools and the mechanisms fascinated me. To put it in plain words, I was hooked on being a locksmith at the age of five or so. The second thing that condemned me, if you will, was that I was a natural. Gifted is what my father said.

"By the time I was ten or eleven, I was going on calls with my father just about all the time I wasn't in school. I played in school and had friends, but I really didn't miss a lot of the other activities that the other kids participated in. In my second year of high school, an event occurred that in many ways changed my life. I got home from school and my dad said he had a call to try to open a safe that was jammed, and he wanted me to go along.

"It was an old Acme safe from around 1920. As it happened we had an old one behind the shop that had been given to us by a customer. He told us that it could no longer be opened, and that there wasn't anything of value in it anyway. When Poppa had nothing for me to do, I worked on opening that old safe. It took me over a year, but finally I got it open. It was just a funny, mechanical problem.

"I said nothing as Poppa tried to open the safe. He spent an hour or so trying the various tricks of our trade but nothing worked. Finally he sat back from the safe and raised his hands along his sides, a gesture that said he was beaten.

"He started to apologize to the owner, but I interrupted him and asked if I could perhaps try something. I'm sure he started to say no, then he gave me a strange look and said go ahead. Hoping I wouldn't look foolish, I tried the same thing that had worked on the old safe at the shop. The safe opened. My father said nothing. When we arrived back at the shop he finally asked how I knew what to do to open that safe. When I explained he just nodded his head. From then on he had me doing more of the work of the shop. For me it was the greatest thing he could have done to show that he believed in me, though he never said a word."

IT WOULD BE an understatement to say that Eddie and Tom were enjoying the story. Eddie said, "Paul, before you continue I think we need a beer and a pee." The other two men agreed.

With a break and a new glass of beer, Paul went on. "One of the things that people in the locksmith business have had to incorporate in their services is security systems. Once again I was lucky in the fact that they too interested me. Mister Able, our next-door neighbor, was a retired electrician who lent me books to read on electricity. When I completed the book, he would test me to see if I had gotten anything into my thick head. Those were his words, always. When he thought I understood what the concept was, he showed me the practical side. Even though he was retired, he still did small jobs for old customers and friends. It wasn't long before I did most of the work, and he supervised.

"I became very good at standard alarm systems and even designed quite a few of my own. We soon added this to our services, sold the products and installed them. By this time I was out of high school and working full time with my dad in the business. When I turned twenty-one, I was a very good locksmith with a talent for opening safes from jammed ones to safes for which the combinations had been lost. I knew just about all the tricks."

Paul paused for a minute, took a long pull from his beer with his eyes off in the distance, as though trying to decide how to tell the next part of his story. Eddie and Tom said nothing.

"You might have guessed that my prison time had to do with safes."

Eddie piped up, "Yeah, we might have guessed that."

Paul smiled. "I do want you to know that I didn't start out to be a crook. It had never entered my mind. I was making a good living, and the business was getting better all the time. What happened was…well, what happened was what happened. My dad's best friend in the world was a German immigrant like himself, named Anton. His granddaughter was diagnosed with a rare form of cancer. The treatment for it was going to cost a fortune, and the money just wasn't there. Even with all the friends pitching in and the state providing some money, it just wasn't going to happen.

"How I came up with the idea, I'm not sure to this day. There was a safe at one of the manufacturing outfits that I knew had cash in it every Thursday for their Friday payroll. I had worked on their alarm system and was there when the money was delivered. I knew it would be enough for the treatment.

"In all my life before or since, I have never been so terrified. I had made up my mind since I knew it would be the little girl's only chance, but terrified hardly describes the next forty eight hours. I did my homework on how I was going to do the job. Even with my good knowledge of the place, the safe and the alarm system, I was still scared shitless.

"I won't bore you with details, but I pulled it off without any problem at all. And I think that was where the trouble began. The next day it was on the news and in the papers. I was, to say the least, apprehensive. Nothing happened. To really show you how scared I was, I didn't even take all the money."

Paul continued, "Two weeks went by and still, from what the papers said, there was no clue as to who had done the burglary. I went to the public library and typed up what I hoped look like an official letter saying that this charity had heard about Anton's granddaughter and was giving this money for her treatment. When they received the money, everyone was so happy that no one thought to check and see if it was legitimate.

"That was, unfortunately, the beginning. I was acutely aware of everything going on while I did that burglary. The adrenaline rush was unlike anything I had ever experienced. It was like I was flying, soaring above everything and everyone. I ignored it for a long time, yet somehow I knew I would do it again, and I did. The same rush was there. The other thing that happened was it turned out I was very good at it. My nerves calmed down to the point where I was almost too calm. I was as good as there was."

Tom said, "If you were really that good, who caught you?"

"No one, really…this is the part I have trouble with. I never kept track of how many times I performed a burglary, though it went on for a number of years. I put most of the money in various accounts and spent very little of it.

"There was a large cash payroll in a business that I knew. It seemed the perfect target, and it was. I planned as meticulously as ever, making sure I knew the safe and the alarm system; it was a cakewalk. The problem was after the job was finished. As I was leaving the building, I knew I had an hour or more before the security guard made his rounds, so I relaxed and started down the stairs from the second floor to the first. At the top stair somehow my bag got in front of me, and I tripped and fell down the entire set of stairs. I hit my head on the way down giving myself a concussion and knocking myself out. That's how the guard found me later; out cold on the floor still hanging onto the bag full of money."

In spite of themselves Tom and Eddie were laughing, the visual in their minds was just too funny.

"I did three years out of a five year sentence and when I got out, I had no idea what I would do for a living. I was barred from opening another locksmith shop, and Dad had long since closed the old one. So there I was adrift with not much in the way of prospects. I was sitting in a bar nursing a beer one day when I decided that I needed to take a walk. As fate would have it, the walk took me by the Smith Lock Company.

"I stood in front of that building for ten minutes wondering if they would hire someone like me. I made up my mind to go in there and tell them that they should hire me because I was good at getting into their safes. I would also tell them that I was one of the few people that could break into almost any safe around. Believe it or not, they agreed, and I had a job. And that, gentlemen, is how I came to work for the Smith Lock Company."

Tom and Eddie now had their laughter under control. They congratulated Paul on a marvelous story. They agreed it was too good to be made up.

Paul left first, and as Tom and Eddie were walking toward the door, Tom said, "Do you realize that Paul turned from a life of crime to a legitimate job, using exactly the same skills. I think that makes him the best safecracker ever."

November 1944

HE STILL REMEMBERS this as though it were yesterday, perhaps it was. His wife came over to San Francisco from Marin County and met him at work. They had planned an early dinner at the *Trocadero* on Geary and then a movie at the Fox Theater downtown. It was a bit extravagant for them, but seemed to be worth doing.

The movie was, as were many in those days, a war movie featuring John Wayne, an actor who he always enjoyed. They arrived with plenty of time; a feat that his wife was extremely adept at. The lobby was crowded for the new picture release, and, with anticipation, they entered the theater. They had the requisite Coke and popcorn and found good seats not too far from the aisle.

They watched the previews of coming attractions, the cartoon and of course the newsreel. The feature began.

As the credits came up on the screen, the music began. It was the Marine Corps Hymn. At first he didn't notice as a few people stood, and then it was a few more. He looked to see who would be so rude as to stand up in front of people trying to watch the movie. At this point he discovered that those standing up were all wearing uniforms, Marine Corps uniforms.

By this time there were at least two hundred men standing; they were all Marines. The people in that audience knew who these men were, who they fought for and who they died for, and they did the appropriate thing. Every person in that theater stood until the Marine hymn ended.

Fate

HE WALKED INTO Harvey's in Tahoe, went straight to the bar and ordered a double scotch over. It was nine in the morning. When it arrived, he downed it in one swallow. He didn't like scotch, and why he ordered it, he hadn't a clue. But he asked for a second. The bartender gave him an appraising look, then poured another. He'd been a bartender a long time, and normally sized up and judged people easily. This guy confused him.

"Bad night at the tables?" he asked as he set the drink down.
The guy's mind was obviously somewhere else. "'Scuse me?"
"I said bad night at the tables?"
"Uhm, no, no, just got here."
"Sorry, thought maybe you were drowning your sorrows."
"I don't think it would work, but I might give it a try. My name is Jack."
"Pleasure, Jack. I'm Tim." They shook hands.
"My dad always told me it was a good idea to be on a first name basis with the bartender."
"Your dad was a smart man." He walked away to wait on some new customers. Jack picked up his drink and walked to a table set by the windows looking out at the street.

How, he wondered, *could a life that was just humming along turn to shit so quickly?* He shook his head; the answer, he knew, would allude him forever. He looked at his glass to find it empty. He could feel his body relaxing as the scotch worked its magic. Not a big drinker, he was surprised at how good he felt at this moment. He knew that he couldn't stay slightly hammered forever, though it was an appealing idea.

The other thing that surprised him is how he got here. He

had jumped into his car with the intention of just going for a long ride to let his mind clear, with no intention of going anywhere.

But here he was in Tahoe. Good thing he liked Tahoe.

IT WAS FOUR in the afternoon. "Hey Jack, have you got a room here?"

He looked up through unfocused eyes. "Uh, no. No room here." He said slurred and stuttering. He felt fine, a little dizzy, but fine.

Tim looked at Jack. "You got some problems?"

"Just one…big one."

"You OK for money?"

"Sure."

Tim made a decision and said, "Wait here. I'll be right back."

A few minutes later he returned. "Jack, there are no rooms available. Do you have any place that you can go?"

Tim couldn't understand what Jack mumbled and realized that he was about ten good breaths from being comatose.

"OK, my friend, come with me."

By the time Tim got him to his place, he could get no more than a mumble from Jack in response to any thing he said. He walked into the house; his wife was at the kitchen table. "Hi, sweetheart," he said as he gave her a kiss.

"Hi, Timmy. How was your day?"

"The usual." There was a pause.

"What?" she said. "You have that look on your face."

"I got a young guy out in the car with no place to sleep. On top of that, he's been drinking all day and he's kinda, you know, passed out."

She smiled and shook her head; it wasn't the first time.

"Nice guy?"

"Yeah, I think so. He's got something big on his mind. I asked him if he had problems and he said 'Yeah, one big one.'"

They brought him inside, mostly carrying him and put him in their spare bedroom. He was asleep before he hit the pillow.

HE AWOKE IN the dark bedroom with a start. The last thing he remembered was sitting in Harvey's, feeling a little drunk. He shoved himself off the bed and headed for the small light in what he hoped would be a bathroom. He barely made it. He knew he was alive because his head wouldn't hurt this bad if he were dead. Finished in the bathroom, he stumbled back to bed.

"Jack?"

He came awake slowly.

"Jack?"

"Yeah, I'm here."

"Hi Jack. I'm Tiffany, Tim's wife. When you're ready, there is something to eat in the kitchen, and there are towels and shaving stuff in the bathroom."

He heard her walk away. He looked at his watch at the same time he looked out the window at the bright day. *Noontime, how is that possible?*

He got out of the shower feeling a little more human. He dressed in the same clothes he had worn yesterday, no choice. He wondered how he even got here. Well, time to face the music. He made his way to the kitchen.

The first thing he noticed was that Tiffany was tall; he guessed close to six feet. Dark hair and a smile.

"Hi, Jack. You are Jack, aren't you?"

"Yes, ma'am."

"Well, sit down, and I'll get you something to eat; Tim's orders."

He sat. She put a steaming bowl of chili in front of him along with an ice-cold beer.

"Ma'am, I…"

"I know you don't think you can eat that, but believe me, you can. It's Tim's recipe for over-indulgence. I've seen it work wonders, now eat."

He ate, slowly at first, then halfway through the bowl, he didn't have to force himself to eat, and the beer tasted cold and good. It worked. By the time he finished eating, and after two aspirins, he thought his head might stay on his shoulders and the chili in his stomach.

"Tiffany, I don't know how to thank you and Tim. I can't think of anyone that I know who would show a perfect stranger, let alone a drunk perfect stranger, so much kindness."

"I won't say it happens all the time, but it happens often enough. Tim's just that kind of person."

Jack stood up. "Is there anything I can do? Can I pay you or something?"

"For heavens sake, no." She paused. "Just be kind to the people you meet. That's Tim's favorite expression."

JACK LEFT AND headed back toward the casino. He was surprised that he actually felt pretty good. Chili and beer. *Who would of thought?*

Yesterday came back to him in a wave of jumbled thoughts. He was surprised that it didn't seem so bad today.

The doctor had been as nice as he could be under the circumstances. But a death sentence is a death sentence no matter how gently it is delivered. Jack had stood and shaken the doctor's hand, then walked outside to his car and decided to go for a ride and sort things out. He ended up in Tahoe.

He remembered that he hadn't called anyone. *Hell, who was there to call?* Work. Even though he was senior on the staff with

- - - - *FATE* - - - -

his company, he had no illusions that he couldn't be replaced without too much interruption. His ex-girlfriend Cicelly would be upset and her new boyfriend would, he was sure, comfort her. His parents were gone, an auto accident had taken them when he was twenty. And last was his best friend Damon, who was in turmoil over his marriage which seemed to be going the wrong way. Damon didn't need any more load on his shoulders than he already had. He was amazed at how short the list was.

All this deep thought had taken place while he sat on a bench across from Harvey's. As he was thinking he was also people-watching. He recognized no one. He had enjoyed, though, the number of people that he had seen smiling; the young people clinging to each other, their love showing through in their expressions, and all the others just going through their day to get to another day. He grinned. That's what life really was, dealing with one day at a time and waiting for the next day to happen.

HE HAD NO idea what he was going to say to Tim. So he said the first thing that came to mind. "Tim, how were you so lucky to end up with someone as special as Tiffany?"

"You said it. Luck, just pure, horseshit luck. How are you feeling?"

"Well, thanks to a recipe of chili and beer, and some aspirin, I actually feel pretty good. By the way, thanks for taking care of me."

"No problem. Speaking of which, how's your 'big' problem working out?"

"Tim, it hasn't changed since yesterday. But it doesn't seem as bad today. I guess maybe that's an improvement."

"That sounds better."

JACK SPENT MOST of the rest of the day walking around Stateline like any good tourist. He had lunch at one of the casino buffets—something he always liked—and did some shopping since the only clothes he had with him were the ones he was wearing. He also did a little gambling, played a few machines and a little bit of craps; he won at both. He was also able to get a room at Harvey's.

A little before four he made his way back to the bar at Harvey's, and had Tim make him a screwdriver.

"Would you and Tiffany like to join me for dinner tonight?" he asked Tim.

"Can't tonight, Jack. We have a birthday party to go to for a good friend. Are you going to be around a few days? We'd love to spend your money on another night."

"Yeah, I am. I'll see you tomorrow then."

JACK WALKED BACK to the bar and ordered another screwdriver. He took the time to introduce himself to Andre, Tim's replacement for the swing shift. He was sitting at what he now considered his table by the window when he saw a couple arrive at the bar. She in her wedding dress and he in his tux; their faces flushed with the excitement of being in love and newlyweds.

He heard Andre take their order for champagne and watched him pull out a small bottle of champagne and two glasses. Jack caught his eye and signaled that he would pay for their drinks, and then shook his head hoping Andre would understand the meaning.

He did. Jack heard him explain to the two when he refused their money that there was a guy who left a standing order for the first newlyweds to arrive at the bar that day. The order specifically said that it would give him great pleasure if they would allow him to buy their first drinks as man and wife.

The girl squealed with delight and the young man reached

- - - - FATE - - - -

across the bar and shook Andre's hand. Jack heard him say, "Would you please thank the gentleman, whoever he may be, and tell him that he made a wonderful day even better."

Andre poured them each a second glass of champagne. They thanked him and wandered off into the casino.

"That was nice of you, Jack."

"It's funny, Andre; I think I enjoyed that more than they did."

"Sometimes it works that way."

"Yeah. I'll see you after I find myself some dinner."

ONCE AGAIN JACK ate at the buffet. Finished, he made his way back to the casino to one of the crap tables. He won steadily, enjoying the action and the people. As they played the table, he glanced at the rail where his chips were and took a quick count. He had about five hundred dollars there. He smiled. *Not bad*, he thought, *for starting with just a hundred.*

He watched her walk up to the other end of the table. She was, he estimated, close to his height, about six feet. Her eyes were wide set, and she had a little too much nose with very high cheek bones, but the effect was startling. He realized that he was staring at her. When she caught his eye, he looked away but not before seeing the deep green coloring of her eyes.

She was greeted by name by a couple of the croupiers, so he gathered that she was probably local and a regular.

Jack was trying not to look at her too much, but he found his eye drawn to her quite a few times. He watched how she played the game. She played well, but it seemed she was afraid to bet too much, and that kept her from winning very much. One mistake he noticed was that she didn't take the odds as much as she should have. The next three people to have the dice didn't make a single point, and a number of players went broke and left the table. Jack saw that she was down to maybe fifty bucks and was looking troubled and nervous.

He heard the croupier ask her, "Still no luck finding a job, Mindy?"

"There just isn't much out there, Al."

"Well, keep looking; you'll find something."

"I have 'til Wednesday to pay rent, or I have to move out of my place. If that happens I'll have to go back and live with the folks. I thought maybe I'd get lucky tonight, you know just kind of had that feeling."

Jack had never thought of it before, but he liked the name Mindy.

The guy next to Mindy busted, and it was her turn with the dice; she was down to about twenty bucks. He watched as she turned the two deuces up on the dice before she threw the come-out roll. Seven, a winner. She had only had five dollars on the line.

Jack had a hunch. "On the Yo," he told the croupier.

"You sure?"

"Yeah."

He had thrown a hundred dollar chip on the table. The croupier placed the bet. He glanced up and found the girl looking at him. He returned her look until she focused back on the dice and turned the two deuces up. She picked up the dice and threw; they bounced off the wall right in front of Jack.

"Yo, eleven. We have a winner." Jack had just won thirty-five hundred dollars. The croupier shoved his winnings over to him with a smile; everybody loved a winner. The croupier's nametag said *Mickey*.

"Mickey, split the winnings with Mindy down there." He nodded at the other end of the table.

"You sure?"

"Yeah." He picked up his half of the winnings, threw two hundred on the table for the crew and walked back to what he

- - - - FATE - - - -

now considered his bar.

ANDRE ASKED, "FIND something to eat, Jack?"

"Good old buffet, my favorite place. How about a screwdriver?"

"Good choice."

Jack started to turn around when he felt a hand on his arm. "Why did you do that?"

He turned to find Mindy standing next to him, looking perplexed. At close range she was even more striking.

"Three reasons, I just had a hunch you were going to throw an eleven and decided that if you did, I would split it with you. The other was I heard what you said about your rent, and lastly, I was ahead so it was the house's money."

She stood looking at him, trying hard to see if what he said was for real. "I can't take your money."

He ignored her. "Would you like a drink?"

"No." She held out a handful of chips. He made no move to take them.

"I'll tell you what; sit down and have a drink or a Coke or whatever, and give me two good reasons why you can't take that money. If you can do that, I'll take it."

"Hi, Mindy. Can I get you something?" This came from Andre behind the bar. "Oh, I see you've met Jack. What would you like?"

The sigh that shuddered out of her sounded like someone a step away from collapse. She sat down next to Jack, her shoulders slumping. "Thanks, Andre. I'll have a Jack and Coke."

Jack said nothing. She sat looking at her hands on the bar. She paid no attention to Andre when he set her drink down. It was easy to tell that she was having a discussion with herself.

"First of all, I don't take money from strangers."

"I see," Jack said. He picked her hand up off the bar and shook it. "Mindy, I'm Jack. Now we are no longer strangers. What else?"

For reasons he didn't understand, he got what he was hoping for, a smile, not a big smile but a smile.

"I didn't earn it."

"Oh, but you did. You threw the perfect number and that is not easy, so in a way you certainly did earn it. So, Mindy, please put the money away, *please*?"

"You are something." She put the chips in her purse and stood before he could say anything else. She finished her drink and held out her hand. He shook it.

"Jack, you've been a life saver. Thank you." She turned and walked away. Jack started to get up.

"Let her go, Jack," Andre said.

Jack turned and looked at him, then slowly sat back down. "What about her, Andre?"

"Let's just say that she is a woman who doesn't need anything else in her life right now." The way he said it left no room for questions.

Jack nodded his head, not really understanding, then looked at his watch; it was only eight.

"I didn't mean to cut you off, Jack. That was a nice thing you did."

"Thanks, Andre. Ya know, it felt good."

JACK DECIDED TO go to the cabaret show. He was still feeling good though he would very much have liked to talk to Mindy more. He shrugged. *That's life*, he thought. Then it hit him again that his wasn't going to last much longer. He decided to not think about that aspect for a while. He didn't know if he could do it, but he would definitely give it a try.

- - - - FATE - - - -

The cabaret show was bad. The music was way too loud to the point where the girl singing could barely be heard, let alone understood. He asked for a booth and, because the place wasn't too crowded, the hostess had given him one by himself.

He started to look around, not really paying any attention to the show. In the booth next to him was a young man who, from snatches of conversation overheard, was trying very hard, too hard, to impress the girl he was with.

She said, "Why don't we go across the street and see what Harrah's is like?"

"Sure, sweetheart." He waved to the waitress for the check.

The girl brought the check, and the young man gave her a credit card. A few minutes later she came back and whispered something to him. He smiled and handed her another credit card. A minute later she returned and whispered in his ear again. He didn't smile this time as he started looking in his wallet.

Now, that had to stink, Jack thought, when he figured out that the guy probably didn't have money either. The cocktail waitress was looking away from the table while the guy looked in his wallet. Jack caught her eye. She excused herself from the other table, glad to be away from the man's embarrassment.

"Can I help you, sir?"

"Yes, you can. The people in the next booth, I'd like to pick up their check. Would you find some way to tell them that the casino is going to comp their ticket? When they leave, I'll take care of it."

The waitress looked at him for a minute. "OK."

She walked a little past Jack's table and then came back to where the man was now looking completely lost, as he tried to decide how to tell the girl he couldn't cover the check.

"Mister Davis, I'm so sorry, but I forgot to tell you that the manager told me the casino would be comping your check tonight. He also said to have a very pleasant evening."

The man just sat there his expression blank; then his face relaxed as he became aware that he had just been bailed out.

"Would you please thank him very much? It is truly appreciated. Are you ready, sweetheart?"

Jack liked the guy for not having tried to play the big man and instead just leaving with good grace.

Jack paid the waitress when she came back, giving her a very nice tip. "That was nice of you," she said.

"I know the guy."

The cocktail waitress smiled and said, "Sure, you do."

Jack laughed to himself. "So much for fooling some of the people some of the time."

IT WAS TEN o'clock. What to do? He wasn't tired. The circumstances were a little crazy if not bizarre. For a dying man, he had never felt more alive.

He walked back to his bar; Andre was still working. "Hey, Andre. How about a screwdriver."

"Sure, Jack."

The drink served, Jack said, "Is there a place nearby to gamble that isn't so big, you know, a little quieter?"

"Just down the road a bit there's a casino that sits in front of a golf course. It's smaller, but they have machines and table games; it's kinda nice. Bartenders name is Al; tell him I said hello."

A SHORT CAB ride and Jack walked into a small casino that fit Andre's description. After saying hello to Al the bartender, he walked over to a blackjack table. Not his favorite game.

The dealer's name was Irene. She was maybe five foot and about ninety pounds, and she dealt faster than anyone he had ever seen. She was dealing single deck blackjack. He didn't like the boot, so he sat down. He knew she was oriental though he didn't know where she was from. She had a mass of black hair and white skin; the combination was beautiful.

"How are you tonight?"

She finally looked at him, "Fine, thank you." Her voice was very soft.

"Quiet in here tonight." Trying to make conversation.

"Yes," she answered.

Jack gave up and turned his attention to the game. A twenty-one right out of the gate, then two twenties and she busted both times. Jack let his bet ride from the first hand where he had started with a hundred dollar bet. He now had almost a thousand dollars on the table. Unbelievable. The irony was too much. What a strange time in his life to get lucky, really lucky. He hadn't lost at anything since he got to Tahoe.

Jack picked up his chips, put a black one on the table for Irene who, for the first time, smiled as she said thank you; then he picked up his drink and walked back to the bar.

"Well, how'd you do?"

"Great. Al, have you got a really good smooth tequila?"

"Yeah, but it's fifteen bucks a pop."

"Sounds fine to me." He downed the shot, it was very smooth, left fifty bucks for Al and decided to walk back to Stateline. It wasn't that long a walk and the night was beautiful.

HE WAS PASSING a gas station when he became aware of his need for a bathroom. Coming out of the bathroom, he bumped into a young girl and apologized for his clumsiness.

She just nodded and walked into the ladies room; he noticed tears in her eyes. He walked into the office to return the key and overheard a conversation.

"Mister, I don't have six hundred bucks to fix the car. Hell, I don't have six hundred bucks for anything."

"I know it's tough, man, but I can't do it for any less."

"I ain't blaming you. I just don't know what I'm going to tell Sharlene."

Jack recognized that accent as coming right out of the heart of Kentucky; one of his best friends from the Corps sounded just like that. The kid sighed, then walked to the side of the station to wait for his girlfriend, muttering to himself.

"Will six hundred cover it for sure?" Jack asked.

"Yeah. If it goes good, might be enough for a full tank of gas too."

Jack handed the guy six hundred bucks. "I don't care what you tell them. OK?"

"Sure, that's damn nice of you.'

Jack walked out of the station and continued walking toward Stateline. He was feeling very, very good.

JACK'S WATCH SAID 12:30. He knew that the bar at the top of Harvey's stayed open till one AM; so one last drink and he would call it a night. He found a table by the window and was immersed in the view when the cocktail waitress asked what he would like. He turned to find himself looking into the eyes of Mindy. Taken aback he said the first thing that popped into his head. "I thought you didn't have a job!"

"I don't," she said sharply, "Tim got me this just for tonight; they were short handed."

Jack caught the sound of resentment in her voice. "Uhm, that was a dumb thing for me to say. Wasn't it?"

"Yes." But this time she smiled.

"Mindy, I would like a shot of what you think is the best tequila in the house with a draft chaser."

"Sure."

He watched her walk away; he liked the way she walked away. He liked her smile; he liked her legs. *Let's face it*, he thought, *you just plain like her.* How can you like someone you haven't really even talked to, but he did. STUPID. Hell, if things were only different he would…what the hell would he do? He was suddenly brought back to reality.

"I hope you like this tequila. The bartender said it was about as good as it gets."

Jack took the shot down and smiled, "Mindy, you tell the bartender that he knows his tequila; that was fine. Mindy, when you get off would you consider having something to eat with me, or a cup of coffee or whatever?"

She paused before answering, "Thank you, Jack, but I have to get home. I promised the babysitter."

"Oh, I see. Well, maybe I'll see you tomorrow."

Babysitter. She has kids? How many kids?

Jack waved as he left. *So much for that*, he thought.

MINDY WASN'T SURE that the way she had treated Jack was right. She wanted to make sure that he didn't start asking who she was and was she available to date etc. Right now she just wanted to get some order back in her life. That bastard Arleigh had screwed up everything. Suddenly she felt as though she were going to cry. She shook her head violently; that wasn't going to happen again, no more tears.

But what about Jack? She owed him something. He had bailed her out of an impossible situation when all she had done was throw the dice. She'd never known anyone do anything nearly that generous.

Yet there was no real way that she could repay him, and the one that came to mind made her ashamed for even thinking of it. That was out of the question. He had not intimated any such thing. He had just asked her if she wanted a cup of coffee, and she had abruptly cut him off.

She realized that she felt like crap and didn't know how to make herself feel better. She walked into her apartment quietly, not wanting to wake the boys. Nancy, her babysitter and best friend, was watching TV.

"Hi, Nance, everything quiet?"

"Yep, the boys are in bed, and there is nothing to watch on TV, as usual."

"If there's nothing to watch, why do you have it on?"

"Keeps me awake." She gave Mindy a hug. "See you tomorrow."

She peeked into the boys' bedroom. Her heart did a little twist as it always did when she looked at her twins. They were absolutely the one constant in her life, the one thing that told her that life was still good.

As she undressed she again thought about Jack. He was kind of cute. He had also done something for her that not many people would do.

TIM KISSED TIFFANY on his way out the door to work as he did everyday. When he kissed her goodbye, he wondered how he had gotten so lucky. Jack had had it right. His old Ford started one more time, and he gave a little thank you to the Lord. He was looking forward to talking to Mindy about her gig last night at the restaurant. She didn't know that the night manager had told him he wanted to replace one of the girls.

He found that he really cared about Mindy. He had never met anyone that was as nice and caring a person as she was, other than Tiffany, of course.

JACK WOKE EARLY, really still the middle of the night. Suddenly the weight of what his condition meant came down to rest squarely and fully in his mind. He knew that he had been escaping through whatever means he could find, but it had changed nothing. He did feel better mentally than when he had arrived. The best thing he could think of at the moment would be to sleep on it. He went back to sleep.

The sun streamed through the window lighting the room and waking him still far earlier than he had planned. He arose and took a shower, shaved and brushed his teeth. There was a coffeemaker in the room so he made a pot, then sat at the window looking at the beauty of the lake. This he decided would not be a bad place to live. There he was back to that living thing again. A living thing, him. If the doctor was right, this living thing wasn't going to be much longer. As he had done the previous day, he decided *To hell with it*. Now was not the time that he was going to worry about it. It was time he would go and do some more gambling, might even have a drink, after all it was already past six in the morning.

He walked past the crap table that was occupied by only three players, and the three girls running the table were trying not to look bored. He didn't know this bartender, so he introduced himself to Sal and ordered a mimosa. He watched for a few minutes and then walked over to the table where the point was nine. He placed the six and the eight, and put a bet on the come line. Just for the hell of it, he backed up his line bet just before the guy rolled a nine.

He tossed three twenty-five-dollar chips on the table for the girls, collared up his chips and walked over to the bar to arrive at the same time as Tim.

With his best Irish brogue, he said, "Is it yourself then, Timmy?"

"'Tis indeed, Jack, 'tis indeed, and how are ya findin' yourself this fine morning?" In a better brogue.

"Foin, foin indeed. Are ya servin' beverages this morning?"

"Aye, and what would be your pleasure?"

Jack dropped the brogue. "How about a nice mimosa?"

"No problem."

Tim set the mimosa down and Jack said. "Tim, did I do something wrong where Mindy is concerned? I thought I was helping her out, but last night I went upstairs to have a nightcap, and she waited on me. I tried to just ask her if she would like a bite to eat or a cup of coffee and, I don't know, she just shut me down. Oh, and she mentioned a babysitter. Does she have kids?"

"Look, Jack. You seem like a good guy so I'll make this as plain as I can. Mindy just went through hell with a complete bastard named Arleigh. One of the last of the great gladhanders. He not only promised her the moon, but he acted and sounded like he could give it to her. Somehow, and I've never asked, he talked her into loaning him all her savings, then poof he was gone. What made it worse was that her two boys really liked him. She fell apart. She just couldn't believe it. By the time she was able to face what had happened, she'd lost her job. There isn't much around in the way of work right now, so I don't think that she wants any man in her life, not even a good one."

"That stinks, Tim. Oh, by that do you mean I'm one of the good ones?"

"We'll see; the jury is still out. Another?"

"Sure, can't walk on one leg." Jack moved to his spot by the window and watched the morning develop on the street outside. He watched people with places to go, and all in a rush to be where they probably didn't want to be, at work.

Work. He had told them he would be back tomorrow. That's what his sense of obligation told him to do. And yet he knew that he just wouldn't be able to handle it if he did. The place would go on without him. He decided to take a walk. He'd call later to tell them he wasn't coming back.

HE WALKED AND thought about his predicament still not fully grasping what he didn't want to believe, that he was dying. He walked along deep in thought, his hands in his pockets, just putting one foot in front of another.

Startled by a voice, he looked up. "Excuse me."

He was looking at a guy with a sign that said, *Anything will help. God bless you.*

"I asked if you had a cigarette."

"No, sorry, I don't use them." They stood looking at each other. The guy had a long face covered with a scrubby beard and a predominant nose; his eyes looked intelligent. He looked to be in his forties.

"How long have you been out here?" Jack asked.

"Does it matter?"

"Yeah, it might."

"You're not a preacher, are you?"

"I've been a lot a things but never a preacher."

"Couple a months, maybe a little longer. Can't find a job. Nobody wants to hire a guy with only one leg."

"You hungry?"

"Always."

"C'mon, I'll buy ya breakfast."

THEY TALKED ALL during breakfast, telling each other a lot about themselves. Milt, Jack's new friend, was a vet who'd lost a leg in action, and since he'd been back, all that he had when he left was gone. Anger was his biggest issue, but lately he was managing it better. He didn't know why or if anything had changed,

– – – – FATE – – – –

but it was better.

They stood out in front of the restaurant. "Your family in San Diego, you think it will work this time?"

"It scares me to think about going home. I screwed things up royally when I got back, but yeah, I think it will."

Jack handed Milt five hundred bucks. "That should get you home OK, and my card is there too. When things get better, you can pay me back."

"Wow! Are you sure?"

"Yeah, see you."

Jack turned and started walking back toward the casinos. He never looked back. The nexus of an idea was rattling around in his head. He felt good, really good.

JACK SPENT THE rest of the day on the phone. He looked at his watch and was surprised to find that it was after six o'clock. No wonder his stomach was talking to him. He decided to shower and shave, then go to the buffet and pig out. He had shopped for new clothes that afternoon and was glad to have something new to change into.

As he left the buffet, he patted his stomach and headed for the casino floor. He had eaten too much, but enjoyed every bite.

High Roller Slots, the sign said. He didn't usually play slots. For him it was almost mind numbing, then again he had never played high roller slots.

He sat down at a twenty-five-dollar machine and fed it three hundred dollars; that would be twelve rolls of the machine. Ten rolls gone and he had won absolutely nothing. He hit the spin button and watched as the three reels lined up. There was a seven and then a double sign and then another double sign. The machine started making all kinds of noise with flashing lights; it was almost deafening. He didn't know what he had won until a woman spoke over his shoulder.

"Hey, that's a big winner. Nine thousand dollars. Congratulations, Mister."

"Uhm, thanks. What do I do now?"

"Just sit there. An attendant will be here in a minute. WOW."

Twenty minutes later, Jack was nine thousand, four hundred dollars richer. Damn, he felt good. He wandered through the casino 'til he came to his bar.

"Hey, Andre. How about a short screwdriver?"

"You got it, Jack. How's it going tonight?"

Jack couldn't suppress a smile. "Really, really good."

Andre hung around as there was only one other person at the bar.

"You been here a while, Andre?"

"Yeah, almost ten years. It's not a bad place to be."

"Kids?"

"Oh yeah, boy and a girl. One senior and one sophomore; the boy is a pretty darn good basketball player."

"I played high school basketball. It was a lot of fun, great memories."

"I did too. You're right; you keep those memories forever. Don't know if my kid's team will finish the season though; someone stole all the equipment and uniforms, even some of the kids' shoes. Unless they can come up with the money to replace everything, the season will probably be over."

"Man, that stinks. What's it cost to replace the gear for a whole team?"

"The coach thinks about a thousand, give or take."

"When did this happen?" Jack asked.

"Night before last. Fortunately they don't have a game 'til Friday night. Maybe by then…who knows?"

"Andre, do you keep your promise when you make one?"

"Yeah, I do. Why?"

Jack took sixteen of his hundred dollar chips and handed them to the bartender. He'd cashed in most of the nine thousand with the idea of a big night on the crap table. "I don't care where you tell people that you got the money, but my name never gets mentioned. Promise?"

"Hell, yes; but…"

"Never mind, Andre; it's OK." Jack picked up his drink and walked away from the bar.

Well, it hadn't started the way he had envisioned, but it was a start.

HE MADE HIS way around the casino just wandering and people-watching. As he neared the Hard Rock Café, the music was so loud it turned him away, and he found himself in the Race Book.

He ordered a drink, then found a racing sheet, and then a chair. He wasn't in any way knowledgeable about horse racing, but he found the form interesting. After a half hour he had garnered all the information that he thought he could from reading, and decided, just for the hell of it, to make a bet.

"I hope you can help me out," he said to the man behind the counter. "I've never bet on a horse before and don't know how to go about it."

"It's always a mystery the first time, but it gets easier. What horse?"

Jack flipped the racing form over onto the counter. "This one, *Dynamite* at Pimlico."

After a moment, the man said, "You sure? He's going off at a hundred to one odds; that is, as they say, a real long shot."

"Look, I know it's kind of crazy, but it's really just for the fun of it."

"OK, what are you putting down?"

"A hundred to win."

The guy looked at him, shook his head at another sucker, punched up the bet and handed Jack the slip. "Well, good luck pal! I hope you picked a winner."

"Thanks." Jack pocketed the slip and walked out of the Race Book. The reason he had bet *Dynamite* was for a friend of his whose favorite expression was "Dynnnnnomite." He couldn't help himself.

He looked at his watch; it was ten thirty. Still at a loss for something to do, he decided to go upstairs, have a final cocktail and call it a night. He saw Mindy the moment he walked into the lounge. He stood at the door until he caught her eye, then spread his hands to ask where he should sit. She nodded to a table by the window.

As he sat down, Mindy came over. "Hi, Jack. What can I get you?"

"Hi, Mindy. Filling in again?"

"Would you believe that this may be permanent? A two-week trial and then the job is mine if I don't blow it."

"You won't."

"I'm glad you think so. I know Tim had a hand in it. Oh, and he said, if I saw you, to remind you that you still owed him and Tiffany dinner. What's that all about? Tim said you'd explain."

"Uhm, yeah. How about a drink first, same as last night?"

"Sure."

He watched as she walked away, and as she came back he couldn't make up his mind which side he liked more. She set his shot and draft on the table then said, "Would you mind if I sit with you? I'm on my break, and I asked my boss if it was OK to sit with my brother while he has a drink and visits with me."

"I'd be delighted. I thought there was a resemblance. I just didn't realize we were that close."

"Jack, I'm sorry if I have acted like I didn't appreciate what you did for me. It's just that I'm going through a rough patch and didn't need anything more to deal with."

"I understand. Tim mentioned a few things."

"Tim looks after me and Tiffany does too, but he shouldn't have…"

Jack looked at her and smiled, "He's a good friend; you're lucky. Listen, now that we are related, I was wondering about a late dinner or snack or coffee or…"

"Look, Jack. It's not that…"

"Whoa. Did you know that I have been known to throw tantrums if I don't get my way? And further more I am not against a little blackmail either if I think it will help my cause. I mean, what do you think that manager would say if I told him I'd never seen you in my life before?"

"You wouldn't!"

Jack just smiled. "Oh, and by the way, your break is over if the way the bartender is looking at you means anything. Now give big brother a kiss on the cheek and go back to work. I'll come get you at twelve thirty."

He stood up and leaned toward her. She had no choice; she gave him a kiss on the cheek and whispered, "You are in big trouble."

He did notice that as she walked back to the bar she was smiling.

AT QUARTER TO one they were sitting in the coffee shop on the casino floor, she with a cup of coffee and he with a chocolate shake. They spent the next hour just talking. To the amazement of both they talked about everything under the sun. He was intrigued and delighted by the animation on her face when she told him about her kids. He knew without a doubt she based her

- - - - FATE - - - -

world on them.

She, on the other hand, couldn't believe that he was ever shy. He told her about having very bad acne, and that when he started high school he was only five foot one and close to a hundred pounds, maybe.

"Oh, God. Jack, I have to go. Nancy was nice enough to stay an extra hour, and that's already past."

"Do you need a ride home?"

"No, thank you. I have my car."

He walked her to her car and as she drove away he wondered about the feeling in his chest and what might have been.

THE FOLLOWING MORNING he woke late, fixed coffee and sat in the window wondering what to do with his day, and enjoying doing nothing. He knew what he wanted to do. He had given it a lot of thought. Money wasn't a big deal for him anymore, so he might as well help a few people out. Besides he liked the feeling he got when he did something for someone. The only dilemma he faced was who.

The thought of breakfast finally pushed its way through his deliberations and said now was the time. *Whoops, it's almost lunch time.* He was in the buffet twenty minutes later. Since breakfast was being cleared and lunch was being brought out, he decided that he was actually having brunch. He enjoyed every bite.

HE WALKED TO his bar to find Tim.

"Tim, I want you to know that I will not take no for an answer. Tonight you and that lovely lady of yours are going to dinner with me at the place of your choice. I won't…"

"Shut up, Jack! We will be delighted; however, there is one condition, and it's very simple. Since the place is our choice, we will pick you up at seven in front of the casino. OK?"

"Anyone ever tell you you're pretty bossy? And yeah that sounds fine."

Jack left Harvey's and made his way down to a small house he passed the day before on his walk. A sign in the window said, *Tahoe Veterans Help Center*, and in large bold letters underneath, it said *Welcome*.

He went through a screen door into an old house that could use a little care, and yet it was clean and neat. This told him that, amongst many others, a Marine lived here.

"Can I help you, young man?"

Jack turned and found a man standing in a doorway to what looked like an office.

"Yes, sir." Jack replied, "I was wondering what kind of help was available."

"Well, son, that depends. Once we used to get good donations and were able to give people a pretty good hand. But now it's very hard to get funds since it's just my wife and I. My son helps sometimes, but we're not an official charity that folks can write off. Right now I can offer you a phone if you need to call someone, a hot meal at a couple of places, and a place to stay for a night or two. And someone who will listen if you need to talk."

"Right now I could sure use a good meal."

"Well, son, come right this way. We were just about to have lunch."

They walked through the house to a kitchen in the back, looking out at a well-tended yard. Jack could see a small lawn surrounded by a path bordered by flowers.

The man turned to Jack "By the way, I'm Allen, and this is my lovely wife, Alice."

"It's a pleasure to meet you. I'm Jack."

Allen Gritsby had helped, in one form or another, hundreds of service men and a few women over the last twenty years. He

- - - - FATE - - - -

started his little service when he retired. He found that though he liked being retired, he still needed some outside interest.

He often saw some vet on a corner or sleeping in the park, and remembered that the help he got when he returned from World War II had meant a lot to him. He was convinced that it often didn't take much to set a person right. As little as a meal, bus fare or just somewhere to spend a night out of the cold worked wonders. Perhaps better than all these things was a person to talk to, especially if that person had been through what you had.

Occasionally he met one that didn't fit in with the average veteran he talked to. Some didn't quite fit the mold, if there was such a thing. Jack was one of these.

Alice served minestrone soup with a tuna sandwich. During lunch Allen observed that Jack didn't really seem that hungry, and that he asked a lot of questions of how they had started helping vets and just what they did for them. They spent a very comfortable hour talking after lunch, and then Jack said it was time for him to go.

Allen showed him to the front door and, as Jack said goodbye, he felt Allen put something in the front pocket of his jacket.

When he had walked up the street from the house, he pulled a ten dollar bill out of his pocket. He stood still for a minute aware that his vision was a little blurry. He was not the least bit surprised.

JACK WALKED INTO the building that housed the Big Brothers and Big Sisters. He could hear basketballs from what he knew would be the gym. The desk was occupied by a woman of indeterminate age with a smile on her face that Jack suspected was there all the time.

"Hi, can I help you?"

"Yes, I'm looking for Larry Martin." Jack hoped that no one

by that name worked here.

"I'm sorry, but no one by that name works here."

"I see. Well, maybe I have the name wrong."

"What did you wish to see him about?"

"Uhm, well, I was thinking about my son coming here sometimes and was just curious to see what the facility looked like."

"As I said I'm afraid there isn't a Larry Martin. I'm Olivia. May I show you around?"

"That would be very nice. Thank you."

The walk took about ten minutes. Jack noticed that the place was well kept and clean, but a good many things were in need of repair. It was obvious from her enthusiasm that Olivia took great pride in the work that they did with the kids, and was very proud of all her volunteers.

When they were back in her office, Jack said, "Thank you for the tour. I guess the biggest problem is funding."

"Oh lord, yes. There never seems to be enough to do half the things that the kids need."

"Well, thank you for the tour."

AS HE WALKED back toward the casino, Jack thought a drink sounded good about now. He had taken care of two things on a list of four. Tomorrow he would finish the list.

"Andre, how 'bout a short screwdriver?"

"Sure, Jack." As Andre set the drink down he said, "You may not want to hear this, but the kids look great in their new uniforms. Everyone wants to know where the dough came from. I told them that the donor wanted to remain anonymous. But I know that they would all like to say thank you."

"They just did."

Jack got up and wandered around the casino drifting generally in the direction of his room. He was looking forward to dinner tonight. He liked T and T; he didn't know where that came from but it was how he thought of Tim and Tiffany now.

He dressed in slacks and a shirt with a pullover sweater. At ten to seven he walked through the casino and out onto the corner of Stateline Blvd. He heard a honk and saw Tim wave from across the street. He walked to the car.

"Hey, Jack. Hop in."

As he opened the back door, the first thing he saw was a great pair of legs on top of which he saw a smiling Mindy. He felt the car start to move.

"Tim said that I had to come along, even arranged a night off for me. He said that Tiffany needed someone to talk to so she wouldn't be bored." This from Mindy.

Jack said, "Thank you, Tiffany. It would be terrible if you were to be bored at dinner. I know that Tim and I will probably do nothing but talk sports or something."

Tiffany smiled. "I knew you would understand, Jack."

They drove over the mountain into Carson City and parked at the Ormsby House.

"Jack, you like prime rib?"

"Tim, that is about my favorite meal in the world."

"Well, Jack, you're in for a treat."

IT WAS AN enjoyable dinner; the conversation was lively and fun as though they had known each other a long time. They had a drink before dinner and enjoyed a good bottle of wine with a dinner that was indeed a treat.

They wandered out to the casino after dinner, the guys playing a little craps with the girls going to the machines. Jack was just ready to throw the dice when Mindy came up, threw her arm around his shoulder and kissed him on the cheek.

"Jack, you won't believe it. I just won two hundred dollars!"

- - - - *FATE* - - - -

He threw the dice, turned and kissed Mindy on the lips, and was thrilled when she kissed him back.

"Seven lines, a winner."

Jack looked at Mindy. "You're something. You're always good luck; I just won two hundred too." They stood looking at each other, both thinking the same improbable thing.

"Hey pal, you going to throw the dice?"

Jack turned back to the table, reluctant to give up Mindy's gaze.

"I sure am, my friend. I sure am."

Jack threw a six for his point; then he bet the back line with the two hundred he had just won and bounced up his odds on the front line.

He felt very lucky especially with Mindy's arm around his waist. His next three throws were an eight, a nine, and a four. He won on the back line each time he let the bets double up.

"Mindy, blow on the dice."

"What?"

"Just blow on the dice." She did, and Jack threw a six. Everybody on the table was happy. Jack threw the dice seven more times, and each time Mindy blew on the dice. He threw his point two more times, plus a seven on a come-out roll. Each time he won, he put the money on the rail in front of Mindy. When he finally busted, he was well over two thousand dollars ahead. What he enjoyed even more was that T and T had gotten in on the action. He collared the chips, then handed them to Mindy as the four of them made their way to the bar for a drink.

When it was time to leave, Jack asked Mindy to cash in the chips while he went to the little boys room. She handed him the cash as they were walking to the car. Jack counted it, then handed half to Mindy.

"Jack, please, I can't."

- - - - FATE - - - -

"Mindy, I swear that when you're on the same table as I am I can't lose. Besides this money is for the boys' education."

"That's not fair."

"I know and besides, I'm not asking."

ON THE RIDE back to the lake, Jack and Mindy sat very close together. He was extremely aware of her thigh against his. She was hoping that he would kiss her and felt disappointed when he didn't. She wondered if she had done something to put him off.

He couldn't get out of his mind, not even for this evening, that he shouldn't start something that would never finish.

She could feel him withdraw from her. She tried to make conversation, but Jack didn't seem to want to talk though he answered politely. He did not, however, let go of her hand that he held almost too tightly.

When they walked to her door, he looked at her in a manner that she couldn't read. It was caring, she could see that, but also with a great sadness that she could not understand.

"Mindy, I had a wonderful time."

"I did too, Jack." She started to say more, but he took her face and cupped it in his hands. He kissed her with the gentlest kiss she had ever felt, then turned and walked back to the car. As Mindy watched the car pull away, she was crying openly.

"Everything OK, Jack?" Tiffany asked. She had picked up on the change in the atmosphere on the way back to the lake.

She heard Jack emit a sigh. "Yeah, everything is just dandy." There was the sound of complete despair in his reply. Jack said nothing more 'til they dropped him off at the casino where he thanked them for a great evening.

JACK WAS AWAKE most of the night with his mind wandering through one painful scenario after another; none of them worked.

"Hi, I'm Jack, I think I'm in love with you. Oh, and by the way, I'll be dead in a few months." There were more approaches, but they all ended up the same.

Finally at five AM he rolled out of bed and took a long hot shower. He then made coffee, sat in the window, and looked at the lake. Today he would finish what he started yesterday; then the best thing would be to go back to San Francisco.

HE HAD A good breakfast at the buffet and, in spite of his bad night and foul mood of the morning, he felt better.

He had decided that one of the things he would check out was his old Marine outfit's charity here in Tahoe.

"Good morning, sir. Can I help you?"

"Yes, Sergeant, I think you can. Do you still do the Toys for Tots Drive?"

"Yes, sir, every year."

"And the toys, do they stay here in the Tahoe area?"

"Yes, sir. A small amount of the money we collect goes to the national drive, but most of it stays right here."

"You can quit calling me sir, Sergeant. My name is Jack."

"Yes, sir, uh…Jack. You a Marine?"

"Yeah, I'm a Marine. When does the drive start?"

"It goes all year, but it gets intense toward the end of October."

"Well, thanks for the information, Sergeant, I'll see you around."

HIS LAST STOP for the day was the Douglas County shelter for abused women. He had been a regular contributor in San Francisco, ever since one of the girls at the company ended up in a Bay Area shelter for abused women. He had worked with the girl for a year or two, and always thought she was cute, but

- - - - *FATE* - - - -

quite withdrawn. She missed almost a month of work after her husband beat her severely, and she fled to the shelter.

He had never asked her about it, but heard plenty from the other girls in the office. She told them that had it not been for the shelter, she would never have made it. Jack started hearing about other women who had had to take refuge in the various shelters. What he had a hard time digesting was that there were so many.

When he arrived at the address for the shelter, he thought he might have the wrong address. The house was old and non-descript with little to let you know its purpose. It occurred to him that this might be an advantage if you were hiding someone from some guy who'd gone off the deep end.

He entered through an open door on the small porch and saw a camera pointing down at him from above the next door. Along side the door was a doorbell outlined brightly in red. He pushed the button.

"Yes, sir. Can I help you?"

"I was hoping to see the director. I'm afraid I neglected to make an appointment."

"Let me see if the director is available."

After a few minutes, the door was opened by a very petite woman with flaming red hair. "Hi, I'm Celia. May I help you with something?"

"I was wondering if I might see the facility. I was thinking of volunteering."

She appraised Jack carefully before answering, "We don't have many male volunteers. Why are you interested?"

"My sister." Jack lied.

"She had need of our services?"

"Not yours particularly, but one that does the same work in Minnesota."

"I see," she paused. "Why don't you come with me?"

- - - - *FATE* - - - -

CELIA GAVE JACK an informal tour and told him about their services and their successes. She remained guarded, as if she couldn't quite understand what he wanted.

"Celia, I can't thank you enough for the tour, all the information and insight. It is still hard for me to believe that there are men who can find it in them to treat women that way. I guess most of us turn a blind eye, preferring not to know. Thank you again."

JACK WALKED SLOWLY back to the casino, glad that he was finished with his stops and glad that he had gone to the women's shelter. It was just after one when he walked up to his bar.

"Hi, Tim. Thanks again for last night. How about a really nice glass of wine?"

"Sure, Jack." Tim set down the wine. "You and Mindy seemed to have a good time last night."

"We did. You were right about her. She is a really nice girl."

"Jack, did something happen last night between the two of you that I didn't notice?"

"No, no, nothing happened."

"Tiffany talked to Mindy this morning and said that she really sounded very sad. Mindy thought that she must have done something to upset you, but couldn't for the life of her think of what."

"Tim, Mindy didn't upset me…it's…it's something I can't explain. Please tell Mindy that I'm sorry if I hurt her in any way; it wasn't intentional. I'm heading back for the city tomorrow. Tim, it was a genuine pleasure to meet you and Tiffany. I don't know of two nicer people in the world." Jack picked up his wine and walked away.

Tim watched Jack disappear into the crowd on the casino floor, perplexed as he wondered what that one big problem was.

- - - - FATE - - - -

JACK FELT GOOD about his choices that he had spent the last two days investigating, and knew that his efforts were worthwhile. However he had not expected to find Mindy. Now his problem that he had been dealing with fairly well seemed much worse because of finding her. Well, tomorrow he would go back to the city, wrap up the details of his life and then…and then what? The doctor had mentioned chemo, and Jack had said no. He'd watched a couple of friends go through chemo. He knew that it was something he did not want to endure on the off chance it might help.

What a conundrum. Maybe, just maybe he'd found the right girl for him. Without time to share, it meant nothing. He couldn't help but smile. Here was a man who had put off many things in his life simply because he had all the time in the world. He wanted to be a success, make some good money and then take care of things like marriage and kids and a white picket fence. *Hell*, he had thought, *I have plenty of time.*

To hell with it, he thought. *I have one more night to gamble and enjoy myself before I leave.* Jack had been sitting on a bench watching the casino floor. He set his empty glass down, stood up and looked around, and noticed the Race Book. He remembered his ticket on *Dynamite* and headed that way.

"Yes, sir. What can I do for you?"

"Would you check this ticket for me?"

The guy took the ticket. "Well, I'll be damned. We wondered if you would come back."

Jack looked puzzled. "Why's that?"

"Oh, it's just that lots of folks bet on long shots and if the odds are big enough, they don't check on the results. We thought you might be one of them."

"I was, sort of. I had forgotten about until just a few minutes ago. You mean I won?"

"Yep, ten thousand dollars."

"Well, I'll be damned. The bet was just for the fun of it."

The guy looked at Jack. "If I were you, I'd keep having fun."

With the paperwork done Jack left the Race Book with the intent of finding a good drink to celebrate. He decided not to go back to his bar, so went to the bar at the back of the casino near the poker room. He felt good. Ten grand in your pocket would make anyone feel good.

The Jack and Coke tasted terrific.

JACK PATTED HIS stomach as he left the buffet, full and satisfied. He gambled for a while with little interest. His mind was on a girl he barely knew, and yet he felt lonelier than he had in his entire life. A few more drinks might take the edge off.

The drinks had not gotten Mindy off his mind. He looked at his watch and saw that it was twelve o'clock. If she was working tonight, she would be getting off in half an hour. He got up and strolled into the lounge, walked to the same table by the window, and sat down. He had seen her at the bar from the corner of his eye.

"Hi, Jack." Pleasant but distant. "What can I get for you?"

"How about a Black Russian?"

"On its way."

As she set the drink down, Jack looked up at her. "Mindy, about last night, I…"

"That's OK, Jack. You don't need to explain.'

"Thank you for that, but I need a favor."

She didn't smile when she asked, "What kind of favor?"

"Would you join me for a few minutes when you get off?"

"Jack, I…"

"PLEASE."

She paused, "All right, for a few minutes."

- - - - *FATE* - - - -

SHE SAT DOWN at his table, but seemed very distant.

"I can't stay long, or I'll lose a babysitter."

"Mindy, I know that I acted strange last night. But if I told you that it was because I like you a lot and that it was the only thing that I could think of to do, would you believe me? And if I told you that there's a reason I pushed you away and telling you that reason might hurt you, would you believe that? And if I told you that the only thing that I want in this world right now is to find someplace that they play nice quiet music so I could dance with you for a while, would I have any chance of it coming true?"

Mindy just stared at Jack and said nothing. She had never in her life heard such utter desperation in anyone's voice. This was insanity.

"OK."

"What?"

"I said, OK. Wait here." Mindy called her babysitter and begged.

JACK AND MINDY went across the street to another casino. In its lounge there was a trio that played easy listening dance music. They ordered a drink, then headed for the dance floor.

They danced slowly paying little attention to the music, holding each other as if they had danced many times before. Neither spoke very much, limiting the conversation to small things about liking a song, that the band was good, and it was a great night. She danced with her head resting on his shoulder aware of the warmth of his body. He held her so tight that he wondered if he was hurting her. They never touched their drinks.

Mindy couldn't believe they had danced for an hour. She turned her head to look up at him. "Jack, I have to go."

"I know."

Jack took her hand; they picked up her purse at the table,

went down in the elevator and walked to the entrance where Jack waved at a cabbie.

He had his arm around her and gently turned her, and once again took her face in his hands. Mindy couldn't fathom or understand the desperation and longing in his eyes. He kissed her again as he had the night before, so softly that she wasn't sure he had kissed her at all. Jack helped her into the cab and said nothing as it pulled away. She watched through the rear window until he was out of sight, sure that she would never see him again.

JACK ABSENTLY NOTICED that it was almost three when he got back to his room. He took off his shoes and lay down on the bed. The depth of his feelings, the emotions pounding through him were far greater than anything he had ever experienced; anything he had even dreamt about. The sense of loss for something that he had never really had was overwhelming. He let the tears roll down his cheeks and wondered when the last time was that he had cried.

He did not sleep, finally giving up the attempt at six o'clock. He shaved, then took a long, long shower, and dressed slowly, putting on a tie and the jacket he had on when he arrived. At the small desk in the room he wrote the four checks that he would deliver this morning. It made him feel a little better.

The buffet had been open for hours when Jack sat down. He was in no hurry, so he had a cup of coffee first before getting breakfast, and he took his time eating. He stopped at the crap table where the three girls were working; again he stayed for half an hour, but this time he lost. He had a waitress bring him a mimosa as he sat at the table by the window; his thoughts running in circles around his brain.

At ten after nine he started for the parking garage, and then decided to walk to the places he wanted to visit. The walk was refreshing. He stopped at each place just long enough to hand the envelope with a twenty five thousand dollar check to the people he had talked to on his previous visit. To say that they were shocked would be an understatement. Finished, he felt better; a feeling he would have a hard time describing.

He was walking back to the casino on the sidewalk when he heard a shout behind him. He was half-turned when the kid on the bike barreled into him, knocking him off the sidewalk into the street.

Jack neither saw nor heard the car that hit him. He was thrown back onto the sidewalk, hitting his head on a steel sign pole before crumpling in a heap.

WHAT THE HELL! Jack woke up in a panic. *Where did those bright lights come from?* He tried to turn his head away from the light beating down into his eyes, only to find he couldn't move his head. He tried to move his right arm to shield his eyes, but he couldn't move that either. Finally he raised his left arm; his hand literally fell across his eyes. *Shit, what the hell is going on and where the hell am I?* He tried to focus but drifted back to sleep instead.

"Hi, do you feel OK?"

Jack opened his eyes to look at the tallest nurse he had ever seen. "I guess so."

"Good, you had us worried. The doctor will be in to see you in a couple of minutes."

"Uhm, what happened?"

"You don't remember anything?"

"Not really."

"You were hit by a car."

Jack mulled it over a minute. *Now how the hell did that happen?* The nurse asked, "Is there anyone I can call for you?"

"You could call Min…No, there's no one to call."

A very young looking doctor walked into his room. "Good afternoon, Jack. I'm Doctor Marsh." Jack shook the doctor's hand with his working hand.

"You're pretty beat up from the accident, but from the body scan I can't see a single thing broken. You do have significant bruising and a couple of small cuts and a mild concussion. All in all, you were pretty lucky."

"What else did you see?" Jack asked.

"What exactly are you referring to?"

"I have cancer."

"You do?" The doctor seemed surprised.

"A large mass in my abdomen."

"I see," Dr Marsh said. "This was a diagnosis from a physician?"

"Yes, in San Francisco."

"Did he say what type of cancer? Did he do a biopsy?"

"He had a name for the cancer, but I'm afraid that I didn't listen. As far as a biopsy, I told him he could do it when I came back. I just had to get out of there." Jack paused. "I'm afraid I was in a state of utter panic. Next thing I knew, I was here in Tahoe."

"Hmm." Now the doctor paused. "Jack, I'll go take another look and see if I can confirm that what you say is correct. I'll be back as soon as I can."

If Jack was confused with all the things going on before, now he was adrift in a sea of what ifs, who knows and a great deal of maybes. *Good lord, now what?* He willed himself to slow down, to just relax and wait to see what the next moments would bring.

"OK if I call you Jack?' This came from his tall nurse.

"Sure"

"Good, I'm Kelly. I'm going to take off that wrap that we have around your right arm and side. You have as beautiful a

- - - - FATE - - - -

bruise there as I've ever seen. The doctor wanted to make sure nothing was broken before letting you move that arm."

Gingerly she removed the bandage. Whatever painkiller they had him on was beginning to wear off. His arm hurt every time she removed part of the wrap. He also noted that his leg was hurting every bit as much as his arm, not to mention the pounding headache that had just made its presence known. He mentioned this to Kelly; a few minutes later she gave him a pill.

HE SLEPT FOR two hours. He lifted his head; the headache was all but gone. He tried lifting his right arm and pain coursed through his whole right side. *Jack, my boy*, he thought, *that was not a good idea.* He moved the rest of his limbs gingerly, one at a time. Everything seemed to be alright as long as it didn't involve the right side of his body.

"I see you're back with us," Kelly smiled encouragingly.

"I'm not sure about that, but at least parts of me are."

"Jack, seriously, how do you feel?"

"The headache is almost gone. I can move everything but anything on the right side hurts like hell."

"That's just about what the doctor expected. Oh, and he'll be in to see you in a little bit."

JACK SLEPT FITFULLY, waking anytime he shifted to his right side. He watched as the darkness crept into the sky through his window. Since the doctor was taking so long, Jack was sure that the news couldn't be good; somehow he had expected no less. The night sky was completely dark when the doctor finally made it to his room. He looked whipped.

"Hey, Jack, sorry I took so long to get back here. We had a bad car crash, and I was in emergency all evening."

"That's OK, Doctor. I don't seem to be going anywhere."

There was the sound of defeat in his voice.

"All in all, how are you feeling after your run-in with the car?"

"I feel like I played ten football games without pads."

"I'm amazed that nothing was broken; you're pretty lucky. As far as that other thing goes, I asked two other doctors beside myself to go over the scan with me, and we concur. You do not have cancer; you have…"

Jack never heard the doctor's explanation of what the mistake had been by the other doctor when he diagnosed cancer. The sense of relief he felt blocked out everything around him.

The doctor was still talking. Jack interrupted, "I'm sorry, Doctor. I missed what you said."

"I could see that; it doesn't really matter. Jack, what you have is a benign condition and not cancer. You can leave here as soon as you want, provided, of course, that you can walk. If you want more clarification you know how to find me."

"Doctor Marsh, right this minute I honestly believe that I could fly."

"I want you to stay the night, and I'm going to give you something to help you sleep. Tomorrow it will be up to you."

"Thank you, Doctor, for everything."

The nurse came in and gave Jack his pill. He thought it was a good idea as his mind was running at warp speed. He was thinking about what he was going to say to Mindy when he drifted off to sleep.

JACK FIGURED OUT that the pill the tall one gave him must be good for four hours because at two in the morning when he shifted position, his side woke him up in brutal protest. He lay still, very still, except his mind once again was getting into high gear. He knew that lying still was not going to work at all. He needed to move, the thought of which actually brought pain.

- - - - FATE - - - -

Slowly he pushed himself up, leaning back against his arms; it hurt, but was tolerable. Nothing ventured, nothing gained. He let his legs go over the side of the bed and sat up. *Not bad. All I have to do is move in slow motion.*

He took his time about the next move, debating whether his leg would hold him up, then turned to the rails at the top of the bed, grabbed hold and put his feet down. *Hallelujah*, he winced, but he stood. Shifting his weight from one leg to the other was a definite adventure but by the tenth time, he felt his right leg would hold. Fear kept him locked in the same place for a few minutes, fear of ending up a heap on the floor. No sense prolonging the agony. He pushed off the bed, took three quick steps to the bathroom door using the knob for support.

His leg hurt a lot, but he knew he could walk. He was surprised how much his arm and shoulder hurt. When he caught his breath, he walked slowly around the room. It took a lot, but not so much that he couldn't take it. *Now what?* He got back to the bed and sat on the edge. He wouldn't let himself think about his reprieve…not yet.

He rang for the nurse. He couldn't believe it when Kelly walked into the room.

"What the hell! Don't you ever go home?"

"I'm working a double for a friend." She noticed him sitting on the edge of the bed. "Have you tried walking yet?"

"Yep, feebly but yes."

"And it felt how?"

"Worse than I thought, but not as bad as I expected. How's that for not making any sense?"

"I've heard worse. Maybe you should get back in bed."

Jack smiled at Kelly. "Nope, I'm getting out of here."

Kelly started to say something, then saw the absolute determination in his face and eyes. She liked this guy.

"What are you going to wear? Your clothes were cut off when you got here."

"Think you could find something?"

"Maybe." She turned and left.

Jack did find his shoes and socks in the closet but nothing else. By the time clothes were found, his release papers were signed, and everything else was taken care of Kelly. She wheeled him to the front exit where she already had a cab waiting. Jack shook Kelly's hand and thanked her for getting him out of the hospital and for the clothes.

Getting in the cab was agony. Jack noticed that it was almost six in the morning.

"Where to?"

"How about the pier where the *Belle* docks?"

"You got it."

IT TOOK JACK a long time to walk to the end of the dock where he found an old chair against one of the pilings. He leaned back in the chair and shut off his brain. He forced himself to just look at the mountains, and watched in awe as the sun started to play down their slopes from a slight hue of pink and purple until suddenly it was daytime, bright and beautiful.

He had a different appreciation of the fact of the new day because it was also his new day. He went back a week, going slowly through the events until he found himself here on this dock, knowing the incredible joy of his life doing a U turn for the second time in a week.

Now what? Seems he asked that question a lot lately. Mindy.

Love. He wasn't sure that he had ever been in love before. The one girl that he thought he loved, and probably did, had hurt him badly. Perhaps that was why he kept a tight control over his heart.

- - - - FATE - - - -

This was different. He wondered how many times he had heard that line coming from other people, and now it was his line.

When he wasn't with her, he wanted to be. When he was with her, he didn't want it to end, and when it did, he felt a loss. Crazy. Sure it was crazy he had known the girl for a whole six days yet…somehow or someway, he was sure. *OK, OK, enough flip-flopping around, now what? Damn, there was that question again.*

The last time she had seen him, she couldn't possibly think he was sane. Here he was with a beautiful girl that he dances with closely for an hour, kisses very gently (no passion, she must have thought), walks her to a cab, then turns around and walks away.

Boy, that must have thrilled her. How fast would she run the next time she saw him? He sat on that dock for another hour kicking himself in the ass, then coming up with a fabulous idea, then discarding it and kicking himself in the ass again. He finally thought, *This is bullshit; there is only one way to find out.*

WHEN MINDY GOT home that night, she cried again, not so much for herself but for Jack. Somehow in her heart she knew, even after only a few days, that she and Jack were in love. She was as sure as she had ever been about anything. She wasn't big on love at first sight, but it had been close to that. What was wrong? What had gone wrong the night they went to dinner when she had felt his kiss all the way to her toes?

There had to be a problem that Jack couldn't tell her about. *God, maybe he was on the run or was really married or…enough.* She shook her head to clear it, took a quick shower after she checked the boys and went to bed.

In the last two years she had had her share of men trouble, deciding that she could do without for a while, maybe quite awhile. When Jack had given her money at the crap table because she had thrown an eleven, her first instinct was *Here's another guy on the prowl* and she wanted no part of it. She still thought she wouldn't have taken it if she hadn't needed it so desperately.

Then she had talked to Tim, and he thought the guy was OK. She put a lot of faith in Tim's judgment. When she and Jack talked, she found him funny, something she had always considered important, easy to talk to and considerate. Then there was the dinner night and last night's dancing and now nothing but confusion. And in some weird way she was longing for him.

She went to work and, on the way in, talked to Tim. He had not seen Jack. She worked with the hope that something would change, and he would walk into the lounge. At the end of her shift, she asked the other bartender, and the answer was the same. He did mention a guy that had been hit by a car almost in front of the casino that morning. She had heard others talking about it while she was working; she went home saddened. She looked forward to getting home; just seeing her boys would cheer her up.

BY THE TIME Jack struggled back to the street, he was exhausted. He took a cab back to the hotel, glad that he hadn't checked out. He went to his room, took a long hot shower that hurt, and fell into bed; he awoke ten hours later.

The look in the mirror was not encouraging. His whole shoulder and arm from the elbow up were black, blue, yellow and purple. He gingerly lifted his arm and the bruise continued from the bottom of his ribcage to the middle of his thigh, skipped his knee and continued all the way to the top of his foot. *Wow, no wonder I hurt.*

A little over an hour and a half later, with a left handed buffet under his belt (Jack was smart enough not to take anything he had to cut), he made his way to a stool at his bar, where he found Tim.

"Well, Jack. This is a surprise. I thought you had left for the big city."

"I started to go and then things happened that stopped me."

Tim held out his hand. "I'm glad. It's good to see you again."

Jack shook his head at the offered hand, then pulled up his sleeve. Tim let out a whistle. "How the hell did that happen?"

"I had a disagreement with a car."

"You were the guy that was hit right down the street?"

Jack nodded.

"Oh man, Jack, that's terrible."

"Tim, believe it or not that was the luckiest thing that ever happened to me. I will explain later. Have you seen Mindy?"

Tim looked at Jack for a moment, then said, "She's been crying and trying to talk it out with Tiffany all morning; I think she fell for you. I couldn't believe it after all she's been through, but I think that's what happened. And Jack, I don't want to see you hurt that girl, understand?"

"You said that before. The last thing in this whole world that I want to do is hurt that girl. You really think she fell for me? You know like she's in love with me?"

"Yeah, that's what I mean."

Jack started to jump off the stool, got halfway and sat back down. "Oh God, that hurts. I need a Jack and Coke, strong."

Tim set the drink on the bar and stood there, waiting for an explanation.

"Tim, when I got here my world had turned pretty much to crap. Between you and the casino and gambling, I was able to put up with it. And then along comes Mindy and in a few days I knew that I was in love with her, but because of the crap in my life, I couldn't tell her. Things have changed, and now I can tell her. I just don't know how. After how weird I've been acting, she's got to think that I'm nuts."

"You're sure?"

"Positive."

"Then just go upstairs and tell her; just tell her."

"She'll probably hit me."

"Jack, if I'm any judge of character, that is the last thing she will do. Now go."

THE PAIN HIS body was experiencing was the worst since he left the hospital. What kept him going was what Tim had said, and the overriding desire to know one way or the other. He entered the lounge, leaned against the wall and surveyed the room. She wasn't there. Unsure, he just stood there.

"Jack?" Mindy couldn't believe he was there. She spoke again. "Jack?"

"I..."

It wasn't what she thought she would do if she ever saw him again, it just happened. She threw herself at him, throwing her arms around him in a huge bear hug. He screamed. She tried to push away from him, scared by his reaction. When she did that, she kneed him in the right thigh. He went down as if he had been hit with a club.

He was still holding onto her, so they landed, wrapped up in each other. He was groaning, and she was trying to get loose, wondering what in the world was going on.

"I...Oh God, that hurts...love you."

"What?"

"Sweet Jesus, Mindy, you're killing me. I said I LOVE you."

With her eyes locked on his, she kissed him the way he had kissed her the last two times, and that didn't hurt at all.

A Rolodex of Memories

SATURDAY MORNING. HE walked outside with his cup of coffee feeling the warmth of the morning sun. He couldn't help smiling when he thought about the coffee cup she had given him labeled, *Just another shitty day in paradise*. He used it all the time.

He adjusted his chair at the table so his legs were in the sun and the rest of him in the shade. He loved the time of year when spring gave way to early summer; *perhaps*, he mused, *the perfect time of year.*

He unfolded the newspaper that he had set on the table and looked at the front page, nothing new there, then the sport page and read about the game the night before, even though he had watched most of it.

After browsing through the rest of the paper he came to the obits. Nope, not today, nobody he knew.

WHEN HE HEARD the door slam, he called out, "Hey Ryan, how are you?"

"I'm fine, Grandpa, really good."

"That, Ryan, is the only way to be." He was at the stove getting breakfast ready for himself and his sixteen-year-old great-grandson. They spend one Saturday a month working around his house, something he always looked forward to.

"Grandpa, are you really ninety this year?"

"Yep, ninety years young this year."

His looks and demeanor strongly belied his age, but what fooled most people was the way he moved. He was still able to do most everything that he wanted to do. He'd had to admit some years back that an eighty pound bag of concrete now weighed at least a hundred pounds. On the other hand, his neighbors thought they would be lost without him. It was generally conceded that he could fix anything.

He looked at Ryan, sixteen and already six feet—*now how in the world does that happen?*

"How does pigs in a blanket, orange juice and fresh cantaloupe sound?"

"Super," Ryan said.

AFTER BREAKFAST THEY did the weeding in the vegetable beds, then went to the front of the house to weed the driveway.

"Weeds really bother you, don't they?"

"I don't think so much that they bother me. It's more that they disturb the order that I like around my house. I guess over the years I got in the habit of seeing things in a certain way, and not having weeds is one of the things I like to see."

"Well," Ryan said "they sure are a lot of work."

"Perhaps that's true, but then, hard work is good for the soul and body."

They had soup for lunch, a good, cold Gazpacho with just enough spice to make it interesting. The warm tortilla chips made it perfect.

After lunch he and Ryan did the side yard, then he showed Ryan what he wanted weeded around the fruit trees while he retired to his office to look at the mail. He only looked at the mail twice a week, and this week he had not bothered to look at it at all. He looked forward to cards or a letter and, surprisingly at his age, he got quite a few.

A letter from the last guy he knew from his Marine Corps days was a pleasant surprise. He opened it with a bit of trepidation, for quite often it was from a family member telling him of their loss. Not this time.

The writing was a little shaky but legible. His buddy Art was alive and kicking, as he said in the letter. He was just putting the letter on his desk when Ryan came into the office

"OK, Grandpa, the fruit trees are weeded. I put the bags of weeds in my truck; thought I would go to the dump on my way home."

"Thank you, Ryan. That'll work out well."

"Grandpa, what do you call that thing on your desk with all the names on it? Yours is the only one I've seen."

He smiled at the thought that he was really showing his age, and how old-fashioned he was. It dawned on him that for Ryan's entire life, you could put all that information in your cell phone.

"That, Ryan, is a Rolodex. It was what we old people used to keep addresses, phone numbers and other information about our friends before the electronic universe took over. Oh, and it worked just fine."

"The other day I was in here, and I looked at it and thought it was actually pretty neat. I noticed that some of the names have a red line through them, and some have a yellow line and some green and blue lines too. Is that some kind of a code?"

He smiled at his great-grandson. "You're pretty observant. Yes, it is a code of sorts, a pretty simple one actually. The red lines are through the names of the people in that Rolodex that have passed away."

"That's sad, Grandpa."

"I don't see it as sad. The first time I did that to a name was a little crazy. I received word that my friend Jim had died. I started to just tear out that card, but for some reason I couldn't do it. Maybe it was because he was the best friend I had in the Marines. I sat there and stared at the card for the longest time. Then I thought that I could just mark it somehow, so that I would know what it meant. That was the beginning of my system."

"What do all the other colors mean?"

"So you want the whole code?"

Ryan nodded.

"OK. There are five colors. Orange, a nice warm color, is for family. Every relative in the rolodex has an orange line. You already know what red is. Now blue is for people that are important in my life, the ones that give meaning to my existence, and who the mere thought of can makes me smile. Yellow is for the people that have disappeared from my life, and I have no clue what happened to them or where they went or even if they're still alive. That color always makes me sad.

"And then there's green, my favorite color. To me green means growth, renewal, beginnings, life. So the green lines are all the new people that come into my little world that keep the cycle going; that means the future is still bright."

"Grandpa, that is really cool."

"Thank you, Ryan. Now I think I'm going to go into the kitchen and see if we have any sweet tea for you and me."

"OK, I'll be in soon. That tea sounds good."

AFTER HIS GRANDPA had gone, Ryan spent a few minutes looking at the Rolodex, now the lines made a lot of sense. Finally he put it back on the desk and opened the door to the office when a thought struck him.

He walked back to the desk and once again picked up the Rolodex and spun through until he came to his name. There was his phone number, his address and his age.

He smiled and then laughed out loud. There were three lines on his card: an orange line, a green line and a blue line.

Just for a Day

HE WAS NOT mean. What did he care if people thought he was mean, especially the kids; he wasn't. Who cares anyway? He had to go pee.

He was old and crotchety. OK, disgruntled with the whole damn thing, sure. Life had not treated him easy. The only two things he had ever had that were his and his alone were taken away when he was nineteen years of age. He had thought about that most of his life, the big 'What If.' However, he knew that it could never have been any different than it was.

Life is what it is. Would it be nice to change some things if you wanted to, if you could? Sure it would. But would those changes change the rest of your life? Sometimes the unexpected consequences will be worse than what you had. Still…

He shook his head and looked in the mirror. Shaking his head had not removed his perpetual scowl. He knew that scowl hadn't been with him his whole life and wondered when it made its presence on his face.

HE WALKED DOWN to the park, a place he liked to be. Without thinking he walked to the practice field of the high school next to the park. It was the end of August, and football practice had been going on for about a week. The new season started in two weeks. He was there almost every day. He had only a few friends, and they were all guys from his time at work.

He sat at the top of the bleachers so he could see the field better. He was a keen observer of the game. A few times he had talked to a player or two about the game. They had been polite but distant, not listening to what he had to say because he was old. The one time he had approached the coach, he had been brushed off. This year a new coach had come in and taken over; he hoped it would help. They hadn't been very good for years.

A GOOD PART of his life, no, a great deal of his life, had revolved around the game of football. When he was young, he never gave the sport much thought. He was a baseball guy; added to that, his mom didn't want him to play. She was afraid that he would get hurt. His dad, who drank a lot, didn't care. Plus in grammar school, he wasn't very big.

That all changed when he started high school. It seemed that he shot up from five-five to five-ten in only a few days. Along with going tall, he went broad. He knew that he was athletic just by the fact that games of any kind came easily to him. At the start of his sophomore year, he was just under six feet and almost two hundred pounds. He ran well with a quickness that was deceiving. He was more than big enough to play, but he still wasn't that interested in football.

"Hey Grief, you coming out for the team this year?"

His name was Willard Grieving; his friends called him Grief. They knew better than to call him Will or Willie; he hated those names.

"I don't know, Red. I don't think it's my game."

Anyone that looked at Michael Grimes' hair knew why he was called Red. "Hey man, ya gotta; we really need some size out there. Just try it for me, OK? If ya don't like it, we'll forget the whole thing."

He thought it over. "OK, OK, but if I don't like it, I'm gone."

He loved it.

HE STARTED ON the JV squad. By the fifth game they had brought him up to varsity, and by the seventh game he was a starter. As the varsity head coach said, "I've never in my life seen anyone that explosive on offense or defense."

He was a linebacker on defense, and a halfback or fullback on offense. As with most great football players, there is some finite instinct that sets them apart from the average player. His sudden love of the game also made him a student of the game. He watched the pro games and the college games. He took books out of the library, all about football. He'd found a real purpose for his life.

His senior year was a year that everyone dreams about. He was voted MVP of his team that had gone ten and one, and become league champions. He was League MVP, played on the league all-star team, and to top it all off, he was elected to the all-state team.

He found himself being courted by four different colleges, with all of them offering a full ride scholarship if he would just play football for them. Life was good.

He had also met the girl with whom he wanted to spend the rest of his life, Diana. They had met at a sock hop. He was now over six feet two and the first thing he noticed about her was he didn't have to bend down to dance with her. She was a very lovely five foot ten. They danced the first dance and then three more after that, then went to the side and sat on the bleacher seats to talk. Never in his life had it been this easy to talk to anyone let alone a girl. Before the dance was over they were hooked, and they both knew it.

HE TALKED THE college offers over with his mother and decided on a university within driving distance. He had tried to talk it over with his father. It was clear that he didn't really care, so the talk was short. His dad was also half in the bag when they talked. It troubled him a lot that his mother stayed with his dad. He was drunk most of the time, he worked seldom and left the load of raising the family completely on her, yet she never said an unkind word against him. When Grief raised the issue, or tried to, all she said was that he would understand some day. He doubted it.

He was on the sideline the first two games of his freshman year in college, played a half in the third and was starting in the fourth. Though the team didn't have a great year, he did. He was the starting tailback and, with his size, he was hard to bring down. But what really surprised everybody was his speed and quickness.

By his sophomore year the team, the coach and he had all matured a little bit. The club had a different feel to it, confidence. Not arrogance, just confidence; they knew they could play. Halfway through the season they were six wins no losses, and he had eleven touchdowns plus he had thrown for two. They were already talking about him as an All-American.

He talked to his mother every Saturday morning early before the game. He loved to hear her voice and how she told him he was in the papers all the time and to be careful. He always laughed and said he would.

They had just won their seventh game and were on top of the world. Everybody it seemed was picking them to win their league title and go on to a bowl game. He was trying not to get too euphoric, yet he couldn't help feeling that life right now was pretty damn good.

THE PHONE CALL came at three in the morning. The keeper of the dorm, as they called him, woke him up with news of an urgent phone call. It was his dad, and Grief could tell he was sober.

"I don't know how to tell you this, Willard, but your mother is in the hospital. She had a fall and hit her head; she's in a coma."

"When did this happen?"

"Sometime early this afternoon. When I came home for dinner, I found her lying in the walkway to the house. When the paramedics got here, they took her immediately to the hospital. They wouldn't tell me anything except that she's in a coma and has a fractured skull."

He heard his father start to cry.

"Dad, I'll be home as soon as I can. You stay at the house; I'll see you there."

He told who he needed to tell at school, then headed for home. He called Diana and told her what had happened. She said they'd meet at the house. When he arrived at home, Diana was already there. His dad was sitting on the couch, his eyes were dry and red.

He gave Diana a hug, and she kissed him lightly on the cheek.

"Are you all right?" she asked.

"I think so, how's Pop doing?"

"He seems OK; just scared, I think."

He walked over to his dad. "Hi, Pop." He knelt in front of him. "You OK?"

His dad mumbled something and started to cry.

"Dad, I'm going to go to the hospital. Would you like to go?"

"I'd really like to stay here; it hurts to see her like that."

"Are you gonna drink?"

"No."

He stood looking at his father, wanting desperately to believe. "OK. Diana and I will be back in a little while."

At the hospital, he gazed down at his mom and told himself she would come out of this soon.

IT WAS THEN Grief decided to stay home until his mom could come home, and things were back to normal. He had no choice.

She came home two months later still in a coma. They could no longer afford to keep her in the hospital. He left school and went back to work. His father had become a recluse in his room, not wanting or unable to see or care about anyone else. If Grief didn't bring him food twice a day, he would probably starve to death. Now he had to take care of both of them at a time when he should be going to college and playing football.

The coach had finally quit calling and imploring him to come back to school. The season was over.

Through all of this, Diana had been a steady comforting source of strength. With her help he had been able to get by with outside help only two days a week. One night after they had checked on his mom and dad, they were sitting at the kitchen table enjoying some time together and the wonderful minestrone that Diana had brought. They were planning what they wanted to do for his twentieth birthday in a few weeks. He said he didn't want to do anything, then out of his mouth popped, "How about we get married?"

She didn't even look up from her soup. "Well, if you're serious, the answer is yes."

"I'm serious, very serious."

THEY WERE MARRIED the next day at City Hall. A few friends joined them at a local restaurant to celebrate. Three days later Diana was dead from a brain embolism. The doctor told Grief that she probably felt nothing at all. It didn't help.

He remembered almost nothing of the next six months. During that time, his dad passed away, and then the inevitable passing of his mother. His nickname had become his life.

At the end of the six months, he came back to his new reality. He rolled out of bed and smacked the alarm quiet. He was already in a bad mood. The day would be a long one. He acted and felt like an automaton; no brain, no soul, no feelings, no hope, and he didn't care. In his mind he had lost everything and everyone that he would ever love.

NOW IT WAS many years later. He had retired from the same job he had held since he came home for his mom. He never remarried or had kids. He couldn't help but wonder why he was alive, and at times he didn't feel that he was.

Football. He found, in spite of himself, that he still loved the game. He lived the game through television and the occasional high school game he went to see. He took out books from the library on offensive football, defensive football, coaching and even the history of the game. The six months between seasons were a complete misery. The game had changed from the days he played. It had gone much more to a passing game, especially the pros and college teams.

HE SAT AT the top of the bleachers watching the practice. He had a small notebook that he made notes to remember later, almost like he was coaching. He liked the new young coach. There was some new hustle to the practices, and the kids seemed to be having more fun, but they still didn't work very hard. When practice was over he stayed where he was, enjoying the late afternoon sun.

"Howdy."

He didn't realize that he had closed his eyes. When he opened them, the new coach was standing a couple of rows below him.

"Oh, uhh, hi."

"I'm the new varsity coach, Bill Sklovas. I see you up here during most of our practices. Thought I'd come over and introduce myself. Did you go to this high school?"

"Yes, I did, Coach, a long time ago."

"You played football right?"

"Yes…yes, I did."

"I played here myself about twelve years ago. What years did you play?"

"My last season was 1958," Grief said.

The coach stood there for a minute then said. "Wasn't that the last time the team went undefeated?"

"No. Actually we lost one game, but it was a hell of a good year."

"Must have been a great time to play; the consummate season, champions. No one can ever take that away from you. I'm sorry; I don't know your name."

"It's Will…just call me Grief."

"Really?"

"Yeah, my last name is Grieving; they've been calling me Grief all my life."

"OK, Grief. I gotta go, but it's been a pleasure to meet you. One of these days you'll have to tell me what's on your pad."

Grief looked down at the pad in his hand and his notes and thought, *Yeah, like he cares what's in my notes.*

That evening for the first time in he didn't know how long, he went out to *Joe's* and had a good steak.

THE FOLLOWING DAY he went to the bleachers to watch practice. Finding his usual seat, he took out his notebook and sat down.

He was saddened to see that the kids still didn't seem to have much desire. They ran through the plays all right, but without zest or enthusiasm. He wondered if it carried over from the last three seasons when they had been cellar dwellers. He liked the new coach. He seemed to have enthusiasm to spare, but so far had not been able to convey that to the players.

"Hey, Grief. Got any notes or advice for me?"

"Hi Coach, didn't see you coming." *That was a stupid thing to say.* "I have noticed a couple of things."

"Let me sit down. You can show them to me."

For the next half hour they talked football. The coach asked a lot of questions, as did Grief. It was apparent that they shared an instant respect for each other. They talked about the team's size, which was good. The kids had some speed at the skill positions, also good. But they lacked discipline; this was not good. One bright spot was a punter who could kick fifty yards; that was really good. The coach worried most about his quarterback. The kid had a great arm and was accurate, plus the ability to move. What more could you ask? However, the kid had not one ounce of confidence.

"Grief, I've gotta go. I'll tell you, my friend; you know one hell of a lot about football. You will be here tomorrow, I hope. I'd really like to talk some more."

Grief found himself smiling. "Sure, Coach, I'll be here. Don't have much of any place else to go.

"That's great. See you then, and thanks for the help."

This became their routine after each practice.

The last thing Grief told the coach was that he needed a leader on the team, someone to get all the rest of them going. Something Grief hadn't seen on the field yet.

GRIEF STOPPED AT *Lollie's* for a drink on his way home; something he hadn't done in a long time. It was a watering hole near where he used to work, where he had stopped many a time on his way home.

"Hey, Grief! Long time no see. The usual?"

" So, you are still here, Mike. I heard you had expired."

"Nah, it was just my wife trying to collect on the insurance."

"Good to see you, Mike."

"Good to see you too, Grief. Ya don't come around much. What's the matter? You don't like us?"

"Long story, Mike, long story."

He stayed longer than he should have. A few friends came in and, of course, he had to have a drink with them. So by the time he left, he was feeling no pain at all. It was a good thing he was walking home.

He lit a fire and pulled up his chair. He felt good for the first time in a while. He felt good about himself. A single malt Scotch would go a long way right now. He got up and made one. He also realized as he sat back down in his chair that he was reasonably drunk.

The fire had a hypnotic affect, and he soon drifted off thinking back to when he was playing. Enjoying the memories, enjoying the feeling of being young again. He wondered what it would be like to be that way once more, already knowing how magnificent it would feel. He posed the question to the air above him, *How about letting me be seventeen again, not forever, you know, maybe just for a day?*

His belief in the higher power had been lost during those six months when he lost his world, and his belief in magical things was even slimmer. *But*, he thought, *couldn't hurt*, then drifted off to sleep.

HE AWOKE WHEN it was still dark, almost morning. He shoved himself out of the chair, shook his head noting the slight hangover. He was surprised that he didn't hear the usual cracks and snaps as his old body protested movement. He wondered if yesterday was carrying over into today. He felt exceptionally good. He passed into the bathroom not bothering to turn on the light. *Why the hell do I need a light on to take a shower?* He knew where everything was.

He let the hot water run on him for a few minutes, enjoying the warmth; something he had started when he played football. His mind was drifting as he scrubbed himself vigorously, rinsed then dried, and decided to shave. He flipped on the light over the sink, looked in the mirror and passed out.

He awoke on the floor. *No, no, it was impossible, stupid; you're having a dream*, he said to himself while still lying on the floor. It occurred to him that it didn't feel like any dream he'd ever had before, so staying on the floor was probably the best idea because he was afraid to look.

But he stood up with his eyes closed, got a firm grip on the sink and slowly opened his eyes. His knees buckled again, but this time he didn't pass out. The face that looked back at him was seventeen; the body under it was seventeen. He jumped up and down, shook his head, yelled and pinched himself, but nothing changed. He was seventeen.

He walked into the kitchen knowing that a cup of coffee would probably wake him up and end this ridiculous nightmare. He made his coffee slowly, made a piece of toast, trying not to notice the young arms that were doing the work. Maybe you could have a dream within a dream; he shook his head. He sat in his chair relaxing as much as his still-racing heart would allow, still sure that this would come to an end.

Finally he could wait no longer. Slowly, he walked back to the bathroom and without hesitation looked in the mirror. *Now what to do?* He was still seventeen. He had forgotten what he looked like at that age; even the zits were there.

Now what? he asked himself again.

He didn't know who to call. What the hell would he tell them?

Again, he found himself in his chair. Half an hour later he was still there. Finally he got the phone book, looked up the coach's number and dialed.

After the coach said hello, he said, "Hey, Coach, this is Grief, how are ya?"

"I'm good, Grief. You OK? You sound different."

"Yeah, yeah, I'm good. Listen, I wonder if you could stop by the house on your way in this morning?"

"Sure. Grief. Any particular reason?"

"Believe me, you'll see when you get here."

"OK, see you then."

GRIEF WATCHED THE coach come up the path onto the porch. He opened the door and stayed behind it, "Come on in, Coach."

"Hey, Grief. I…uhm, oh, I'm sorry. Are you a friend of Grief's?"

They stood looking at each other for a minute. He could see disbelief and recognition on the coach's face.

"Grief?"

"Yeah, Coach. It's me, Grief; at least I think it is. I woke up this morning, and this is what I found. It's me but I'm seventeen years old. And before you ask, no, I don't know what happened."

"But my God, Grief, how could this happen?"

"I wish you'd tell me."

"I think I'll sit down." The coach sat in Grief's chair, a look of total wonder on his face. "Anything strange happen last night? You know, different?"

"Not really. I stopped at the bar and had a couple, then came home and had a couple more; nothing terribly unusual. I do remember asking or maybe just wondering how it would feel to be seventeen again, even for just one day; to be able to play again, and then I guess I went to sleep."

"Well, someone heard you 'cause you're definitely seventeen again. WOW, I mean, WOW. What are you going to do?"

"I don't know."

The two sat there both in awe of what appeared to be happening, unable to believe and unable not to believe.

The coach said, "You think it's for just one day?"

Grief thought for a moment then said, "Well, if all this is because of what I asked for last night, it should be."

"What if it isn't?"

"We won't know that until tomorrow."

'What are you going to do today?"

Grief didn't answer for a few moments. "I've been thinking about that since before I called you. How about letting me practice with the team? I know, I know. It's crazy, but it's the only thing I can think of that I want to do. I think it would help me complete my life."

"God, Grief! I don't know if that's a good thing to do."

"You could introduce me as a new transfer from out west. What could it hurt?"

Now it was the coach's turn to think for a few minutes. "Why do I have an awful feeling that I'm going to regret this?"

"You'll do it?"

"Yeah. Show up at the gym around two-thirty. I gotta go, and besides, if I stay here I'll probably change my mind. See you at two-thirty."

"Thanks, Coach."

GRIEF COULDN'T STAND still. He wandered around the house finding himself over and over in front of the mirror. He wanted to make sure the situation hadn't changed, but still kept thinking it was a bizarre dream. Finally he could take it no longer. He had to find out if this body functioned the way it did when he was really seventeen.

He walked out through the back gate to the street behind his house; it was half a dozen long blocks slightly uphill to the end of the street. He started slowly at a light jog letting himself feel how things were working. At the end of two blocks he was running at a good clip and feeling his stride lengthen. When he got to the last block, he went into a pure sprint hearing the air rush by his head. He rounded into the cul de sac and came to a halt looking down the long street. He wasn't even breathing hard. He started to laugh, a crazy, wonderful laugh that was filled with pure giddiness. He still did not know what had happened or how. Yet he was filled with a feeling he hadn't enjoyed in over fifty years.

HE WALKED INTO the gym at two twenty. The place had changed completely. It was a new building with all the facilities new and modern. The coach's office was large with a small room attached for a secretary or an assistant. He looked through the glass wall and saw the coach with the two men he recognized as his assistants.

The coach looked up and caught his eye. He waved for Grief to join them.

The coach was talking when he entered, "Dave, Allen, this is the transfer that I told you about. Greg Jensen, these are my two assistant coaches."

They shook hands all around and then talked to him about his experience. It took him a minute to get used to his new name; he wondered why the coach had changed it.

He found the locker room, then the equipment manager and got set up with gear.

HE WAS TAKING his time putting on the gear, enjoying the feelings that were being awakened every time he did something that seemed so familiar and had been so long ago. He had bought a new pair of cleats and worn them all afternoon to break them in. The only other item he brought was from a long time ago. It was the sweatshirt that he had worn when they won the league championship. Why he had kept it all these years, he never knew. Now, perhaps he did.

"Hey, how ya doin'?"

He looked up to find himself looking at the team quarterback, who he noted was almost his size. "Hey, I'm good. I'm Greg, Greg Jensen" He held out his hand.

The handshake was strong. "I'm Charlie Parker, the QB on the team. Nice to meet you."

"Nice to meet you, Charlie."

"Coach said you just transferred in. What position do you play?"

"Line backer and running back."

"You play both ways?"

"The school I came from is small."

"Cool. It will be nice to have a good size running back."

While they finished dressing he met half a dozen other players curious about the new guy.

He went through the warm ups with a lot of energy, running as fast as he could, doing jumping jacks like they were the most fun thing in the world. He was wound up, really wound up. They did some one on one blocking, and soon no one wanted to go up against him. He was once again in his element.

The team was having a full scrimmage getting ready for their first game this Friday night.

"Hey Jensen, get over here."

"Yeah, Coach."

"Look at this play book for a while."

"OK, Coach."

Grief sat on the bench and studied the playbook. He already knew most of the plays after all his talks with the coach. It was interesting too, because some of the plays could have come right out of the playbook he used in high school.

"Jensen, you familiar with most of that?"

"Yes sir, Coach."

"Get in there for Williams and let's see what you can do."

He ran into the huddle. His heart was going ninety miles an hour, yet his breathing was easy and he was completely calm. Just like it had always been.

"Hey, lookie here, Hollywood's gonna play."

That was Kronsky. Ever since he found out in the locker room that 'Greg' was from out west, he had started calling him Hollywood. He was as big as Grief and a good player who played offense and defense line. But he had a big mouth; he thought the team belonged to him. Worse, he was by nature a bully, and he didn't know when to keep his big mouth shut.

Grief looked at him, and they locked eyes. It lasted for just a few seconds, and then Grief winked at him. Kronsky's face turned into a frown. Grief turned back into the huddle.

Charlie said, "OK, listen up. We're gonna run trap right three on two. Go."

It was an off-tackle play that ran right at Kronsky, and Grief carried the ball. He couldn't help but smile.

Grief took the handoff cleanly from Charlie Parker, aimed at the three hole. He saw Kronsky break off his blocker and come right at him. He shifted slightly to the right and saw Kronsky do the same. He couldn't believe the move still worked. He shifted back to his left, lowered his shoulder and hit Kronsky just below the shoulder. With his weight over shifted to his right, Kronsky didn't have a chance. Grief drove him right back through the line and dropped him at the feet of the linebacker, and he was into the defensive backfield.

The scrimmage lasted another fifteen minutes with the same personnel. Grief carried the ball almost every play. He punished people. He drove through them, he ran over them, he dragged them along. It was impressive. He ran Kronsky's side a lot. After the first two or three times he heard no more of the Hollywood bullshit. He did however gain a lot of respect for Kronsky, because he learned quickly and seldom made the same mistake twice.

The whistle blew. "OK, everybody take a breather." This from the coach.

GRIEF MADE HIS way over to the sideline to stand by the coach.

"You OK, Greg?"

"Yeah, I'm fine. There aren't many breaks during a game, Coach." He said this under his breath.

The coach gave Grief a hard look, then nodded his head with a small smile. "OK boys, times up."

Coach called for a new group of personnel, and this time he had Kronsky playing on the offensive line with Grief still in the backfield. The first play ran over Kronsky's position. The hole was beautiful; Grief had to admit the kid knew how to play the game. On the way back to the huddle he patted Kronsky on the shoulder. "Great block, man, great block." He got a smile in return.

Back in the huddle, "OK, red sixteen, three right on two."

"Hey Charlie, how 'bout blue four?" Kronsky asked.

"I don't know Kronsk, I…"

"Hey, Parker, are you the quarterback?" Grief interrupted.

"Course I am."

"Then call the damn play!"

"Right. Red sixteen, three right on two."

The huddle broke; Kronsky gave Grief a dirty look. He was not used to being second to anyone.

The play worked well.

"Hey man, don't interfere; got that?"

Grief turned to face Kronsky. "In the huddle, there is one man calling the signals, and that's the quarterback. If you're not the quarterback, keep your damn mouth shut, got *that*?"

The two stood nose to nose. Finally Kronsky blinked, and Grief turned his back on him into the huddle. Grief noticed a slight smile on Parker's face.

A few plays later Williams came in for Grief, and he found himself on the sideline next to the coach.

"Well, what do you think, Greg?"

Grief gave it a second, then said, "Good practice so far."

"So far?"

"Were you about to end practice?"

"Yeah, it's quarter to five."

"You know that play we talked about?" The coach nodded. "Why don't you let Parker try it?"

"OK, anything else, Greg?" This said with just a touch of sarcasm.

"Well, since you asked," With a little more sarcasm. "Special teams, kick off practice and returns, a little running up and down the field is a nice way to end a practice."

The coach looked at him for a moment, "You don't want this to end, do you? You're enjoying it too much."

"You'll never know, Coach; you'll just never know."

THEY RAN THE new play at least ten times. Grief could see that Charlie Parker really liked it; they also found that Charlie really did have a great arm. He was easily throwing the ball between forty and fifty yards and on target.

The special teams practice went for more than half an hour. By its end the whole team was ready for the showers.

"OK, OK, gather round. Gentlemen, that was a good practice. I think we are ready for our first game. I don't want anybody running around and screwing off tomorrow. I want everybody well rested for tomorrow night's game. See you in the locker room no later than four tomorrow. Hit the showers."

The coach called out, "Parker, hang around a minute. Greg, you hang around too."

He continued, "Charlie, for the first time you looked like you were in charge out there; keep it that way."

"Got it, Coach, I will. Hey Greg, some of us are going to get pizza. Want to come with us?"

"Thanks, Charlie, but I've got something else to do."

The coach turned to Grief when everyone else was walking to the lockers. "Let's sit on the bleachers."

Once seated, the coach turned to Grief. "Well?"

"TOO short. I wanted it to last a long time. For whatever reason I know that it was just for this one day, that tomorrow I will be Grief again, the old Grief…but it was worth every second. Somehow it made all the rest of it OK."

"I don't think many of us ever have that opportunity," the coach said.

"I'm surprised I did."

"Grief, maybe whatever power made this happen thought you should. What are you going to do the rest of today?"

"I don't know…I think I'll go for a long walk, then find a good hamburger joint— one that makes good shakes—then I'll go home."

HE FOUND THE hamburger joint with the right shake, and it tasted just like it should. Once home he turned on the TV, sat in his chair and watched the news. He found that today when every-thing had been so different for him, the world had gone on its way as usual. There had been no profound changes in the world as there had in his life, nothing remarkable at all. The news couldn't offer a thing as momentous as this day had been for him.

He started to get up and get himself a nice tall Scotch and soda, then burst into a fit of laughter when the thought came to him that he was too young to drink. It felt good to laugh. Later he started a fire and made himself that Scotch after all, it tasted funny. He must have dozed for the next thing he knew the eleven o'clock news was on, and his day was coming to an end.

He thought about staying up to see what would happen, then decided against it; he was a little scared. He was debating with himself when he quietly fell asleep in his chair.

HE AWOKE TO darkness. He pushed himself out of the chair hearing the snaps and cracks of his old body reminding him that he was no longer a young man. He found his way to the bathroom but didn't turn on the light as he got into the shower. He let the water run on him for quite a while, enjoying the relaxing warmth. He was sore today, sorer than he could remember being in quite a time, then he remembered yesterday.

Could it have been? Could it really have been?

He took his time finishing his shower, spending so much time that the water started to turn cold. He grabbed the big towel letting it drape around him. He felt his beard and told himself he should shave.

He sat down on the toilet with the light still off, letting his mind wander through the day before. He luxuriated in remembering his run up the street behind the house and the pure feeling of being young. There were no words; there was only the feeling.

Well, you can't put it off forever, he told himself.

Slowly, he got to his feet in front of the vanity. He took a deep breath and flipped on the light. It was, as the Irish say, himself again.

Nothing had changed although he knew that for whatever he had left to live, he would cherish yesterday

"Well, 'ya old goat you're back where you started," he said to the mirror. He stood looking into the mirror. Something had changed, but what? A low, slow chuckle made its way out of his mouth. His scowl was gone.

A Million Times

HE WALKED INTO the house, stopping just inside the door. He stood there for quite a while just looking around the house, noting things he had paid little attention to in the past. His first thought was to go pour a stiff drink yet he did not move. He just stood there.

Finally he walked over to his leather recliner and sat down, picked up the remote out of habit, but did not turn on the TV. The old chair felt comfortable and some of the tension that held his body lessened as he sank deeper into the chair. His gaze kept wandering around the room; other than the chair he felt like he had never been here. The sigh escaped his lips with a whooshing sound that surprised him, which made him sit up a little. He turned his head toward the dining room, his eyes fixing on the picture of Babe, his favorite picture of her. It was, he knew, impossible that she had been gone eight years, almost nine. Time flies when you're not having fun. *Yeah, right.*

He made his way into the kitchen and found the biggest glass in the cupboard for the large bourbon and seven he intended to inhale. Instead he drank slowly, surprised at how he was enjoying the taste of the drink. He never turned the TV on that night; instead he sat in his chair getting up only for a second drink, then going to bed.

HE WAS UP just before dawn, a habit he was unable to escape since he was a teen, dressing quickly and heading for the kitchen to turn on the kettle for coffee. He wondered how many times he had done the same routine over the years, knowing that it had to be many. That thought ran through his mind bringing the question, *How many times have I done a thousand different things?*

He went through his day, doing the things that needed to be done. Starting with breakfast, sweeping the front walk, getting the paper and the mail, talking with Art, his neighbor. And all that while, he kept thinking about all those things that he had done over and over, a million times. It was that expression: 'I've done that a million times.' How many times had he heard it? How many times had he said it?

ONE THING HE hadn't done a million times was fix his own meals; Babe had always taken care of the meals except maybe breakfast. Now, however, it was lunchtime, and he was going to make a nice bologna sandwich. With the sandwich plate in his left hand and a Budweiser in his right, he pushed the screen door open with his hip, took the two steps down to the patio and sat at the picnic table with his lunch.

He thought about yesterday then decided that this wasn't the time to dwell on it, so he looked around his back yard. Now, mowing the lawn was something he thought he'd done a million times, at least it felt like it. The smile crossed his face unbidden; he had enjoyed mowing the lawn more often than not. It was one of those chores that you didn't have to think about, you just followed along behind the mower, no sweat. When you were done, your wife said how nice the yard looked. Win, win.

He looked at his sandwich on the table that had a bee on it; he picked it up—the bee decided to leave—and took a bite, it was good. The Bud that washed it down was a fine brew, made the sandwich taste even better.

He looked at the fence he built along the back the month after Babe had passed; he had needed something to do. He could see some of the deep hammer marks on the fence; the nails hit far harder than they needed to be as he let out his anger and frustration. Probably a stupid thing to do, but it had helped. The one thing that he was sure of was that in his lifetime he had driven more than a million nails.

The sun went behind the trees and without its mid-summer warmth, he felt cold. He picked up the plate and went into the kitchen. He put the dishes in the sink and, as a smile worked its way across his lips, he thought, *Here's another thing I've done a million times, the dishes.*

Finished with that little chore he wondered what he would do the rest of the afternoon. He decided to watch some baseball. Again in his chair, he clicked on the game. The Giants were playing in Florida today. Six to four, Giants. He turned off the TV. The Giants were good, but the little leaguers up the street at the school were more fun to watch.

"HEY, BILL. HOW are you?" This, from his old friend Jimmy, who never seemed to miss a game at this field.

"I'm fine, Jimmy. How's with you?"

"Great, just great."

He sat at the top of the bleachers and looked at the scoreboard to see it was the top of the fourth inning. After a while his mind came back to the thought of a million times. He shook his head, deciding to give it some real thought and count the things he had done a million times, or at least those things that it seemed he had done that many times.

He couldn't help but wonder how many games Jimmy had watched. *OK, this is serious.* Brushing your teeth, easy a mil. Washed the car, combed his hair, thought of Babe, wondered how the kids were, walked down the same streets, driven down the same streets, put his clothes on, taken his clothes off. He paused; *this was kinda fun.* Written his name, said I love you, hugged someone he loved, smiled, frowned, laughed so hard it hurt, cried.

"You OK, Bill?" He turned to find Jimmy next to him.
"You seemed to be lost in thought."

"Jimmy, I was lost in thought, but thanks, I'm fine." He hadn't been aware that the game had ended. "You gonna be here tomorrow?"

"You know me, Bill. Where else would I be?"

"Good, then I'll probably see you tomorrow."

WALKING BACK HOME, he again started on his list of millions. Steps, forward and backward, songs he had sung, women he had ogled—when Babe wasn't looking, of course—dishes of ice cream, pieces of cake eaten, the things he had wondered about, ants he had sprayed, mosquitoes he had swatted, mosquitoes bites he had survived.

He stopped suddenly and couldn't help but laugh; he had walked right past his house. Once again in the kitchen he made himself a large Jack and Coke, and settled into his chair in the living room. He turned and looked at his favorite picture, then turned on the TV.

What a difference a day could make. He felt happy. He had really enjoyed his game with the millions. It somehow had brought him some solace and had taken away the dread he had been feeling. It took a long time to do all those millions of things, which of course meant he had enjoyed a pretty full life. He *had* enjoyed a pretty full life: four good kids, a woman who had loved him more than he could ever have hoped for, and work he had done well.

The day before when the doctor had told him he had only a few months, he had sunk to the bottom of the pit, the second time in his life that he had felt despair. The first time was when Babe died.

But the millions had made it all right. He *had* done millions of things in his life. A life full of joy, of sadness, of triumphs and failures. He had always found that the failures taught him more and explained more of life than had the triumphs, and here he was, perhaps not for much longer, if the doctor was right.

He switched off the TV, picked up his drink and went out onto the front porch. There he found a comfortable chair and put his feet up on the railing. He took a sip of his drink. The sun was falling behind the trees across the street as it had done forever.

He would have to call the kids soon and let them know what was happening, happy in the solid knowledge that they would be able to handle it.

But for right now he decided, he was going to enjoy all of the millions of seconds he had left.

The Anniversary Card

THEY WERE NEWLYWEDS; well not really, it was one year today. He was tired. It had been a long and hard day. He thought about not stopping at the store, but knew that he could not do that. How had a year gone by so quickly?

He struggled with the thought of what this first ever anniversary card should say. He wanted to tell her all that he felt, but he didn't want it to be too mushy. Instinctively he picked up a card that had little writing on it and read what it had to say. He started to put it back, then stopped and read it again.

He smiled as he turned and headed for the check stand. The card said just what he wanted her to know.

She was setting the table when he came through the front door. Without looking up she said, "Hi honey, how was your day?"

He walked up behind her just as she finished, wrapped his arms around her and pushed against her butt.

She smiled and said, "Mmm, that feels good."

He couldn't believe how lucky he was. He handed her the card and said, "Happy anniversary."

"Well, what do you know, according to my friends you wouldn't remember."

"How could I forget?"

Taking her time, she opened the envelope and removed the card. The front of the card read: "TO THE GIRL I LOVE." Just as slowly, she opened the card to find, "AND ALWAYS WILL."

His name was in its usual scrawl at the bottom. He had added beneath his name. "YOU ARE MY WORLD."

They had an elegant dinner by their standards including a bottle of wine. They went into the living room after dinner and watched some television, but he couldn't help noticing that she kept picking up the card and looking at it. A little later she said she was going to take a shower and go to bed. He joined her in the shower. It had taken most of their first year together to get over being nervous with each other when they were naked. In bed they made love, enjoying every moment and the pure magic of being together. He felt, unbelievably, that it was better than the very first time a year earlier.

She was up and gone by the time he got out of bed as it was his late day at work. He poured a cup of coffee from the pot that she had made and saw the anniversary card on the counter near the phone.

He started to throw it away then stopped and opened it to read the words that meant so much to him. Alongside his signature he saw that she had put her initials. He couldn't help smiling. He put the card back on the counter where he had found it.

THE TWO SIBLINGS were in the middle of a search.

"Jean, didn't Dad say that he wanted us to find a greeting card that he kept in his top drawer and bring it to him?"

"Yes, he did."

"Well, it's not here."

"Look in all the drawers. Sometimes Dad doesn't know top from bottom."

Steve started through all the drawers starting at the bottom first. He found it in the second drawer down, of course. The envelope was almost in tatters and turned slightly yellow with age. He pulled out the card and read the cover.

Without knowing how, he knew that there was something special about this card. He opened the card and read what was inside.

"Jean, come take a look at this."

"What?"

"Come here and take a look at this card."

"What card?"

"Jean, get your butt over here and look at this card!"

"OK, OK."

Steve handed her the card. She read the front, "TO THE GIRL I LOVE." and then opened the card and read "AND ALWAYS WILL." inside. She stared at the card for a minute before saying, "That's really beautiful, but what's all the rest?"

"I don't know for sure but it looks like it's their initials starting almost from the beginning."

"Beginning?"

"You know, from their first anniversary."

"How many?"

"Let me see." He started trying to count the initials.

"I can't keep it straight, Jean. Give me a hand and maybe we can figure this out."

Their parents had been married forty-four years. When they got done counting for the fifth time, they could only come up with forty-three.

"We will have to ask Dad. Somehow we are not doing this right," Jean said.

They finished removing the things from the house their father had asked them to save. Tomorrow the movers would be here to take the rest to storage and the Goodwill, and the house would become a new home for a new family.

Jean had tears in her eyes as they left the house and her brother was the same. They had been raised in this house by parents they both gave thanks for, who had raised them with discipline and unending love.

The ride to the rest home seemed to take forever. They talked about the card and just what it meant. They speculated about many things, finally giving up and deciding to just ask Dad. They didn't want their father in a rest home. Both had offered to take him to their homes, but he steadfastly refused. He said they had enough going on in their lives; they didn't need him hanging around.

HE CALLED UP the stairs, "Honey, you ready?"

"Be right there."

He had made arrangements at a fine restaurant down town for a dinner with some champagne, her favorite poached salmon, and strawberries and cream for dessert. He waited by the door thinking, almost with disbelief, that they had been married ten years tomorrow. How was it possible that ten years had passed? There were reminders he thought as he smiled, in the form of their two wonderful kids, Steve and Jean. Also the fact that they now had a house. When he thought of it that way he could see the ten years.

And yet there was Diana, his wife. It was always the same feeling with her, that it was new, just starting, a beginning, it was in a word, wonderful.

Later, he said, "I really thought dinner was super."

She smiled as she answered, "I thought the company was good too."

She was sitting very close to him so he took her hand and gave it a squeeze. "Not bad, not bad."

She punched him in the shoulder.

The next morning she found the card on the kitchen counter. When she opened it she saw his initials and made hers alongside, then took the card and put it back in his sock drawer.

STEVE SAID, "WHY just one anniversary card?"

"How would I know? But I'll bet you it had to be for some

romantic reason, you know how Mom was."

Steve smiled as a memory flooded through his mind. "Do you remember Mindy?"

"Mindy, your prom date?"

"Yep, that's the one. Mom was sure that was the girl for me. On prom night she made everything as romantic as possible including having Dad put up that ridiculous flowered arch by the front door with candles in the entry and a double orchid wrist flower! It was really something."

"She *was* a romantic. When I was dating Arnie Davis he came over to the house for dinner one evening. As soon as dinner was over, she had to go over to Tina's house for some emergency. I found out later that she and Dad just went for a ride so Arnie and I could be alone."

HE HAD ONE of those days that can ruin a week or a month. He came in the door in a foul mood not wanting to talk to anyone, not even Diana. He was not a big drinker, but on this day he went directly to the liquor cabinet and made himself a stiff drink that he proceeded to finish quickly. It didn't help. He poured another just as Diana came in from the garage. She was, he noticed, nicely dressed.

He barely acknowledged her, then went into the living room and turned on the news. The evening went downhill from there. Diana finally quit trying to talk to him. Every time she tried he had something nasty to say. By this time she was getting pissed off herself. The last thing she said to him was that he was being an asshole and went to bed. She had no idea what time he came to bed.

He propped himself up in bed so he could see the alarm clock. "Oh, God," he thought, "I have to get up in twenty minutes." He rolled over as he remembered what his dad used to say, he felt like five pounds of shit in a two pound sack. Last night was fuzzy. In his whole life he hadn't been drunk more than half a dozen times, and last night was a doozey.

He left for work after a shower and two cups of coffee. He felt better, but not a lot. He was halfway to work when it dawned on him that yesterday was his anniversary.

AS HE ENTERED the room, he said, "Hi, my love. How are you feeling today?"

"Like I'm dying." Her voice was barely audible.

He said nothing, instead went and pulled the shades to let the sunshine in. She was dying. She wasn't saying anything maudlin. She had a habit of confronting the truth.

"What would you like for breakfast?"

"Just some…" She broke off and went into a coughing fit.

He held her till it subsided. He waited till she caught her breath. "Well?"

"Just some orange juice."

He leaned over and kissed her cheek. "It's on its way."

He started for the door and heard her say something. "What was that, honey?"

"Bring the card, you big goon." Her voice, he noticed, was stronger.

"Sure." He could barely hold back the tears. It was their anniversary. He brought the card with the orange juice.

THEY WERE NEARING the rest home when Steve said; "Do you think he'll tell us?"

Jean thought for a moment. "Yeah, yeah, I think he will. I don't think it was a secret as much as it was just something that they kept between themselves. You know, something they just thought was private."

THE ANNIVERSARY CARD

"Why did he have to pick a place so far from where we live?" Steve asked his sister.

"Probably for just that reason, so we wouldn't be out here bugging him every day."

Jean parked the car and grabbed the cookies off the back seat. They were her dad's favorite. The two walked to the room that their dad jokingly called his suite, only to find it empty. They walked back to the desk and asked if anyone knew where their father was.

"Oh, sure." the girl said. "He's in the kitchen fixing the stove."

Steve turned to Jean with an obvious smile. "Wouldn't you know it!"

Jean returned the smile as they started for the kitchen.

THEY ENTERED THE kitchen and found their dad talking to the chef. "Hi, Dad." They said in unison.

"Billy, that oven gives you anymore trouble, you know where to find me." With that he turned and took his two kids by the arms and said, "Let's go back to my suite where we can visit."

When they got back to his room, Jean asked, "Dad, about those things in the box, all the stuff you asked us to get for you, we were wondering…"

"About the anniversary card?"

"Yes. We know that there has to be a story that goes along with it."

"I was hoping that you would look at it, and that you would ask me what you just did. The story is really quite simple, but because the card meant so much to your Mom and I, I wanted you to hear it."

He pulled the box open and found the card. He sat on the couch, and the two kids sat in the chairs opposite. They could see that he was close to tears, but he composed himself and began, "When your Mom and I got married, we knew that we were truly in love. Some people never find that, but we knew from the beginning.

"On our first anniversary I brought that card home to Diana. It was, she said, the most beautiful card that she had ever seen or read. I thought that she was exaggerating, but all that evening she kept picking it up and looking at it. The next morning when I was getting ready to go to work, I saw the card and picked it up to throw it away. I opened it for a last look and saw that she had put her initials alongside my signature. So I left it on the counter.

"The following anniversary as I was leaving for work, your Mom turned to me and said, 'Honey, don't buy me an anniversary card, OK?' I looked at her with what was probably a blank expression so she said, 'I'll explain later.'

"That night when I got home with a beautiful dozen red roses and no card, I asked her why. This is what she said, 'When you brought me that card last year, it meant everything; more importantly it said everything, everything that I could ever hope to hear. I don't want a funny card one year and a mushy card the next year and whatever else the next year. That card is the only card I ever want for my anniversary. It says all that I will ever want to hear. So, if it's all right with you, each year we will just add our initials, and it will be our card forever.'

"I had never been so overwhelmed. I didn't quite know what to do, let alone what to say, so I said nothing. I took her in my arms and kissed her forever, then picked up the card and put my initials alongside hers. Every year we did that on our anniversary, every year but one."

"What happened that year, Dad?" Jean asked.

He handed her the card. "You see that little scribble on the right side about halfway down?"

"Yes."

"Well, it's hard to read now but it is just one word, 'Fight.' Your mom put that in there so we would not miss a year. The reason was simple. I came home in a lousy mood and acted like a jackass all night. So for the first and last time, we didn't initial the card. Your mom never mentioned it. I didn't know about the word 'til the following year when we added our initials.

"The last time was the week before she died, our last anniversary. She was so weak she could barely hold the card, yet her initials are surprisingly clear. So that is the story of the card; I thought you might like to know."

Jean blinked through her tears. "That is so beautiful! I can't imagine a more beautiful story." Steve said nothing as he wiped at his eyes.

"Oh, there is one more thing. Your mom asked for a headstone with nothing on it but these words: YOU ARE MY WORLD."

A Written Mystery

THE YEAR 2122 was just beginning and already James had a mystery to solve. He was sure that he had a pretty good idea what he was looking at, but just wasn't sure. It was a letter from an estate that included him in the will, but he could not read it. It was from the father of a man who had just died at the ripe old age of one hundred eleven.

By the standards of 2122 that was not particularly old. James turned the letter this way and that, even upside down without understanding even who it was addressed to. Frustrating.

James was twenty-five and in his second year with the Smithson law firm. He was bright with an intent mind, but what he held in his hand was a complete conundrum. To whom should he turn for enlightenment?

"Ron, this is James on seventh floor. I have a letter here that I can't read. It was written over a hundred years ago, and I haven't a clue what it says."

"What's it look like?"

'To me it looks like a lot of funny loops all tied together."

"OK, well, I'll be up in a while and take a look."

"Thanks."

A VOICE OVER his shoulder said, "Well, let's see this mystery letter."

James had not seen Ron as he approached his desk. He was still studying the letter. Without looking up he held the letter over his head and felt Ron take it.

"I've seen a few of these before and, like you, I could never make heads or tails of what it says. Until he retired and then died, old Ben Schwartz could read this stuff. Now I don't know who to turn to."

James sat for a moment, then said, "Do you remember what this writing is called? Maybe we could find someone at the college who could decipher it."

"Hmm, that's not a bad idea. It's late now, so maybe I'll try to call someone in the morning." Ron said.

"OK, I'll just leave it here on my desk." James stood up getting ready to leave when, on impulse, he took a sheet of white paper, put a big question mark on it and attached it to the letter. *Time to go home*, he thought to himself.

IT WAS MIDNIGHT. Arthur was halfway through his shift. He sighed as he got off the elevator on the seventh floor. Arthur was still working because he liked working and, since Amelia died, he couldn't bear being at home alone at night.

He was a janitor. He had always been a janitor and, though this seemed to amaze those who knew him, he liked being a janitor. That being said, he was an educated man. His mother was an English teacher who had impressed on him the value of education.

He had completed a degree while working evenings as a janitor to help pay for school. After graduation he had gone to work for a firm in Los Angeles. The pay had been good and although he didn't mind the job, he knew that he really didn't enjoy it. So he started working part time as a janitor again, soon realizing that it was what he wanted to do.

When he got married, he worked a shift and a half for more money and, since Amelia worked too, they got along just fine.

Over the years Arthur had developed a system that he used to make the time go faster. First, he emptied the wastebaskets, then mopped the linoleum, followed by vacuuming the rugs, and then straightened up the desks. The routine gave a rhythm to his nights and a time to clear his mind, and with this he was able to notice things that were out of the ordinary.

It caught his attention right away—how could it not?—the question mark took up the whole page. He knew the young fellow who sat at this desk was new to the firm, and his first name was James. He moved the paper to the side and was greeted with a letter written long ago.

The question mark now made sense. He read the letter. It was sad. It was written by a man almost on his death bed to his children. When he finished reading, Arthur had tears in his eyes. The letter was beautifully written.

Arthur took a fresh sheet of paper and translated the letter, then attached it to the letter and the question mark. His mother had made him learn to write in the special script because she said it was a dying art, and that it was beautiful. He had agreed.

Arthur stood up, straightened the desk and moved on to the next desk. After a moment he returned to James' desk. On the paper with the question mark he wrote the following: "It's called cursive."

Just Another Marine

A FULL MONTH had gone by and Ryan and Ralph were getting used to the new gunny. He was, in their opinion, an idiot that couldn't do anything if it wasn't by the book. He was, in the wisdom of their knowledge of the Corps, a throwback who just didn't understand the new Marines.

However, things had calmed down considerably when the lieutenant returned from leave and, for the moment, at least there was polite cooperation amongst the four men in the recruiting office.

Once in a while, normally on payday, the lieutenant would invite the office out for a beer after work and, since this was the first time that the sergeant was in the office on a payday, the lieutenant made a point of asking him.

"Thank you, sir. If you don't mind, I think I'll pass."

The lieutenant felt a little rebuffed, but said, "No problem, Gunny. I just think it's a good idea once in a while to get together when we're not in the office. Maybe next time."

Gunny was non-committal. "Thank you, sir."

RALPH ASKED, "LIEUTENANT, what do you think of the new gunny? If you don't mind my asking, sir?"

The lieutenant didn't answer right away, then signaled the bartender for another round.

"Ralph, how long have you been in the Corps? Three years?"

"Four, next month, sir."

The lieutenant looked at Ryan. "How about you?"

"Four, the month after next, sir."

"Well, for me it will be seven years in August. Let's see, that gives us fifteen years between the three of us. The gunny has been in for thirty-seven years."

"You're shittin' me!" Ryan said. "That puts him in the Corps before World War II!"

The two corporals were in disbelief. "Ralph, would you believe that shit?" Ryan said. "He doesn't look that old."

FROM BEHIND THEM, "Mind if I join you?"

The three men swiveled around in unison, startled by the gunny's voice.

The lieutenant said, "Gunny, it would be our pleasure."

Not knowing what the gunny had heard of their conversation, he added, "Matter of fact, we were just talking about you. We were talking about years in the Corps, and I was telling Ralph and Ryan that you have been in the Corps for more years than the three of us combined."

"Hell, Gunny, you've been in the Corps longer than I have been alive." Ralph said.

"Don't remind me."

The lieutenant continued, "Gunny, I joined the corps because of John Wayne, know what I mean? Anyway, what made you join?"

Gunny didn't answer for a minute. It was easy to tell that he was thinking of another time and place from the look on his face.

"I didn't have the best family in the world. Being raised in an era when a man was proud if he put a roof over his wife and kids' heads and decent food on the table with maybe a few little extras; it meant he was doing okay. It was different than now. My tenth birthday was two weeks before the crash of '29," he paused, "and then things just got bad.

"My dad was soon out of work, and there really wasn't anything he could do 'cause it seemed that everyone was out of work.

Soon my two brothers and I were working more than going to school. We would do anything we could find to make some money. It stayed that way for what seemed forever. The day I turned sixteen I went to see the Navy recruiter. He turned me down, but the Marines took me; and that, gentlemen, is how I came to be in the Corps."

"Sixteen isn't old enough to get in the Corps, Gunny," Ralph said.

"So, I lied a little."

The lieutenant and the two corporals were astonished. In the two months that they had worked with the gunny, they had never heard him put more than two sentences together.

"Gunny, that photo on your desk, you said someday you would tell me about him. Is this the day?" Ryan had had just enough to drink to ask the question.

The lieutenant chimed in, "I have wondered the same thing, Gunny. I've seen the picture on your desk."

Gunny looked at the three men sitting at the table with him. They were all fellow Marines. He looked at each one of them, aware that they were waiting for an answer.

"That picture on my desk is a picture of someone who taught me a lesson about what the Corps is and what it means to be a Marine. His name was…

HALF ASLEEP, HE heard, "Williams?"

"Yo."

"You're wanted in the duty hut."

Billy Williams sat up slowly in his rack and swung his legs over the side. He couldn't believe how tired he was. It had been a struggle this morning just to get up and go to chow.

Slowly, he put his boots on; tying the laces was a chore. He was on light duty for the rest of the week after the doctor had diagnosed that he had valley fever, whatever that was. He shook himself to get a little loose, then stood up, squared away his cover, then headed for the door to the barracks. Outside was a brilliant Southern California day that normally he would have enjoyed to the fullest, but today he hardly noticed.

THE DUTY HUT was of the quonset variety straight out of World War II. It was the same shabby green that all the buildings on Camp Pendleton were except the ones that were painted desert beige.

"Lance Corporal Williams reporting, Sergeant." Billy said.

"Oh yeah, Williams. The doc down at the hospital at mainside wants you to report there ASAP. In other words, get your ass down there now, *capice*? Radiology department."

"Right, Sarge. What do I do about transportation?"

"Corporal, the bus comes by every hour, catch it."

"Okay, Sarge."

Billy went back to his barracks. He grabbed his field jacket and walked to the bus stop in front of the slop chute. It was warm out, but he felt cold. The music from the jukebox in the mess was restful. He sat on the bench and was soon asleep.

"Hey, you going somewhere?"

Billy crawled out of sleep slowly. "Yeah, I'm going down to mainside to the hospital. Thanks for yelling at me."

"No problem, corporal. We all get tired sometimes," the bus driver said.

Billy looked at the driver. "My friend, you wouldn't believe how tired I am; you just wouldn't believe it."

MAINSIDE WAS THE center of Camp Pendleton; it was where the business of the base was conducted. It was also where the hospital was. Billy made his way to the main reception desk where a very stern-looking, blond nurse sat, scowling as though she hated the whole world.

"Ma'am, I'm Corporal Billy Williams, and I was told to report here to see the doctor in radiology."

The nurse looked at him for a moment, then looked at her appointment log on the desk. In contrast to her forbidding look, her voice was southern, soft and quiet. "Here we are. You're due to see Captain Morris in Room Two Twenty; that's down the hall to the right."

"Thank you, ma'am."

BILLY STRODE UP to the desk. "Captain Morris, sir, I'm Corporal Billy Williams."

"Corporal, sit down; we have a few things to discuss."

Captain Morris was large; by any interpretation of the word, he was large. At six foot four and two hundred and sixty pounds with shoulders that looked an axe handle wide, he was imposing. He didn't remotely look like what most people think of when they think of a doctor.

"Corporal, what exactly did the doctors here tell you is wrong with you?"

"They said I have valley fever, some kind of a lung infection."

"I see. You're sure that's all they said?"

"Yes, sir."

"Very well, I'm going to keep you here today and run some more tests and get a few more x-rays. You'll probably have to stay overnight. After I get the results back, I'll know a lot more. I'll see you in the morning."

Billy pushed himself to his feet, "Thank you, sir; I'll see you in the morning."

The rest of the day Billy spent being x-rayed, prodded and tested for one thing after another. He would swear that the one corpsman had turned into a vampire as he couldn't imagine them needing that much blood for testing.

BILLY APPROACHED THE office of Captain Morris wondering if he had found an answer to this lung infection, and when he would quit feeling so tired. He entered the waiting room, gave his name, and was shown immediately into the doctor's office. Captain Morris got up from behind his desk, set the x-rays down that he had been looking at, and came around to sit on the front of his desk.

"Corporal Williams, what I have to tell you is something that I hate to tell anyone. Since there is no way to make this easy or nice, I'll tell you straight up. You do not have valley fever; you have cancer of the lung. Now…"

"Wait a minute, sir; how could I have lung cancer? I'm only twenty years old and I never smoked 'til I joined the corps, and even now I only smoke a few cigarettes a day. How could I have lung cancer?"

"Corporal," The doctor sighed and leaned back. "I don't have an answer to that question. What I can tell you is that long before cigarettes, people got lung cancer. What we need to talk about is what we are going to do about your lung cancer; how we are going to treat it."

"Is it bad, sir?"

Again the doctor sighed, "Yes, Corporal, it is. From what I can see from the x-rays and from my consultation with the radiologist, it is quite advanced."

Billy stood up and started walking in a circle in the small room. His head was down and the doctor could see that he was as deep in thought as he probably had ever been. The doctor said nothing.

"What you're telling me, Doctor, is that I don't have much

of a chance?"

"Well, Corporal…"

"Doctor, my name is Billy. My dad told me that most sentences that start with the word 'well' are mostly bullshit. So that being said, tell me the truth."

"Very well, Billy, I'll tell you the truth. The cancer is in both your lungs and, as I said, it is advanced. It is amazing to me that you went so long without symptoms. Your records say that you told the doctor you didn't even have a bad cough; that's unbelievable. If the doctor you went to hadn't taken an x-ray and sent it down to us, we probably wouldn't have caught it even now. It is beyond my comprehension that he didn't see it. The cancer is bad enough with what we know, and I'm sure that it has metastasized to other places in your body. The only way to be sure is to do a series of more x-rays. I've ordered that for today. When I have the results, I'll be able to tell you more."

"Doctor, they took lots of x-rays yesterday. Why more?"

"I want to look at your lungs from as many directions as I can to get a better picture of the extent of the cancer."

Billy looked at the doctor. "So I'm right? I don't have much of a chance?"

"Yes, Billy, I believe you are."

"Shit."

Billy continued to walk around in his little circle. He always walked when he was nervous or scared; right now he was both. The thoughts in his head were going a million miles an hour. He didn't seem to be able to keep everything from running together, and right now he needed to concentrate on what to do about what the doctor had just told him.

He took a deep breath and stopped walking. He raised his head up to look the doctor directly in the eye.

"Sir, if it's as bad as you think, then I really don't have much time, do I?"

"Probably not."

"How much?"

The doctor knew that this kid deserved the truth. "It could be a few months, or it could be less."

"Will any kind of treatment help?"

"You said you wanted the truth; so in my opinion, no."

"Shit," was all Billy said.

The room was silent for a few minutes as Billy walked around in his circle. The doctor again remained silent.

"Sir, you've probably been through this before. What does the Corps do with me now? I mean I'm still a Marine. Do they just throw me out?"

"Billy, I've been in the Corps for quite a while. They make lots of mistakes, and they screw up a lot, but one thing I do know is they take care of their own. I'll put in for an immediate leave for medical reasons, and they will send you home. When you get there, I'm sure that you will have to report in at your local reserve unit or the local recruiter, and that's about it."

"What will my duties be?"

The doctor didn't answer for a moment. Here was a twenty-year-old kid who happened to be in the Marine Corps, who he had just given a death sentence, and all he wanted to know was what his duties were going to be.

"Billy, I haven't the faintest idea what your duties will be. I doubt if you'll have any. You'll just have to ask at your next duty station. Remember, you will be on medical leave."

The doctor studied the young man as he slowly walked in his circle. It was impossible for him to imagine what was going on in his mind, yet he knew he was looking at an exceptionally strong person. One of the few that was okay within himself.

Billy looked up and walked over to the doctor's desk, "Thank you, sir, for being so honest. I'm sure it wasn't easy to tell me."

Billy held out his hand; the doctor did the same. The handshake was firm. Billy turned and left the room as the doctor went behind his desk and sat down. He sat back in his chair in wonder at how the human condition could allow one man to completely fall apart at the kind of news he had just given Billy, and how some, like Billy, could just accept the knowledge of their fate and go on.

He was sure that Billy had understood what he was telling him. Was he in denial? Some, maybe, but he didn't think that was the case. Instead he realized he had just met a remarkable person.

THE GUNNY SAT behind his desk reading one horseshit recruiting report after another, all written by idiots. He considered everyone in this office to be a certifiable idiot. He hated being a recruiter. Problem was he was good at it.

He picked up a message from his desk, read it and put it in one of the baskets. He had a marine reporting in who was home on medical leave; some jackass who had managed to get the docs to send him home to Mommy for a while so he could sit around on his butt. They didn't make Marines like they used to.

The gunny rose from his desk and went out into the front office.

"Miller, I'm going to see the Ciocci kid so I can tell his parents what the skinny is. Tell the lieutenant that I should be back in a couple hours."

"Right, Sarge."

The gunny started for the door, picked a set of car keys off the board, then stopped. "Miller, if that kid that's reporting in from Pendleton gets here, tell him to hang loose until I get back."

"Got it, Gunny."

- - - - JUST ANOTHER MARINE - - - -

THE SERGEANT SPENT a little over an hour with the Ciocci kid's parents and when he was through, he knew he had a new recruit. The parents in an indirect way let him know that their son had caused them some trouble, and that they hoped the Marines could improve him. He also learned from them that the boy was quite intelligent.

He was amazed to find a parking spot directly in front of the recruiting office as he slid the car to a stop. On the way back he stopped and grabbed a sandwich at the nearby deli so it was almost exactly two hours since he had left.

He tossed the keys to Miller. "When you get a chance, Corporal, would you see that that thing gets some gas in it?"

"Sure, Gunny. There is your kid from Pendleton."

The gunny turned in the direction that Miller had nodded his head. In the corner of the office a Marine in summer uniform sat with his head against the wall snoring softly, oblivious to what was going on around him.

The gunny studied him for a few minutes. He could see that the kid was skin and bones, and his skin had a lousy color. He wondered if it was from the illness that had him on medical leave, or if he had been born that way. He remembered his name was Billy Williams.

BILLY LEFT THE doctor's office and went back out into the bright California day. Across the street there was an open area with a few benches under a scrawny tree offering a little shade. He walked to the nearest bench and sat down.

The whirl in his mind had slowed as he began to come to grips with what the doctor had told him. His first thought was how much this was going to hurt his mom. His dad died when he was ten. From then on it was just his mom, he and his sister. His sister was now married with a baby of her own. The baby had been really good for his mom. It seemed to add a great deal to her life. It was easy to see because she smiled more.

He and his sister were also very close. The two could talk to each other about anything and always had. She told him that he was her ace in the hole; that no matter what happened in her life, she knew he would always be there.

Billy leaned back against the bench and let the tears run down his face; he made no move to wipe them away. He didn't mind the idea that he was going to die. He had been in Korea the last year of the war and had expected to die at any moment. He just didn't know how he was going to tell Mom and Sis.

He sat there for an hour or two; he would never know, time it seemed had almost stopped. He came out of his reverie only when the same bus driver yelled at him to see if he wanted a ride back to camp.

"Hey, yeah, thanks."

If the bus driver noticed the marks from the tears, he said nothing.

When Billy got back to his barracks there was a note from the first sergeant on his bunk, informing him that he wanted to see him at seventeen hundred. A glance at his watch told him it was sixteen hundred; he decided to take a short nap.

"Hey, Billy, wake up. The top wants to know where the hell you are; it's seventeen-thirty." This came from Billy's best friend, Ski, short for Kablonsky.

Ski knew something was going on and knew his friend was sick, yet he had no idea how serious it was. "Top says to get over there as soon as you can. He added that means now."

Billy rolled off the rack and stood up, then picked up his cover, squared it on his head and started for the door. "Thanks, Ski."

Kablonsky walked with him. "You went down to mainside

yesterday and got back this afternoon. Did they tell you anymore about what's wrong with you, Billy?"

Billy was walking slowly. He turned his head and looked at his friend. He wondered if Kablonsky could read anything in his face. "Yeah, Ski, they gave me the straight scoop. After I'm done with the top, I'll tell you about it. You gonna be here in the barracks?"

"Where else?"

"Okay, I'll see you in a few."

"YOU WANTED TO see me, Sarge. I'm sorry I'm late, I fell asleep."

"No big deal, Billy."

From the top's answer Billy knew that he was aware of what Billy had been told by the doctor; otherwise he would be getting his ass chewed out. He would have preferred the latter.

"I've got orders here for you for sick leave home, plus travel vouchers and your paycheck. When the Corps wants to, they can get things done pretty fast."

"You get the scoop on me, Sarge?"

"Yes, Billy, I did."

"Look, Sarge, I was pretty sure you did when I didn't get my ass chewed for being late. If it's all the same to you, I'd like you to keep it under your hat. I'll tell Ski. The rest of the guys don't need to know right now, they'll find out soon enough."

BILLY WAS ON a plane waiting for take-off; he was thinking of his friend, Ski. When he told him what the doctors said, Ski just sat there looking at him. His mouth worked a few times, but nothing came out while the tears just ran down his face. Billy put his arm around his buddy's shoulders, and they sat that way for a while.

"Billy, you're my best friend in the world. You saved my life in Korea. What am I going to do if you're gone?"

The plane's motion brought Billy out of his reverie with a jolt. Soon the plane was in the air with the earth passing beneath the wings. Billy wondered if this is what angels saw.

"Excuse me, ma'am."

The stewardess stopped. "Can I get something for you?"

"Yes, ma'am. I was wondering if I could get a Vodka and orange juice?"

"For a Marine, you bet. My brother is in the Corps. I'll be right back."

"Thank you, ma'am."

She returned with his drink. "There you are. Anything else I can get you?"

"No, ma'am, thank you, this is just fine."

The stewardess smiled and walked away leaving Billy looking out the window of the plane taking him home.

THE GUNNY STOOD looking at the kid in the corner fast asleep, waiting for him. He knew that the kid had been in for a couple of years plus, and wondered if it would be worthwhile getting his service record or not. He decided not to. He walked over to the corner. "Hey Corporal, time to wake up."

Billy opened his eyes and came to his feet. "Sorry, Gunny; guess I'm just tired."

"That's all right, come into my office."

As the gunny went behind his desk, Billy put his orders on the desk and took the chair in front. Once seated, the gunny picked up Billy's orders and glanced through them.

"What exactly is your medical leave all about, Corporal?"

"They didn't tell you why I was…I mean…they didn't tell you what's wrong with me?"

"No, Corporal, they didn't. They just told me that you were

on medical leave until further notice."

"What are my duties while I'm on this leave, sir?"

"That's just it, Corporal. You don't have any duties other than to get better."

"Gunny, if it's all right with you, I'd like to find something to do while I'm home. I can't just sit around the house all day. I'm a Marine, so I don't just sit around on my ass. I'd probably go crazy. My mom works, and my sister is married. She lives in another town, and she works. Okay if I stop by in a few days? You know, see if maybe you have some running around for me to do?"

The gunny looked at Billy. He'd been around for a lot of years, been through two wars, and he was a good judge of character. For the most part he read people well. This one he wasn't sure about.

"All right, Corporal. You come around when you're ready, and we'll see if there is something for you to do."

"Thank you, Gunny."

With that Billy left the office, picked up his duffel bag and headed for the last place on earth he wanted to be—home. He had deliberately gone from the airport to the recruiting office in order to prolong going home and facing his mom with the news. He had called her to tell her he was coming, but had not given her a time.

The gunny went into the front office. "Johnson."

"Gunny."

"Will you please get me Corporal William's complete jacket ASAP?"

"Roger that, Gunny."

"Gentlemen," the gunny said, "I'm going to call it a day."

OF ALL THE scenarios that Billy had run through his head, none of them came close to what happened when he told his mom what was wrong with him, and what the prognosis was. He had imagined everything from her falling completely apart to total denial, and everything in between. His mom stood there saying nothing; just held his hand and looked him in the eyes. Finally she led him over to the couch, and they sat down.

"Billy, you know what you just told me. You told me that I'm going to lose my son. That there is nothing that either you or I can do about it. When I lost your dad, you were too young to remember. I fell apart completely. If it hadn't been for your sister, I don't know what would have become of me. She held me up, explained to me that I had to go on, and I did. When you just told me that you are going to die, I saw in your eyes that you are not afraid; that your concern was more for the people around you, for me and your sister. I knew you were strong; I just didn't know how strong."

Billy put his arms around his mom. The two of them sat there rocking back and forth like two people trying to calm a baby.

SHE COULDN'T HELP herself. "Billy, you look awful."

"Well now, Sis, is that any way to greet your baby brother?" Billy was feeling strong today, and he picked his sister up off her feet for just a moment. "Boy, it's good to see you," he said.

"What's going on? You were here on leave just five months ago. How come you're on leave again?"

"I'll tell you in a few minutes." He knelt down and held out his arms, and his little niece ran into them. "How's the sweetest girl in the whole world?"

"I'm fine, Uncle Billy."

While holding his niece he shook hands with his sister's husband, John. They talked while he carried his niece into the house.

"John, if you'll excuse us, I'm going to take my sister down to the ice-cream parlor and buy her a treat. We haven't done that in years, OK?"

"Sounds like a good idea to me. Just bring one back for the rest of us."

On the way to the ice-cream parlor Billy told his sister. With the calm and grace that he always expected from her, she listened, asked some questions and then asked what she could do to help. God, but he was a lucky man.

TWO DAYS HAD gone by and the gunny had gotten Billy's records and read them through. The kid had done well in his time in the Corps. Then came this death sentence. The gunny sat behind his desk and wondered what he would do under the same circumstance. He hadn't a clue. Through two wars he had known that dying was a distinct possibility. During that time he had watched too many of his friends die not to be aware that it could happen to him. Yet in all that time no one had ever sat him down and told him he was going to die. That his time was finite, measured, finished.

"Gunny."

He looked up at Miller in the doorway. "What?"

"That kid Williams is here; says you thought you might have some things for him to do."

For a moment the gunny was silent. "Tell him to come in."

Miller left. A moment later Billy Williams appeared in the doorway.

"Good morning, Gunny."

"Come in and sit down, Williams. How you feeling?"

"I've been better, Gunny, but okay. Would you mind calling me Billy?"

"I'm supposed to call you Corporal according to the manual. But Billy will work."

"Thanks, Gunny."

The gunny smiled. "Just don't get used to favors. Now tell me what the hell you're doing here. You're on no duty for medical reasons; so you're not supposed to be here at all."

"Gunny, I spent the last two days with my mom and my sister, and it was great. However my sister had to go back home, and my mom had to go back to work. She said that she could take some time off, but I told her to go to work. I'd be waiting for her when she go home. On top of that all my friends still have jobs, and I'm stuck sitting around the house screwing the pooch. So here I am."

The gunny quickly made up his mind. "I've got to go over to the reserve unit in the next county. Feel like a ride?"

"Sure."

They were about halfway to their destination. The gunny was getting to like this kid; he didn't talk his ear off. "What made you join the Corps, Corporal?"

When there was no answer, he looked over at Billy to find him with his head against the door, asleep. The gunny spent about two hours at the reserve unit. While there he introduced Billy to a good friend of his, Dutch Giannini. While the gunny did what he came for, Dutch showed Billy around the facility.

Billy and Dutch hit it off. Dutch was a gunnery sergeant also and had known Gunny since World War II.

"Hey Dutch, your last name is very Italian. How'd you get the nickname Dutch?"

"Ha, that's a joke. You remember boot camp, I suppose?"

"Sure," Billy replied.

"Well, the day we were marched into receiving barracks, this DI named Stobie walked up to me and asked me my name. Anthony Aurelious Giannini, I answered. He stood staring at me nose to nose, and all the other recruits were waiting to see what was going to happen. Finally he took a step back and said, 'You don't look like a wop, you look like a damned Dutchman.' And that is how I got to be named Dutch."

With a frown Billy said, "I always wanted a nickname, you know it seemed kind of cool; never had one."

Dutch said, "When you get one, let me know."

"Hey kid, time for us to *adios*."

"Okay, Gunny."

"Thanks for the tour, Dutch. See you next time."

"My pleasure, Corporal."

THE NEXT DAY Billy stayed home; just too tired to get down to the recruiting office. And the pain that the doctor had told him would come had arrived. The doctor had given him pills for the pain with the warning that if the pain got severe, he was to go to the nearest hospital and give them the file that the doctor had sent along. Billy took a couple of the pills and slept most of the day. The night before he and his mom spent the evening going through her picture albums, something he really enjoyed. The next day was Thursday, and he felt a hundred percent better. So after his mom left, he headed for the recruiting office.

"Good morning, Gunny; anything going on?"

"Not much, Billy. I've got one appointment that I need to take care of, maybe a couple of hours. After that, why don't we go someplace and have lunch, you can buy?"

"Sounds good to me. I'll hang here till you get back."

WHEN THE GUNNY walked back into the office, Miller said, "Gunny, what's the skinny on this kid Williams anyway? After you left, he started cleaning stuff, emptying wastebaskets, whatever he could find to do. I thought he was on full leave."

"Corporal, I don't know what to tell you exactly. Maybe he

just doesn't like to sit around on his butt."

The gunny looked around and didn't see Billy, so in his best parade ground voice he growled; "Williams, get your butt front and center. I'm hungry."

"Roger that, Gunny," came from the back storeroom.

THEY WERE SEATED by a very pretty, dark-haired girl at the nearby IHOP; it was the gunny's choice. They looked at the menu without conversation and then gave their orders.

"You know, don't you, Gunny?"

"Know what, Corporal?"

"About why I'm here on medical leave."

"Corporal Williams, I received orders to check you in so the Corps knows where you are. I'll receive orders telling me at some point to send your sorry ass back to Pendleton or wherever, and I will do that. Does that answer your question?"

Billy didn't know whether to believe the gunny or not, so he didn't say anything for a few minutes then, "Sorry, Gunny, didn't mean to be pushy."

"Forget it."

Their meal arrived and while they ate the conversation was stilted. They talked about the Giants and, of course, the weather and a little about the Corps.

"You like the Corps, Williams?"

"You know, Gunny, you've been in the Corps a long time since before World War II. I, on the other hand, have only been in for a little over two years. Yet it feels that this is where I was meant to be. Growing up with my mom and sister was great, but my sister is seven years older than I am, so even though we are really close I... Let me put it this way, when I was starting seventh grade, she was graduating from high school. You know what I mean?"

"Yeah, I think so." The gunny replied.

"My mom made our home nice. We didn't have much, still we ate well, and I knew I was loved as much as anybody in the world. I hardly remember my dad. So when I got in the Corps it was like…I don't know, it was like being someplace I always should have been. I want to say home, but it was more than that. Oh hell, Gunny, I don't know what I'm trying to say, except from the first day, it just felt right."

The gunny nodded. He didn't speak for what seemed to Billy a long time. The gunny had been taken back to how he had felt when he had been in the Corps only a short while. He heard himself trying to tell his brother what Billy had just tried to tell him. He wasn't sure if he did even as well as Billy.

"I know what you're trying to say, Corporal."

Somehow the gunny was sixteen again; he could feel the pride and strength he had felt then. It was a very good feeling.

Billy smiled. "I'm being philosophical, how about that? My mom always told me to watch out for that; she said it was a sure sign of age."

It was the gunny's turn to smile. "I guess she's right at that, you being past twenty and all."

The conversation died for a few minutes then Billy said, "Gunny, you can tell me to stow it if you want, but I gotta ask, you know, curiosity. You ever been married?"

"Jesus H Christ, what the hell brought that up?"

Billy put his hands up in surrender, "Sorry I asked; forget it."

The gunny couldn't help but smile, "What about you?"

"What?"

"You, nimrod, you ever been married?"

"Oh no, Gunny. I'm too young to be married."

"I'll have you know my parents were married when he was seventeen and she was sixteen."

"I think they were lucky people then." Billy said.

"You might be right, Corporal. Now, are you going to tell me what brought up all this married crap?"

"Forget about it, Gunny; it's no big deal."

"Spit it out, Corporal."

"You're gonna think I'm an idiot."

"I might already."

"Okay, okay, it's just…" Billy stopped in mid-sentence. The gunny could see the pain flow across his face. He'd seen it too many times before; he waited.

Billy had gone two shades paler. "Man, that hurt.'

"You got anything for the pain?" the gunny asked.

"Yeah, the doc gave me a bottle of pills."

"Take one."

"I…"

"I said, take one."

Billy pulled the bottle from his pocket, shook out one of the pills and took it with the water on the table.

"Can I go on now?"

"Sure, tell me about the girl."

"What girl?'

"The one you were going to tell me about before you were interrupted."

"How…never mind. When I was home on leave last summer, I met this girl up at the Russian River. Gunny, she was fabulous. Did I tell you she's Portuguese?"

"No Billy, you didn't."

"Oh, anyway, we met at the dance on Friday night, and oh, did we dance. Gunny, I never held a girl that fit in my arms the way she did; it felt like I'd been holding her like that my whole life long. Then the next day she ditched her friends, and we met at the beach. We stayed on the beach until the sun went down, and in all that time we never stopped talking. Her name is Nicki, at least that's her nickname. Her last name is Russo. We met at the dance again that night and…Gunny, it was so special, there is no way I can even describe it. The bad part is she was leaving the next day."

Billy stopped talking, and the gunny thought he was in pain again. "You OK, Billy?"

"Yeah, Gunny, the pill is working. It's just that she gave me her address, and I told her I'd write and give her mine 'cause they said I might be transferred."

There was a long pause. "Gunny, I lost her fricking address. Shit. Now she thinks I'm some inconsiderate asshole that didn't really give a damn about her; you know, just another loser."

"Do you know where she lives?"

"Somewhere in the East Bay, Antioch or Pittsburg, I think. Gunny, I told her I'd write. I told her that when I got leave again we would spend the whole time together; she said that she could hardly wait. Gunny, how could I screw up like that?" Billy was close to tears.

"Shit happens, kid."

"Can you believe I don't know her first name? I called her Nicki. I just love the sound of that, but that isn't even her real first name. Gunny, I knew that girl for two days, not even, and as sure as I'm still breathing, I know that I love her."

"Corporal, I don't know what the hell to say. I'm sorry for what happened, and if there was something I could do I would. But now I've got to get back to the office."

Billy only lived a short distance from the recruiting office, so the gunny dropped him off in front of his house. He watched as Billy walked to the door; he was having a hard time. The gunny knew the pain had returned.

On his way home that evening the gunny was thinking of a

young, blond girl from years back, someone he tried not to think of at all. *Damn you, Billy Williams.*

BILLY DIDN'T GO to the recruiting office for the rest of the week. He had a feeling that maybe he had bent the gunny's ear a little too much.

On Monday he called Captain Morris. The good doctor was kind enough to not ask him how he felt; he probably knew. He did ask him about his symptoms. Billy told him that he was coughing more, that the pain had moved to include his stomach. He couldn't figure out why, if he had lung cancer, that he should hurt around his stomach.

They talked for another five minutes about a number of things, then the doctor asked him if the pills were enough for the pain. When Billy hesitated, the doctor told him he would send him another prescription, just in case he needed it.

Billy spent some of his time fixing little things around the house. He always tried to have something ready for dinner for his mom, even if it was only pizza. He wasn't much of a cook, but he was a salad gourmet. Both kinds he knew how to make, he made well. His sister spent a lot of the time on the phone with him, always able to ease the pain he felt with just the warmth of her voice.

BY WEDNESDAY HE decided that he had had enough of the house, so he walked down to the recruiting office. To his delight the sun felt great. He turned his face up to the sky and walked that way for a few strides. He decided that wasn't a good idea when a parking meter hit him in the side.

He had, by now, been home a little over two weeks. He knew he was losing weight plus the pain was coming more frequently. The pills, on the other hand, weren't helping as much.

The new pills from the doctor were in his pocket. Billy so far had only tried one; the last thing he wanted to do was walk around like a zombie. He slowed as he approached the office wondering still if he had over stepped the boundaries with the gunny. He still wasn't sure why he had told all that stuff about Nicki to the gunny. He hadn't told anyone else, not even his best friend, Kablonsky. Well, he would soon know.

"Hey, if it isn't Corporal Williams. How are ya?"

"I'm good, Corporal Miller. How about yourself?"

"You know, better than nothing according to my girl friend. Johnson and I were just thinking about getting some lunch. Want to join us?"

"Sounds good. I'll even buy."

Miller smiled. "I knew there was a reason we wanted you to go to lunch with us."

Johnson looked up from his desk, "Hey Miller, anybody ever tell you you're a jerk?"

"All the time. I'm getting to where I like it."

That got a smile from Johnson and Billy. Billy asked, "Is the gunny around?"

Johnson answered; "Nope, won't be back till Monday. You need something?"

"No" Billy replied. "Just had a couple questions for him."

They had lunch at a little diner two blocks from the office The food was good, and Billy found himself relaxing with the other two corporals. The conversation was mostly about where they came from, their high school days and whatever other bullshit that came to mind. His pain was better today, so he skipped the new medication the doctor had sent him mostly because it made him too sleepy.

THE GUNNY ENTERED the office Monday morning with his

head down in thought. When Miller said hello, he only grunted a reply. During the four days he had been off, he had given a lot of thought to his conversation with Billy about the Corps. Of all things, a snot-nosed, wet-behind-the-ears corporal had reminded him what it was to be a Marine. It wasn't just in combat that you stood for each other or in a bar fight started by some Navy guppie; it was all the time. It was just because the other guy was a Marine. Period.

The gunny had also decided to do something for Billy. He had never in all his years seen the look he had seen in Billy's eyes when he had talked about Nicki, the girl he had found and lost. If that look wasn't love, then the gunny knew he would never see it in his lifetime.

He opened the phone book picked up the receiver and dialed. Ten or more phone calls later, he put the receiver back in the cradle and looked at the clock. It was taking too long; at this rate he would never get it done.

"Miller, Johnson, get in here."

The two corporals walked into his office. From the tone in his voice, they were sure they must be in some kind of trouble.

"You wanted to see us, Gunny?" Johnson asked.

"Yeah, is the lieutenant in yet?"

"Yeah, Gunny, he just got here." Miller said.

"Johnson, shut the door.'

Johnson turned and shut the door while Miller sat in one of the chairs at the gunny's desk. Johnson sat down.

"All right, listen up. There is a girl I want to locate."

The two corporals glanced at each other. The gunny picked it up. "No, it isn't for me. It's for Williams."

Briefly he told them what Billy Williams had told him, though he shortened the story.

"I've been looking through the phone book for this county

and there are forty two entries under her last name. Billy said her name is Nicki Russo but he says that Nicki isn't her real first name, just a nickname, and he can't remember the real first name. That's what makes this tough. We have a last name and nothing else. On top of that he thinks she lives in Pittsburg or Antioch, but he isn't sure. That means she could live anywhere in the whole Bay Area; that also means it could involve a whole bunch of people.

"Today I started making phone calls and realized very quickly that I'd never have time by myself to call everyone with that last name, so I'm asking your help. One last thing, do you guys know how sick he is?"

Miller answered. "Not really, Gunny. He's never said anything other than he was on medical leave."

"I didn't think so."

The gunny paused considering whether to tell Miller and Johnson just how bad it was.

"Williams has about a month to live, maybe less. I didn't say anything; I figured that it was his place to tell you guys. I finally woke up to the fact that he won't tell anyone that he thinks doesn't need to know. He doesn't want any of that 'woe is me' shit."

"Jesus, Gunny. I mean he looks kinda sick but...What's wrong with him?" This from Johnson.

"He has lung cancer."

The three men sat at the gunny's desk in silence. Finally Miller said, "Count us in, gunny." Johnson nodded his assent.

"Just one more thing, I got a phone book for Contra Costa County, and there are over two hundred Russos listed. Since that is where Billy thinks she's from, we'll start there. If she's not there, there's probably a thousand Russos in the Bay Area. Let's hope we get lucky."

BY NOON THE next day the three men had made ninety phone calls. For half of them, they got no answer so they would have to be called again. Half of the other half they had gotten a kid or someone who didn't have an answer, so they would have to be called back. That meant that in reality they had made thirty calls.

Corporal Miller was about to go tell the gunny it was hopeless. He started to get up from his desk then abruptly sat down; he had a gem of an idea.

"Hey Johnson, you still know that recruiter in the Berkeley office?"

"Sure."

"Arkin is still working in the Santa Rosa office, and I know a couple of guys in the office in San Jose. What do you think if we just call around to the different offices and see if we can get some help?"

"Miller, most of the time you sit around on that lump you call a brain, and then out of the blue you scare the hell out of me by coming up with a good idea. How about this? Let's get all the phone books we need and make up a complete list; then when we call these guys we can give them a certain number of calls to make."

"Uhm, just one thing."

"Yeah."

"What do we tell them is the reason for this?"

"Just tell them it's Marine Corps business and mention that the gunny wants to find her. If they do, they're to call one of us and we will tell Gunny."

Johnson and Miller spent that night putting together the lists. The next day they started phoning the other recruiting offices around the Bay, giving out the lists and the reasons for them. They didn't, however, mention it to the gunny. By that afternoon there were more than eighty Marines making phone calls looking for Nicki Russo.

BILLY FINALLY HAD to admit things were getting worse. The pain was now a constant thing. The periods of relief were getting fewer, but he still went down to the recruiting office to say hello, though he didn't stay. He had the feeling that the gunny was avoiding him; so he came to the conclusion that he had indeed said too much at their lunch.

It was curious to him that he wasn't afraid of dying. He wondered all the things that everyone wondered; whether there was a heaven, or for that matter, hell. What it would be like. Yet he wasn't afraid. If he felt bad about anything, the worst was that he wouldn't be around to see the people around him grow old. He also worried that, with some of the tough things that had happened to his mom in her life, now she was losing her only son.

The one true regret is that he would not see Nicki again. He had beaten himself half to death for being a complete idiot and losing her address; he still couldn't believe it.

Then he beat himself up some more for not remembering her first name. He couldn't remember if he had even heard the names of her mother and father.

He shook his head violently; he was not going to cry anymore. He pushed himself up awkwardly from the couch and walked slowly out to the back yard. He felt that some fresh air might make him feel better. He sat down and a coughing spell grabbed him. It took minutes for it to stop. He coughed a lot now, to the point that his chest hurt a lot. He was supposed to see the doctor today and had instead skipped the appointment and stayed home. What were they going to tell him? That he was looking better?

His sis had called that morning, and they talked for a while.

She caught him up on all the things his niece was doing; it seemed trivial and totally unimportant, yet he looked forward to her calls.

He suddenly felt cold, something he noticed happened a lot lately. Maybe a nap would feel good.

IT WAS FRIDAY. The gunny was at his desk getting ready to make what seemed like his ten thousandth call when the phone rang and he jerked it out of the cradle. "Marine Recruiting Office," he answered.

"Gunny?"

He recognized the voice of Colonel Davis. "Yes, sir."

"Gunny, you had better have a good answer for what's going on down there. I've been told that every recruiter in my whole district is using government phones to try and find some girl. Now, you know damn well that is not authorized use of our time and material, not to mention the cost. I want that stopped now, you hear me, or it's your ass." With that the good Colonel hung up.

"Miller." It had to be Miller.

"Yo, Gunny."

"In here, now!" Miller appeared at the door but did not enter the room.

"The colonel just called me and informed me that every recruiter in the district is trying to find a girl and if that shit didn't stop, it would be my ass. You wouldn't happen to know anything about that now, would you?"

"Gunny, there was no way we were going to make all those phone calls, and then make all the callbacks we didn't complete the first or second or even the third time. On top of that when Johnson and I completed our list of possible numbers, we were over a thousand. So I rallied the troops."

"And just exactly what did you tell them was the reason for

us finding this girl?"

"Uh well, I told them it was Marine Corps business. I mean it is in a way. I told them that you personally were involved, and if they found the girl to call Johnson or me, and we would tell you."

Miller stood there waiting for the gunny to chew his head off.

To his surprise the gunny nodded his head and said, "Good idea, Miller. I should have thought of it myself."

Miller felt like someone had lifted a weight off his shoulders. "The bad news, Gunny, is that we haven't gotten any positive results. It's been almost a week and we've made one hell of a lot of calls and so far nothing. What are you going to do about the colonel's order?"

"I'm going to have a talk with him."

THE GUNNY DIDN'T particularly like Colonel Davis. He was a ninety-day-wonder out of the end of World War II who had seen no combat duty then or even later in Korea. He was a by-the-book Marine without a lick of common sense.

The order to stop looking for the girl had gone out to all the various recruiting offices from the colonel's office. And now all the recruiters were calling Johnson and Miller, telling them what had happened. They were told to stand by until the gunny had a chance to talk to the colonel, that he was already driving to the colonel's office.

It was almost five when the gunny came back to the office and to his surprise, found Miller and Johnson still there; most Fridays they were gone around four.

"What did the colonel say, Gunny?" Miller asked

"After I explained to the colonel the reasons for what we are doing, he decided that what we are doing is a legitimate Marine activity."

They could tell that the gunny was surprised by this, but Miller and Johnson could see that he wasn't going to say any more about it, and they didn't ask. They got back on the phones, however, and spread the word that the search was still on.

It was seven that night when the gunny left the office. He was as frustrated as he had ever been. The day had been long, and the talk with the colonel had been draining. For one of the few times in his life, he was tired, really tired. The last thing he had done was to call Billy's house. He spoke with Billy's mom who told him he was sleeping, but that he was doing pretty good. He thanked her and left the office.

SATURDAY MORNING THE gunny had gone for a run. He had run for almost an hour trying to work out his frustration. He was shaving when the phone rang.

"Yeah."

"Gunny." It was Miller. "I had an appointment this morning and when I got here, the phone rang. One of the guys over in Pittsburg is pretty sure that he found the girl. Her first name is Nicolina. Here is her address."

The gunny copied down the address; there were even some directions. He finished shaving, then dressed in uniform making very sure that everything was correct. *What do you know*, he thought, *there is a God*. He checked his appearance in the mirror. Satisfied that he was looking like a Marine, he went out to his car and started the drive to find Nicki Russo.

As he neared Pittsburg he found to his surprise that he was nervous. What would he do if she didn't want anything to do with Billy, or if she already had another boyfriend? Well, he would deal with that when it happened. One thing he had learned in the Corps, you couldn't deal with a problem until it was one; imaginary problems were just that.

HE PULLED UP in front of the address he'd been given. It was a well-cared-for house, set a little back from the street on a nice sized lot with a huge Liquidamber tree in the front yard. He got out of the car and straightened his uniform. When he was at the front door, he hesitated then knocked. A moment later, the door was opened by the girl he had come to find. There was no doubt; Billy had described her to a tee.

He said, "You have got to be Nicki."

She looked at him candidly and said, "I'm sorry, do I know you?"

"No ma'am, but I know someone who knows you and, if I could have a few minutes of your time, I will explain why I'm here."

AN HOUR AND a half later they were driving back to San Rafael. The girl was in a world of her own, not needing to talk but needing to come to grips with all the things that the gunny had told her, so he didn't offer conversation. He had told her the whole bitter truth. He admired the depth of her fortitude. She was a very strong person; someone who matched the character he found in Billy. He had watched her as he had told her about Billy losing her address and not even knowing her real first name. She smiled when he told her how Billy had been kicking himself in the ass for eight months and agonizing over his inability to get in touch.

She didn't cry, at least she didn't make any of the sounds that most people make when they cry; the tears just poured down her cheeks as he told her all about Billy's illness and the prognosis.

She told him that she knew it was impossible that she had misread the way she thought Billy felt about her because she felt the same. Then no letter and no letter and no letter… Her voice had drifted off, and she had gone into that place all of us have when we just have to be alone with our thoughts.

Gunny had decided not to wait for the ferry across the bay and had driven through Vallejo and across to Black Point, then down to San Rafael.

"Does he look the same?"

"Yes ma'am, I believe he does. I'm sure he has lost weight. Other than that I believe he would look the same."

"Will you please call me Nicki?"

"Yes, ma...uhm, Nicki."

Before they left her house, he called Billy's house. To his delight Billy had answered the phone.

"Hey, you gonna be around for a while? I was thinking about dropping by, in a couple hours maybe...OK, see you then."

THE CAR PULLED to the curb in front of Billy's house. The gunny looked at the girl; she was scared to death.

"Nicki, I think you're worried about this reunion. Let me just tell you this; inside that house is a man who wants to see you more than he wants to breathe. It is going to be wonderful."

"Thank you, Gunny. Are you going to come in?"

"No, ma'am."

She smiled, turned and walked to the door. As he drove away, he was thinking about the blond girl; the memory was pleasant.

"SO NOW YOU know who the person in that picture on my desk is."

The three men at the table with the gunny were quiet for a few minutes. Then the lieutenant asked the question that all three wanted to know.

"What happened next, Gunny?"

"Billy died ten days later. The first eight days were amazing.

It was as though somewhere he had gotten a shot of life and maybe that's what it was. He came into the office the next day with Nicki and introduced her to everyone. I would have sworn he wasn't even sick.

"From his sister and his mom I heard about the last days of his life. He and Nicki were together for the entire time. They went places and did the things that young people in love do, yet the most important thing was that they were together. Their time together was short, and they made the most of it. On the ninth day his mom called to tell us that they had taken him to the hospital; he had suddenly gone into a coma.

"He died the following morning. There were not too many civilians at the funeral; just those that were family and some friends. The rest were Marines. Every single Marine from the recruiting district was at the funeral. I don't know that I was ever prouder of the men of the Corps than I was that day. We buried Corporal Billy Williams with full military honors. I was amazed when the colonel showed up for the ceremony and gave the flag to Billy's mother. It was one of those days that you know will stay with you for a long, long time."

"How'd you get the picture, Gunny?"

"Three days after the funeral his mother came into the office. She handed me the picture and asked if I would like to keep it. I said I would. She said that the graduation from boot camp was probably the most important moment in Billy's life, and she would like me to have the picture."

"That's one hell of a story, Gunny. I want to thank you for sharing it with us."

"It was my pleasure, Lieutenant. I haven't told that to anyone for a long time. Speaking of time, it is time for me to get myself out of here." The gunny rose and started for the door, stopped and turned around, "I'll see you on Monday."

JUST ANOTHER MARINE

A MONTH OR two later, the father of one of the new recruits that they had just signed was leaving the gunny's office when he noticed the picture on the gunny's desk.

"Is that your son, Gunny?"

"No…just another Marine."

Made in the USA
San Bernardino, CA
27 July 2016